DON'T BE CRUEL

Cassie Miles

Harlequin Books

TORONTO • NEW YORK • LONDON
AMSTERDAM • PARIS • SYDNEY • HAMBURG
STOCKHOLM • ATHENS • TOKYO • MILAN
MADRID • WARSAW • BUDAPEST • AUCKLAND

To Marya Hunsinger-McConnell.

ISBN 0-373-22285-8

DON'T BE CRUEL

Copyright © 1994 by Kay Bergstrom

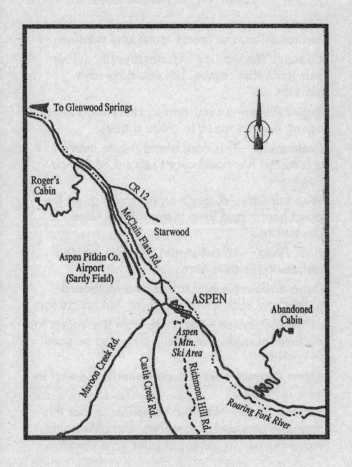

To Glenwood Springs

N

Roger's Cabin

CR 12

McClain Flats Rd.

Starwood

Aspen Pitkin Co. Airport (Sardy Field)

ASPEN

Abandoned Cabin

Aspen Mtn. Ski Area

Maroon Creek Rd.

Castle Creek Rd.

Richmond Hill Rd.

Roaring Fork River

CAST OF CHARACTERS

Gina Robinson—On a search for Elvis memorabilia, she found crime and passion.

Conner "Hound Dog" Hobarth—His career was mountain rescue, but could he save himself?

Roger Philo—a semi-retired Hollywood talent agent, he was quick to make a deal.

Lydia Philo—This cool blond Aspen matron contrasted her flamboyant second husband, Roger.

Wendell Otis—Roger's ex-partner's quest for good health and Elvis memorabilia were obsessions.

Alex Philo—An assistant D.A. who wanted justice on his own terms.

Dean Philo—He had talent as a keyboard player and rock-and-roll singer, but no career.

Michael Penrose—He came from Las Vegas to perform at a glitzy Aspen party, and he paid the price.

Norm Garrett—As a deputy sheriff, he was in over his head.

Jerome Sage—Was it a coincidence that this reclusive Broadway composer from Memphis made his rise to fame just after Elvis died?

Prologue

To Gina Robinson, a business trip to Aspen in February was a pleasure. Her memories of the Colorado resort town glistened like champagne powder snow under blue skies. Nothing ugly could ever happen in Aspen.

Yet, when she disembarked from the Aspen Airways plane, Gina felt strangely apprehensive. The panorama of the surrounding peaks was almost too beautiful, too pure. She inhaled huge gulps of clean air, hoping to erase the grit of Manhattan from her lungs. Still, the sense of impending disaster clung to her.

Her stepuncle, Roger Philo, the man she'd come to Aspen to see, met her at the baggage pickup. She'd never been comfortable with Roger, her aunt Lydia's second husband.

"You've grown into a beauty," he said with an admiring look.

He'd grown, too. Roger had bloomed in the full flower of middle-aged spread. He was a big man who seemed even larger because of his expansive personality. Now semiretired, he had once been a full-time talent agent who blustered his way around Hollywood and loved to make a deal.

"All that red hair." He stroked the dark auburn curls that fell past her shoulders. "It's fabulous."

"Roger, please stop." She recoiled from his touch. "I hate to be patted on the head. I'm not a child."

"That's obvious, honey. How old are you now?"

"Twenty-eight—the same age as your oldest stepson, Alex."

As his gaze slithered up and down her body, she reminded him of the purpose of her trip. "We need to talk, Roger."

"Yeah?" He brightened.

"About Elvis," she said.

ROGER PHILO OWNED one of the finest collections of Elvis Presley memorabilia west of Memphis, and Gina wanted to sell it on consignment through Berryhill's, the prestigious Manhattan auction house where she worked. Berryhill's was staging a special auction of rock-and-roll souvenirs from the estates of two recently deceased rock stars, supplemented with items from other legends.

Though there were huge quantities of Elvis memorabilia, ranging from plastic key chains to motorcycles owned by the King himself, the true collectors refused to part with their treasures. The auctioneers had despaired of finding any really good "Presleyana." That was when Gina had remembered Uncle Roger.

If she could convince him to offer some of his Elvis memorabilia for sale, she would take a giant step forward in her career. Though discovering a source of Elvis toys wasn't in the same category as finding a missing Rembrandt, it was Gina's job to appraise and acquire items for auction, and the rest of the staff had come up empty-handed.

When she first mentioned the sale to Roger on the phone, he had encouraged her; but now that she'd arrived in Aspen, he seemed reluctant. After a night and a day of listening to his excuses, Gina had reached the end of her patience. "When, Roger?"

"Soon."

They had just finished dinner with Wendell Otis, Roger's former partner, who now lived in Los Angeles and had an Elvis collection of his own. Gina appealed to him. "How about you, Mr. Otis, do you have photographs of your collection?"

"I have a complete computer inventory." He held up a slim leather briefcase, then snatched it away so that she couldn't touch it. "But I won't sell unless Roger does," he added peevishly.

She glanced back and forth at the two men, who were so totally different that Gina couldn't comprehend how they had ever worked together. Roger boomed like a big, loud bass drum. Otis whined like a skinny oboe. At the moment, however, they harmonized in their intention to give her a hard time. "Before the night is over," she said, "I want this matter settled."

"Sure," Roger said. "Anything for you, babe."

He directed her down the staircase from the restaurant to an Alpine-style tavern. She squinted through the dim light. The band had just set up, and she recognized Roger's younger stepson, Dean Philo, standing at the keyboard.

"Hey, Dean!" Roger bellowed.

When he looked up and waved, Gina admired his poise. If she lived in the same town with Roger Philo, she would have killed him long ago. But Dean was cool, very laid-back. He was the exact opposite of his fussy older brother, Alex.

When Roger directed them toward a small, round table near the band, Gina repeated her demand. "We need to set a time, Roger, when I can inventory the items you wish to sell."

"Most of the stuff is in my cabin, over toward Glenwood." He signaled the barmaid. "How about you, Otis? Want a beer?"

"I think not. Beer makes me gassy." He glanced at Roger's gut and added, "I'm watching my weight. You might do the same."

"Why should I? Lydia says there's more of me to love."

The two former partners started bickering. Again.

Gina leaned back in her chair and tried to ignore her companions. Looking around the tavern, she decided the patrons must be locals for the most part; there was a lack of glitter, and a lot of cowboy in their style of dress and manner. Her gaze caught on one man who stood by the pool table, leaning on a cue and waiting his turn. He was tall and lanky. The sleeves of his plaid flannel shirt were rolled up to reveal a white turtleneck underneath. When he smiled, she was sure she'd seen this brown-haired, well-tanned man before. Was he a celebrity? Aspen was a mecca for the beautiful and famous.

Dean Philo made his way through the crowd to their table, and Roger thrust him in front of Wendell. "Here's my boy. He's got the talent, and I'm going to make him a star. Bigger than Michael Bolton. Richer than Elvis. Right, Dean-o?"

"Whatever." He pushed his long, scraggly hair off his forehead and winked at Gina. "How're you doing?"

"I'm fine, Dean. Thanks for asking."

Roger was still bragging. "My other boy, Alex, works for the district attorney's office. He's brilliant." His chest puffed out. "I adopted both boys, gave them my name and raised them like my own. Didn't I, Dean?"

He nodded complacently. "I've got to get back to the band."

Gina knew that once Dean started playing she'd never be able to talk with Roger. Propping her elbows on the table, she leaned forward. "Tomorrow, Roger. I'll come to your cabin and inventory your collection. Pick a time."

"I don't know. Tomorrow's kind of busy for me."

"Pick a time," she repeated.

"Four o'clock."

She looked over at Wendell Otis. "Would that work for you? Can you be there with your computer list?"

"I suppose so," he whined.

"Good." She repeated, "Four o'clock. Do you need to write it down, Roger?"

"I won't forget." His eyes flashed an unreadable message. "When you get there, babe, my stuff is going to knock you out. You're going to believe that Elvis lives."

From the bandstand, Dean announced, "Okay, we're going to get started here. It's oldies night. And I've got a song for my redheaded cousin. Here's to you, Gina Robinson..."

The guitars twanged to life and Dean leaned into the microphone at the keyboard to sing the opening words to one of Elvis's greatest hits, "Don't Be Cruel."

Roger shouted over the music, "I asked for that one!"

"Why?"

"Loosen up, honey. Relax a little bit. Don't be cruel to me." He ordered another beer. "Want to dance?"

"No."

After ten minutes, Gina's head was throbbing with the loud beat, but she didn't want to insult Dean by leaving too quickly. She excused herself and headed toward the ladies' room.

Much to her dismay, there was a long line at the door. Nothing was easy for her tonight. She leaned against the wall and sighed.

"Excuse me."

"Yes?" It was the man in the flannel shirt.

"Would you like to dance?"

"Yes."

When he took her hand, she felt a shiver. This interesting and pleasant reaction intensified on the dance floor when Dean's band segued into a slow song. The tall stranger held her lightly but firmly as they moved together. They were the only couple on the floor who were really dancing. Gina didn't consider herself graceful, but the man's lead was easy to follow. They seemed to be floating, drifting. When he looked down at her, she saw that his eyes were as blue as the Aspen skies. It was as if he'd stepped out of a dream to remind her that all men weren't obnoxious like Roger or cranky like Otis. Real men still existed, and she was dancing with one.

Then Roger cut in. Before she could tell him she didn't want to dance, her dream man had faded back into the crowd by the pool table. Though she would have liked to stay and find out the name of the blue-eyed man, there wouldn't be a chance, not with Roger hovering over her. She gathered up her parka and said her good-nights. "I can walk from here. My hotel is only about four blocks away."

"I'll see you to the door." Grandly Roger escorted her to the staircase leading up from the tavern to the street. "You're really something, Gina. Oh, my, I tell you. If I was a couple of years younger—"

"You'd still be married to my aunt," she said. When would he get the point? "Good night, Roger."

As she ascended the staircase in front of him, he reached out and patted her bottom. Gina whirled and smacked him so hard that he fell down the two stairs and sprawled flat on his back, like a huge fat cockroach.

For a moment, he had the wind knocked out of him, and he lay there, completely immobile. It seemed to Gina that everything else stopped, too. Her world had frozen in a tableau of sheer embarrassment. Conversations ceased. The barmaids halted, trays raised. The blue-eyed man stared. Then Roger flailed his arms, laughed and said, "I like a gal with spunk."

Spunk? "Dammit, Roger. I could just kill you."

Chapter One

The dead weight of the body fell heavily into the woodbox, and the man who had carried that burden stepped back, breathing hard from his exertion. He bent the arms and legs to fit the body inside the four-foot-high, five-foot-wide box. Then he took a single-shot derringer from the pocket of his parka, held it to the chest of the still-breathing unconscious man and pulled the trigger.

There might be blood spatters, but it didn't matter. He'd remember to dispose of the gloves. One more detail. But he wouldn't forget. He was on a roll, had done everything else right. It was perfect. He was going to get away with murder.

The sound of a car engine cut through the mournful drone of the mountain wind. He listened.

The engine strained in second gear to climb the last stretch of snow-packed road leading to the A-frame cabin near Glenwood Springs, and he watched until he saw the nose of the red Jeep through the conifers. It was Gina, all right. He pushed up the cuff of his parka and checked his wristwatch. Seven minutes before four o'clock.

She was early.

He shivered, more from anticipation than from the cold.

The trap was set. All he needed was for Gina Robinson to step inside, and she'd be caught. Helpless. No matter how she struggled and protested, she wouldn't escape. She couldn't. He'd thought of everything.

The lid of the large woodbox closed with a slam.

"Sleep well," he said as he rolled down the black ski mask to cover his face. "You're Gina's problem now."

He almost felt sorry for her. Beautiful Gina. Sophisticated Gina, with her flaming red hair and her cold Manhattan attitude. She thought she was better than everyone else. Smarter. More successful. But not this time.

The rumble of the Jeep went silent as she parked at the bottom of the steep, winding path that led to the deck and the front door of the A-frame.

He hid in the shadows, behind the clutter that was stored beneath the overhang of the deck. She mustn't see him, mustn't suspect what was happening until he had completed the last detail, until he had tightened the noose around her slender throat. When would she guess what was happening to her? He wished he could stick around and watch. Would she try to escape? The nearest neighbor was two miles down the road—a long hike. He shrugged. She might try to run, but it wouldn't matter. Her fingerprints would be here. And her car. He'd see to that.

When he heard the car door slam, he stiffened. There was one point on the steep path leading to the cabin where she could look through the open space between the steps and see him. He must remain motionless, must not be tempted to look out and attract her attention to him.

But he couldn't resist watching her. Her breath came in little frozen puffs as she climbed the snow-packed, icy path. Her boots slipped, but she caught herself on the handrail.

When she reached the staircase, ten wide wooden steps that led up to the deck, his eyes bored into her, playing with fate, daring her to glimpse him.

She paused. Her long auburn hair, partially hidden by a lavender beret, flared around her shoulders when she turned her head and peered down the steep hillside toward the Jeep. Checking her route of escape? Like any good quarry, she must have sensed the presence of the trap.

Silently he urged her forward. He ducked lower behind the junk beneath the overhang—a grill, a picnic table, a mountain bike with wide tires. He eased back against the covered box that was used for storing wood—*and other things,* he thought. Dead wood. Dead bodies.

A nervous laugh caught in his throat, and he pressed his lips together to hold it back. Not now! He was so close to the perfect crime. He had to be careful! There was too much to lose, too much at stake.

Gina continued up the stairs to Roger's cabin.

He heard the thud of her bootheels on hard-packed snow and bare wood as she crossed the deck over his head. When she knocked at the door, he tasted the sweetness of victory.

GINA BANGED on the door again. This place was amazingly desolate. A thick blanket of clouds obscured the afternoon sun, creating a weird flat light across the slopes and in the forest of dark, snow-laden pines. She shouted, "Hello? Uncle Roger? Is anybody here?"

Nobody answered, but she heard noise from inside. Why was he taking so long to answer the door?

Gina slapped her gloved hands together and stamped her feet to dispel the chill seeping into her bones. Her annoyance simmered, the only bit of warmth in this frigid landscape. If this four-o'clock meeting didn't turn out well, she intended to catch the next plane back to New York. Or maybe, if the sun came out, she'd forget Roger and take a vacation day for skiing. What a shame to visit Aspen and never once get on the slopes!

"Come on, Roger! Open up! It's cold out here!"

When she grasped the door handle, it turned easily. Gina stepped inside. The two-story wood-paneled room was warmed by a crackling blaze from the moss rock fireplace. On the ebony coffee table was a pair of leather ski gloves with the fingers in the grasping shape of the hands that had worn them. Against the far wall was a stereo, designed to cheaply replicate a jukebox. An LP record clicked down and fell into place, filling the air with the twang of a ukelele and the baritone of Elvis Presley singing the title song from *Blue Hawaii*.

"Not Elvis again," Gina groaned.

Though she expected accolades and career advancement from obtaining Roger's world-class collection, Gina was *not* pleased with this assignment. Her usual work involved fine art and antiques. She had a master's degree in art history. For the past four years at Berryhill's, she'd worked on appraisals for oils by Monet, Fabergé eggs, furniture designs by Mies van der Rohe and jewelry that had been worn by duchesses and queens.

And now...the "King."

It was quite a comedown. After much research, Gina had formed the opinion that Elvis artifacts represented the epitome of vulgar taste. Which suited Roger Philo to a T. The decor of his cabin included a great deal of crushed velvet and ghastly plaster lamps; the carpet was orange shag.

But there should have been even more tackiness. Where was the Elvis stuff? Roger had promised today would be the showing. And Otis had agreed to bring his inventory list. So, where were the two men?

They had to be nearby. Someone had placed a stack of LPs on the record player and built the fire. And they couldn't have stepped out for a moment. Roger's cabin was seven miles from nowhere, and the weather forecast predicted heavy snowfall.

She went through the open front room to the kitchen at the rear of the A-frame. On the counter, there were an Elvis whiskey decanter and two freshly rinsed glass tumblers.

She returned to the front window and looked out. The wind swirled flurries of snow. But otherwise the scene was devoid of activity. Nothing but trees and sky and snow. Looking out from this angle, she couldn't even see the road, or her Jeep parked at the bottom of the hill.

"Dammit, Roger. Where are you?" Looking for a clue, she went to the desk that stood against one wall. The surface was clean except for an appointment book and a bulging padded envelope. Her name had been scrawled in the upper right corner beside a doodle of hearts and a notation of the time: four o'clock. Maybe Roger had thought to leave a note. She reached inside and pulled out a banded stack of hundred-dollar bills.

"What's this?" She spilled the contents of the envelope across the desktop. There were twenty bills to a stack. Each band was marked $2,000. And there were twenty of these little packages. Forty thousand dollars in cash. Why?

Over the sound of Elvis crooning, she heard a creak from upstairs. Was someone there? Maybe Roger was up there, hiding for some idiotic reason, waiting to jump out and say, "Boo!"

Her irritation heated to full-fledged anger as she climbed the wrought-iron spiral staircase to a balcony that overlooked the living room. In the large bedroom, the angled walls of the A-frame disturbed her sense of proportion. The black satiny sheets on the king-size bed were askew. Roger's clothing had been carelessly discarded on a chair.

The second bedroom, decorated with floor-to-ceiling closet mirrors and a florid bedspread, looked untouched, as if no one had inhabited it for weeks. There was only one thing out of place: a bronze statuette of Elvis Presley, circa 1957, tossed carelessly on the bed. Including the pedestal, the replica was eighteen inches tall. From her research, she knew the style at a glance. The base value of the piece was three hundred and fifty dollars.

Downstairs, the last notes of "Can't Help Falling in Love" faded and the stereo clicked off. An eerie silence flowed through the cabin like a cold draft.

"I guess," she said with a shiver, "Elvis has left the building."

She leaned across the bedspread and picked up the statuette for a closer look at this product of a sloppy mass-production casting. The dark bronze felt strangely sticky and wet.

"Oh, my God..." The statuette was covered with blood. She set the Elvis on the bedside table. Her hair fell forward, and she pushed it from her face. Glancing up, she saw herself reflected in the closet mirrors. Dark red blood was smeared across her cheekbone.

Something terrible had happened. She needed to get out of here.

But what if someone was downstairs? She stood very still and listened. There was the snap of burning wood in the fireplace. The creak of wind outside. The rap of a tree branch against the house. Gina crept to the doorway, to the balcony that ran the length of the upstairs. From where she stood, she couldn't see anyone in the downstairs, but the kitchen area was hidden. Was someone there? Someone who had used the statuette as a bludgeon? Maybe she should force a window up here and climb out. The house abutted right up to the hillside—she could easily reach the ground.

Through the window, she glimpsed a movement in the gathering darkness outside. A squirrel? A chunk of snow falling from the eaves? Or something else? *Someone* else?

Taking a deep breath, she ran along the balcony and fairly flew down the corkscrew staircase. She slammed out the door, onto the deck. Though the long path and stairs leading up the hill had been shoveled, it was slippery and she had to descend with care. When she grasped the handrail, her hand made a bloody print in the frozen snow. She'd left her gloves in the cabin, and the cold bit into her palms.

When finally she reached her Jeep, she dived into the driver's seat, locked the door and strapped on the seat belt. Gina turned the key in the ignition, and was rewarded with a harsh grinding noise. The engine did not turn over.

"Dammit." She tried it again. And again.

Still the engine did not engage. Was the battery dead? How could it be? She hadn't had a problem while she was driving up here. The Jeep she'd borrowed from her aunt Lydia hadn't given her a bit of trouble during the past two days. Why now?

Gina closed her frozen fingers into a fist and hammered against the steering wheel. Again she tried to start the car. The grinding sounded faint. "Please, please start."

She popped the hood and went around to the front of the Jeep to stare at an assortment of wires and belts, a square battery and a round thing with a winged nut. To Gina, the engine looked like an ominous and exotic sculpture. She'd lived in Manhattan for the past five years, and didn't even own a car.

After jiggling a couple of wires, she slid behind the steering wheel and offered up a prayer to whatever gods reigned over dead batteries.

Her prayers went unanswered. This time there wasn't even a click. The Jeep wasn't going to start. She should call a mechanic, but that meant returning to the cabin to use the telephone. Renewed fear shot through her. She had to go back. What else could she do? Stay in the Jeep and freeze to death?

As she climbed back up the hill, she heard a whimpering sound and halted. Her glance darted across the bleak landscape, where snow had begun to fall in a steady, light drift. She almost cried out, "Who's there?" Then she realized that the small cry had come from her own wheezing throat. If she hadn't been so cold, she would have sat down on the path and sobbed.

But she couldn't. She would not allow herself to be beaten so easily. She fought her way up the stairs, onto the deck and inside. The fire still blazed. The lamp was still lit. Nothing had changed. No one *seemed* to be here. But Gina sensed danger, a presence that lurked beyond her peripheral vision.

She went to the desk and picked up the telephone. It was dead. Not even a dial tone. She was trapped here, stranded. The last cabin she remembered seeing on the drive up here was quite a distance back. Too far to walk.

"Skis," she said.

Roger must have skis up here. Or snowshoes, or something.

Charging through the house and the kitchen, she found a separate room with several parkas hanging from pegs. And skis. Three sets of cross-country skis. And boots in varying sizes.

She ignored the dark sense that someone was watching her, the prickling at the back of her neck. She jammed her feet into ski boots. The fit wasn't perfect, but it would do.

Outside, she fastened the bindings and raced the wooden cross-country skis back and forth in the snow. She'd found heavy gloves and slipped into a warmer parka, but her socks were too thin. She'd dressed for a business meeting, not a ski excursion, and the snowfall was coming heavier by the minute. She'd heard reports of blizzards. The bitter wind blew down the collar of the oversize parka and penetrated her light cashmere sweater.

Digging in her poles, she thrust forward, took a few strides and caught an edge. With a loud cry, she fell. Her beret went flying. The snow crusted on her jeans. And the wind seemed to echo with eerie laughter.

Gina scrambled upright, positioned herself again and tried to find her cross-country rhythm. Years ago, her parents had always vacationed in Aspen, and she'd been a better downhill skier than Dean or Alex, who lived here year-round. But that was ancient history. And her skill was in Alpine-style skiing, going fast down a long slope, reacting by instinct. She'd never been great at the Nordic style of cross-country. With uncoordinated strides, she crossed a wide clearing, seeking higher ground and a vantage point. She expended a huge amount of effort to progress to a small promontory.

On a clear day, she might have seen for miles, but now her view was limited by darkness and a thick curtain of snow. Beyond the sheltering trees, everything was white. Following a path through more trees, she came onto another wide, clear area. Halfway across, enveloped in blinding snow, she fell again. Damn! She lay there, immobile and hopeless. She'd never find help in this blizzard. She could barely see the trees on the other side of the clearing. Her lungs heaved. Behind her was Roger's cabin, with that warm fire blazing within. She was so cold. Freezing cold. It might be better to return to the cabin, to face the blood and danger. Out here, she'd surely die of hypothermia.

Her wet hair was plastered against her forehead and cheeks. Her toes were already numb. She couldn't give up, had to keep moving, had to keep the blood circulating. She forced herself up and forward. This snowfield was her last chance. She'd ski across and through one more thicket of trees. On the other side, she might see something. The lights of another cabin. The road. Headlights. Something.

"Hey!"

The shout came from behind her, and Gina turned, startled. A man, dressed in black, came through the trees, taking the small incline in a few powerful strides.

Instinct told her to escape. Run from the stranger. Never talk to strangers. With a frantic effort, Gina propelled herself forward. Her arms and legs pumped furiously. Why wasn't she going faster? This was a nightmare, in which she was moving as fast as she could and not getting anywhere. She didn't see the icy patch until her skis skidded and she fell again. Her boots slipped their bindings.

He stood uphill, at the edge of the trees, where there was some slight shelter. His voice was calm. "Are you all right?"

She was so cold, so damned cold. But she hadn't given up, not yet. Sitting up, she aimed her ski pole at the center of his chest. "Who are you?"

"I'm with the Aspen Ski Patrol and Rescue Unit." He offered what might have been an encouraging smile, if half his face hadn't been covered with goggles. "Need a hand?"

She regarded him suspiciously. "If you're with the ski patrol, why aren't you wearing their parka?"

"Didn't bother." He shrugged. "I got a call from the rescue dispatcher that some idiots were out here trying to ski, and I was heading across the hill to Roger's. I saw you cross the clearing near the house."

"You know Roger?"

"I'm his neighbor. My cabin is about a mile and a half uphill and to the west."

He slipped his goggles up on his head. His intense blue eyes flashed, and she recognized the man from the tavern, the man who had danced with her. Unfortunately, he didn't look friendly right now, and she wasn't sure she could trust him. "Why were you going to Roger's place?"

"I was looking for someone dumb enough to take off on a cross-country ski trip with a blizzard coming in. Roger has more than his share of idiots for houseguests at this little hideaway cabin."

"I'm not a houseguest."

"Whatever you say, Gina."

"How do you know my name?"

"Last night I asked Dean. He said you were his cousin Gina Robinson from New York City."

"Who are you?" she demanded.

"The name's Conner. Conner Hobarth."

Gina took a closer look at the tanned face behind the goggles. Conner Hobarth? The famous *Hound Dog Hobarth?* She'd seen his face in ski magazines, heard his voice in television interviews. Conner was a local legend, almost as renowned as Billy Kidd and Jean-Claude Killy. Ten years ago, Conner "Hound Dog" Hobarth had been on the Olympic downhill ski team, and he'd been nicknamed for the Elvis-like "Hound Dog" way he swiveled his hips when he went through the slalom gates.

She was safe. This man would help her. She dropped the ski pole onto the snow. "I'm glad to meet you, Hound Dog."

"I prefer Conner."

Relief made her giddy, and she said teasingly, "But that doesn't do justice to your Elvis swivel."

Inadvertently she glanced down at his hips. He was wearing tight-fitting ski pants that outlined his muscular thighs. His legs looked incredibly powerful, as if he were one of those cartoon superheroes who could leap over tall buildings in a single bound and carry her away.

Carry her away? Where had that thought come from? She was a mess! Sprawled in the snow, wearing an oversize parka and no hat. Her auburn hair, usually her best feature, must look as stylish as a soggy mop. No male in his right mind would dream of sweeping her off her feet.

"Okay, Gina. Let's get going."

He knelt beside her and worked to fit her boots back into their bindings. Instead of helping, she lay back in the snow and allowed the wet flakes to fall on her face. Like falling lace, the snowflakes caught in her eyelashes, touched her lips and froze the tip of her nose. She was now so cold that she could hardly feel the chill. She was also feeling pretty light-headed.

At her feet, Conner gave up what he was doing. "You screwed up the bindings, Gina."

"Did not." She struggled to push herself to a sitting position. "These skis are ancient. They were probably defective."

He glared across the snowfield. His blue eyes narrowed. "There's no way you can walk. As soon as we get away from the natural snowpack by the trees, you'll sink up to your hips in powder."

"I'll make it." But when Conner pulled her to her feet, her body felt as limp as a string of cooked linguine. She was glad for his support as he held her upper arms, keeping her upright. "Where are we going?"

"Back to Roger's."

"No."

He felt her arms tense beneath his hands. Her small hands in overlarge gloves shoved at his chest. Her brown eyes showed a flicker of fear, and her voice was weak as she repeated, "No. I won't go back there."

"You won't make it to my cabin, Gina. You're too cold. This is a blizzard. We have to go to the nearest place where you can get warm. That's Roger's."

"I can't. It's too dangerous. I have to tell you what happened. . . ." Her knees buckled, then straightened.

He'd seen enough people in the first stages of hypothermia to recognize the euphoria and incoherence that overcame the sensation of cold. If left on her own, Gina would stand in the snow until she froze into a delicate marble statue. He needed to get her warmed up. "Come on, Gina, let's go. I won't let Roger hurt you."

"Not Roger." Her breathing was ragged. "It's Elvis."

Now she was making no sense at all. Might be hysterical. Might be in shock. He wasn't going to try to reason with her. Though she was putting up a good front, she was exhausted and weak. He picked up his ski poles and fastened them across his back, using the belt from his parka.

"What are you doing?" she demanded.

"This." He scooped her up into his arms. Beneath the bulky parka, her body was lithe. She fought him for only a moment before her strength failed. "Stay still," he said. "You'll be all right."

"Okay." Gina had to trust him. There was no other choice. She couldn't possibly make any sort of trek through the snow. She was too cold and wet.

She closed her eyes and snuggled against him, drawing warmth from him as he carried her. She listened to his heavy breathing as he plowed through the thick snow back to Roger's cabin. She heard the pounding of his powerful heart. A muscle, she thought. Conner's heartbeat was strong and hard, like everything about him. He must be in excellent physical condition to carry her. She wouldn't have thought he could keep his balance. But Conner was an incredible skier, an Olympic skier.

Gina opened her eyes and saw only white. Her body jostled in Conner's arms, and her bones rattled against each other, as if she were a marionette whose strings had been cut.

They were back at the cabin. He set her down on her feet, propped her back against the cedar wall so that she wouldn't collapse when he opened the door. Inside the cloakroom she was aware of the heat. Gratefully she inhaled the warmed air.

"Roger!" Conner shouted as he pulled Gina into the kitchen and sat her down at the table. "Hey, Rog!"

"Not here," Gina mumbled. "He's not here."

"Where is he?" Suddenly alarmed, he leaned close to her. He spoke slowly, as if to a child. "Is Roger outside?"

"Don't know."

"Did Roger go out skiing with you?"

She stared blankly, confused by the anger in his voice.

"My God, Gina, tell me. If he's out there in a blizzard, I've got to find him before it's too late."

"He wasn't here when I arrived." She'd revived enough to respond. "I searched the whole—"

"What the hell possessed you to go skiing?" He unzipped the front of her parka and roughly pushed the material aside. "Look at you! You're wearing a lightweight sweater and jeans. No hat."

"When I came here, I didn't intend to ski."

"Are you even aware that there's extreme avalanche danger?"

"Of course I am. They've been saying that all week on the radio."

"But you never thought it would happen to you," he said. That was the typical flatlander attitude. They swarmed the mountains every weekend, setting out for a ski or a climb or a hike, thinking the Rockies were their own private Disneyland. When the reckless fools got into trouble, the rescue teams came out, risking life and limb to find them.

"Nobody believes they'll be caught," he said. "But it happens, and when the blizzard does come, you don't have time for regrets."

She spoke through chattering teeth. "If it's so dangerous, why were you outdoors?"

"Because somebody's got to watch out for people like you."

"People like me?"

"That's right, Gina. Irresponsible people who take chances."

"I'm not irresponsible." Her backbone stiffened. When she stretched out her neck and shook herself, her red hair stuck out in all directions. She looked like a furious banty rooster.

He remembered that in the tavern Roger had called her a spunky gal and that was a fair description. Spunky. It wasn't a word that Conner used, but it suited Gina.

"Listen, Conner. We have to get out of here."

"Not a chance." He went down on his knees, unsnapped her boots and pulled them off. She was going to survive. No question about that. If she'd actually been hypothermic, it was fading fast. Still, he wanted to warm her up as soon as possible. Her feet felt like frozen little stubs under her thin socks. He peeled away the material.

"Ow," she complained. "Did you have to do that?"

"We could amputate."

"Oh, my gosh, I don't have frostbite, do I?"

"No, you're going to be fine." He knew the drill. Cover her up with blankets, raise the core temperature nearest her heart, then worry about the extremities. "First, you need to get out of these wet clothes."

He reached for the waistband of her jeans and she slapped his hand away.

"Stop it!" she said. "Would you please listen to me? We've got to get out of here. Right away."

"Why? What's wrong?"

She thought of the statuette. "There was blood. A lot of blood. If you don't believe me, we can go upstairs and I'll show you."

"Okay, fine." He braced his arm around her waist and pulled her upright. "After we go upstairs and I check for monsters under the bed, you get out of the wet clothes. Okay?"

"This isn't a joke!" She wrenched herself away from him but her feet felt numb and her legs weren't working properly. She stumbled across the kitchen and caught herself on the counter. Clumsily the palm of her hand skidded across the tile and she knocked the tumblers beside the Elvis decanter into the sink. One of them shattered. The other cracked.

Though the destruction of two cheap glasses was not a tragic loss, her eyes filled with sudden, spontaneous tears. Angrily she dashed them away. Crying would affirm Conner's opinion that she was a helpless dope. Bracing herself against the kitchen counter, she turned and faced him.

"I came here for a business meeting with Roger and his ex-partner, Wendell Otis. But when I arrived, nobody was here. There was a fire going and a lamp lit. Music came from that jukebox stereo. Elvis Presley singing 'Blue Hawaii.'"

"Elvis?"

"When I went to the desk, I found an envelope with my name on it, and a lot of cash. Forty thousand dollars. I got scared. I tried the phone." She looked into his eyes, underlining her words. "But it was dead."

"That happens a lot up here," he told her. "The phone lines are aboveground, and they get knocked down. If you were so nervous, Gina, why didn't you leave?"

"That's what I was trying to do." Her voice raised, near to a shout. "That's why I was skiing."

"How'd you get up here? Didn't you drive?"

"Of course, I did. I ran down the path to my Jeep. But it wouldn't start."

Again he nodded, calm and unperturbed. "Dead battery."

"I haven't had any problems with it. Not until now."

"Cars can be unpredictable in mountain weather. It's probably twenty below zero right now, colder with the wind chill." He strolled toward the front room. "Well, come on. Take me upstairs, Gina, and show me what scared you."

"I'd feel better if we were armed."

"But you thought the house was empty."

"I didn't see anyone, but I had a sense... I felt like somebody was watching me." A shiver crawled up and down her spine. "What if they're still here?"

"Well, we'd better find out, because neither of us is going anywhere tonight. We're stuck in this cabin, like it or not." He started toward the staircase. "Come on, Gina. Let's go."

"Don't patronize me, Conner. I've lived in New York City for years and I know how to take care of myself."

"Okay, city girl, show me how tough you are."

When she strode across the room, Gina tried to move with confidence, to show him she wasn't an irresponsible ditz who was scared of her own shadow. But her body ached with the sensation of physical warmth returning. When she reached the second bedroom, she barely had the strength to point at the bronze Elvis standing beside the bed. "It's covered with blood."

"I don't see any blood."

"I didn't notice it, either." She shuddered. "Until I picked it up."

Conner nodded. On the off chance that she actually had something to be scared of, he didn't touch the statuette. He'd worked with the local sheriff often enough to know that this might be evidence and they should leave it alone. "This is what you meant when you said you were scared by Elvis."

Gina had recovered enough to regain her wits. Archly she said, "Elvis terrifies me. I can imagine his tackiness destroying the world."

"Not a fan, huh?" He turned on the bedside light by the statuette and studied it closely. There was no blood. "Gina, this little statue is completely clean."

"That's impossible." She'd stood right here, seen herself in the mirror with blood on her face. Outside, she'd left a bloody handprint in the snow. But when she inspected it beneath the light of a bedside lamp, the statue appeared to be clean. That could only mean one thing. "Somebody was here. Somebody wiped this statue."

"Or maybe you accidentally wiped off all the blood when you touched it before."

"No, there was too much. He came back."

"He? Did you see a man?"

"Conner, he might still be here." Again, she sensed the danger. Her gaze flew to the closed closet doors. He could be hiding there. Or under the bed. Or behind a door.

"I don't think so," Conner said. "But you're not going to relax until I make a search, right? Secure the perimeter?"

He was nonchalant, casually opening doors and peering in dark corners of the upstairs. Gina followed, cautiously testing the locks on all the windows.

Downstairs, after they'd checked the closets, he turned to her. "Satisfied? There's nobody here."

"But there was."

"You know, Gina, you said this wasn't a joke. But it might have been. Has it occurred to you that Roger might be playing a trick on you?"

"Why? It doesn't make any sense."

"Roger can be pretty weird. He has a strange sense of humor."

Not that weird, Gina thought. But last night Roger had promised a surprise. Maybe this was his way of repaying her for the slap that knocked him down. "But why would he stay in hiding? Why wouldn't he come out and gloat about how he'd tricked me?"

"Don't know. Ready to change clothes now?"

"I guess so."

Conner went to the jukebox stereo, lifted the lid and turned it on. "How about a little Elvis to lighten the mood?"

"Not that record," she said. "The one on top is 'Blue Hawaii,' and I don't feel like ukeleles."

But he'd already lowered the needle.

She heard the intro for a different record. The 1968 Elvis comeback special. *Someone had been here. They'd changed the records.* The first line Elvis sang was "You looking for trouble?"

Chapter Two

The switched order of the records on the jukebox stereo confirmed her worst fears. Someone had been here, and he wanted Gina to know it. That was why he'd changed the music. He wanted her to know he'd been watching.

But why would someone go to all this trouble to frighten her? It didn't make sense. She'd only been in Aspen for two days, not long enough to make enemies. Except for last night, when she'd fought with Roger. This bizarre scenario had to be his doing. But where on earth was he now?

"Gina? Are you all right?"

The sound of Conner's voice calmed her. If she'd been alone, Gina would have been screaming; if not with fear, with the sheer frustration of not knowing what was happening. But Conner made her feel safer, more secure. They had thoroughly searched every inch of the small cabin. Whoever had been here was gone now.

But could he come back? She turned toward Conner. "Nobody could travel the roads through this blizzard, right?"

"Not on foot. Not for any distance."

"So, the person who was here before is gone now, and he won't come back. Right?"

"Right," he said firmly. "You were kind of hard on old Roger last night. This is probably just his idea of a practical joke."

"But what's the punch line?" She frowned. "There really was blood on that statue. What if somebody came in here and bludgeoned Roger?"

"It's more likely that Roger clubbed somebody else."

She glanced up sharply.

"Sorry, Gina," Conner said. "I didn't mean to imply that your uncle killed somebody."

"Stepuncle."

"But I ought to tell you that your *stepuncle* and I aren't friendly neighbors."

Not a surprise. She would have been amazed if anyone was terribly fond of big, blustery, obnoxious Roger Philo.

"How are you feeling now?" Conner inquired. "You're not scared anymore, are you?"

"No." Especially not when she noticed the beginning of a smile in his eyes. Gorgeous eyes, she thought, sapphire blue and ringed with dark lashes that would have been pretty if his face hadn't been so rugged.

His thick brown hair was trimmed short, almost as short as a military cut. Efficient, she thought. This was a man who didn't bother with making himself handsome, who probably only looked in the mirror to shave. His ski pants, and the turtleneck he wore under his sweater and parka, were a simple black, nothing with a designer label.

Looking at him soothed her. The broad angle of his shoulders fascinated her. He stood straight as a ramrod. The muscles in his legs bulged against the snug black pants. Nobody was going to mess with this tall, strong Olympic hero.

With a gentleness that contrasted with his strong appearance, he touched her arm and guided her to the sofa in front of the fireplace. "You still need to get out of those wet clothes. But just sit here and relax for a minute."

The sofa was more comfortable than it looked. Gina frowned at the long sofa, with its ornate curlicue arms in ebony that matched the coffee table. The coffee table, she remembered. There had been a pair of thick gloves lying upon it when she first came inside. The gloves were gone. Another indication that someone had returned to the cabin. He'd wiped the blood off the statue, changed the records and picked up the gloves.

There was a sinister feeling to these clues, but Gina pushed aside her dark suspicions. Right now, she was safe. They'd searched everywhere. The doors and windows were bolted. Maybe tomorrow morning, if the blizzard passed, Roger would show up and have his big laugh at her expense.

She trailed her fingers across the bloodred velvet of the sofa. "Do you believe this furniture? And the orange shag carpet? Roger must have used the same decorator who did Graceland."

"Elvis did his own decorating," Conner informed her. "And it was the seventies, remember? Bell-bottoms and lava lamps and psychedelic paisley. Not exactly an understated era. Graceland was right in step."

"You sound as if you've been there."

"I have."

"So you were called Hound Dog because—"

"Because I like the King. Always have." Effortlessly he sang along with the jukebox stereo to the tune of "Lawdy Miss Clawdy," ending the phrase "You sure look good to me" with the famous Elvis sneer.

Gina raised an eyebrow. "Is this where I applaud?"

"This is where I get you a drink."

"If this was an Elvis movie," she said, "we would almost kiss, but twenty-seven bad guys would charge through the door and you would defeat them with a couple of swift karate moves."

"Hey, baby—" he called out the rough Elvis impersonation from the kitchen "—don't knock the King."

"I wouldn't dream of it. All those movies made money, you know. Elvis was a top box office draw in the 1960s."

"With good reason," he said. "Those were great flicks."

"Sure, Conner. Academy Award material."

Gina settled back with a sigh, stretching her bare toes toward the fireplace. She was tired, but not exhausted. Considering the fact that she'd nearly frozen to death in a blizzard, she was feeling pretty good, and she expected to improve when Conner placed a tumbler of amber liquid in her hand. "I really hope this isn't from that Elvis decanter on the counter. As cute as those bottles were, the stuff inside was dreadful."

"Agreed." He pulled aside the fire screen and fed the flickering blaze with chunks of pine from the hopper beside the fireplace. "Roger's got a fully stocked bar behind the counter. That's peach brandy."

"Of course, Uncle Roger would be well supplied with booze." She sipped and shuddered. Gina wasn't much of a drinker, and the brandy burned all the way down her throat.

He finished stoking up the fire. "We're going to need more logs if we want to keep the fire going all night. Do you know where Roger keeps his wood?"

"This is the first time I've been here."

Conner sat beside her. Not too close, she noticed. Gina had been single long enough to recognize every step, glide and dip in the mating dance... not that this was a date.

He sipped his own brandy. "So, why's a nice girl like you hanging around in Aspen with Roger Philo?"

"You really dislike Roger, don't you?"

"Let's just say that you don't seem like his type."

"Does Lydia?"

Nobody in Gina's family could understand why Lydia had married a slob like Roger Philo in the first place. And why had she stayed married to him for nearly sixteen years? Lydia was much too classy for a creep like Roger, who drank too much, talked too loud and asserted his masculinity by slobbering over anything in a skirt. Gina couldn't think of a single reason why Lydia would endure her husband's crass flirting. Though Roger Philo was richer than Midas, there was plenty of family money that Lydia could count on, not to mention the income from her own successful Aspen-based real estate brokerage. Nor was Lydia staying with Roger for the sake of her children from her first marriage, because Alex and Dean were twenty-eight and twenty-three years old. They were fully grown adults. And, as far as Gina could tell, the boys had never liked Roger that much in the first place.

She shook her head. "Must be some kind of beauty-and-the-beast thing with Roger and Lydia."

"How so?"

"Do you know my aunt?"

He nodded. "She sells real estate."

"I always admired her," Gina said. "My family used to come out here and ski every winter, and Lydia always seemed so cool, with her smooth blond hair and perfect clothes. She wanted to be an actress."

"She's still involved in that stuff. Film festivals."

"And Lydia was one of the only people in my family who advised me to pursue a career in art."

"You're an artist?"

"Not hardly. But I majored in art history." She took another dose of the medicinal brandy and wrinkled her nose at the taste. "I work for an auction house in Manhattan, doing appraisals of artworks and antiques. I help put together the sale brochures and set up the displays."

"You like your work," he said.

"I love my career. The reason I'm out here in Aspen is because Berryhill's, the auction house, is putting together a rock-and-roll-theme sale. Nobody could get hold of good Elvis memorabilia. Then, I remembered Roger's collection." She shrugged. "He's been a major pain in the rear to work with. But if I can go back to New York with some classic Presleyana, it'll all be worth it."

"Even the bloody statuette?"

"As long as he didn't use it to kill somebody." She gave a nervous laugh. "Actually, that might increase the value. You know, like auctioning off Lizzie Borden's ax."

"Aren't you the cold-hearted career woman."

"Maybe it runs in the family. Maybe I'm like Lydia." She wouldn't mind that comparison at all. Lydia was an admirable woman, except for her taste in husbands. "What do you think about Roger and Lydia? You must know the family pretty well. Are they happy?"

"Don't know," he said.

"Come on, Conner. You're Roger's neighbor."

"It's like this," he drawled. "Aspen is a small town, and if you're interested, you can gossip all day. I'm not interested."

"Small town, huh?" She stood. "With all the celebrities who live here?"

"I know it sounds corny, but they're just people."

Gina found that bit of homespun wisdom hard to believe. These incredibly beautiful mountains drew incredibly beautiful people. And Gina was impressed by celebrities. Not only the film stars who lived here, but the artists and writers and musicians, too. Yesterday, when she was prowling an art gallery and waiting for Roger, she'd sighted the most famous ballet dancer in the world. She'd almost swooned.

Stiffly she dragged herself off the sofa. "I'm going to clean up. Never can tell when one of those 'just folks' might decide to drop in."

In the upstairs bathroom, she peeled off her cold, clammy clothing and stepped into a hot shower. Though she told herself that she was only getting herself cleaned up before going to sleep, Gina knew herself well enough to recognize her other motivations. She wanted Conner to see her looking more like herself and less like a drowned rat. After all, he was a celebrity of sorts, too. When she was sixteen and he was skiing in the Olympics, Gina had cherished a small crush on him. She remembered ogling his photograph in the newspaper, feeling devastated when he came in ninth in his event.

In the guest room closet, she found a navy blue velour robe that fit fairly well and a pair of soft slippers that were close to her size.

When she came down the staircase, Conner nodded with approval, and she decided that cleaning herself up had been a good idea, indeed.

He pointed to the coffee table. "I found some food and made sandwiches. Hope you're not vegetarian."

"I eat meat."

"Dig in, city girl."

Gina didn't realize she was hungry until she took the first bite. It was ham and cheese and heavenly. She swallowed and said, "I'm really not a city girl, you know. I was brought up in the suburbs of Boston."

"But I'll bet you fit in just fine in Manhattan."

"So you've got me figured out, have you? What am I like?"

"You like art," he said, "so you're probably a snob."

"Wrong!" She was insulted. "Maybe I was like that when I first graduated. But not anymore. I like selling art. Selling. That's fun. I love to watch the bidding."

"Had any big sales at Berryhill's?"

"Lots of them. The most exciting one I remember was a small Monet. It went for $968,550, and the auction was unbelievable. One of the bidders was a collector herself. And the other guy was bidding for somebody else. When they got past five hundred thousand, he kept checking on a cellular phone."

"Who won?"

"The lady. And she hardly even batted an eye. Just a tiny smile, and she sat and watched the rest of the auction. I was more excited than she was." She nibbled at the sandwich. "Anyway, I'm not the snob you think I am. So, Conner, what else do you think I am?"

"Impetuous."

"Wrong again. I'm very well organized, and I seldom make decisions on the spur of the moment."

"You have a temper."

"Not really."

This time, he knew she was lying. "Not only have you got a hair-trigger temper, but you back it up with a mean right hook."

"What's that supposed to mean?"

"Last night in the tavern, you were a sight to behold." She'd been amazing. All that red hair flying, and her eyes flashing with dark fire. Right now she was bundled up in a robe, but he had a vivid memory of her slim waist, her long legs and the sexy roundness of her buttocks that poor old Roger had dared to grope at. "If I remember correctly, you told Roger you never wanted to see him again, and you could just kill him."

She groaned. "Close enough."

"So, why did you come to his cabin?"

"I told you, Conner. I want that Presley collection. We were supposed to do an inventory today. And, as a bonus, I'd get a peek at the computer list of Wendell Otis's collection."

They finished their sandwiches and tidied up the kitchen and Conner flipped the stack of Elvis records. Then, nourished and content, they were back on the sofa again. "I wish I had more time for vacation here. I used to like Aspen a lot."

"What part of Aspen?"

"The skiing, of course. But I've got to admit that it's fun to catch glimpses of famous people."

"You're not one of those?" He groaned. "An Aspen groupie?"

"I don't pester for autographs. But I do stand and stare." She turned toward him. "Speaking of celebrities, I had a crush on you when I was a teenager. You were the famous skier in town."

"That's me, all right." He left the sofa and adjusted the logs in the fireplace with a poker. "Should I get more wood or let it die down?"

"Didn't you like being famous?"

"I didn't like promoting. Your uncle represented me, and I did exactly three commercials for ski equipment. I hated it." He stood before her, looking down, and the blue of his eyes sparkled with breathtaking warmth. "I like being a small-town boy. Doing my job. Skiing in the winter. Hiking in the summer."

"Occasionally saving a life here and there," she added.

"No big deal."

When he sat back down, he was closer to her than before. His muscular thigh stretched out beside hers. He placed his arm on the back of the red velvet sofa, and Gina found herself leaning into his embrace. Her cheek snuggled into the crook of his arm. Their nearness should have been comforting and calm, but an excitement began to build within her.

"Okay, Conner, here's the million-dollar question—if I'm an impetuous snob groupie with a bad temper, why did you ask me to dance?"

"Because you're beautiful. I wanted to touch you."

"That's terribly shallow and sexist," she said teasingly.

"Why? Because I wasn't attracted to your mind? I didn't know you then, hadn't talked to you."

"And now?"

"You're even more beautiful."

On the jukebox record player, Elvis sang "Love Me Tender," and his voice described her mood exactly. Her head tilted back. Slowly she gazed up through her eyelashes and studied the planes of his face. He was the handsomest man she'd ever seen. Every character line, every shading, even the dark stubble on his chin, suited her idea of the perfect male.

Her lips parted. She knew he was about to kiss her, and the instant of waiting was sweet. When his mouth slanted across hers and his grasp tightened, all her senses came to life, overwhelming her with an unquenchable, uncontrollable desire.

She pressed against him, craving more, wanting to make this kiss last into the next century. They were alone here in the cabin, stranded all night. The blaze in the fireplace crackled. Elvis sang. Outside, the night was a cold, hard blizzard. Within...

He broke away from her. The expression in his eyes asked a silent question.

"No," she said, albeit reluctantly.

When he shifted his weight and moved slightly away from her, Gina longed to change her answer. She wanted to make love with Conner all night and into the morning. But she knew better. She wasn't accustomed to even kissing on the first date . . . not that this was a date.

She exhaled and leaned back against the sofa. Her eyes stared up at the rafters and the balcony. Her instincts urged her to throw caution to the four winds, to take advantage of this marvelous romantic moment. They'd been thrown together by the forces of nature. He'd saved her life.

But Conner would be gone in the morning, and she'd be left with emptiness and hurt.

"City girl, you're one hell of a good kisser."

He pushed himself off the sofa, stretched, yawned, and glanced down over his shoulder. On the jukebox, Elvis was singing "Don't Be Cruel." Conner extended his hand to help her to her feet, and Gina caught hold.

With slight exertion on his part, he pulled her to her feet and into his arms. His embrace was strong and commanding as he pulled her body against him and claimed her lips with a hard kiss that left her dazzled.

He scooped her off her feet, like Rhett preparing to carry Scarlett up the sweeping staircase of a southern mansion. But they were in a small cabin in the rockies. Conner eyed the narrow spiral staircase leading to the second floor and ruefully set her back down. "No way," he said.

"None." Then she asked, "Which bedroom do you prefer?"

"Which one has the biggest bed?"

"That would be the master bedroom." She thought of the rumpled black sheets and imagined Roger's imprint upon them. "You can have that one."

He looked doubtfully at her. "That means you sleep with the statuette. Will that bother you?"

"Not if I can put it in a drawer. But I guess I shouldn't do that. I mean, if it's some kind of evidence or something, and the police need fingerprints."

"Do whatever makes you comfortable," he advised.

Gina was stubborn enough to treat the statuette as evidence, even if she was pretty much convinced that this was all some stupid, elaborate joke on Roger's part.

"You know, Gina, we could both sleep in—"

"Goodnight, Conner." She headed up the spiral staircase.

DESPITE HER UNEASINESS about the day's events, Gina slept peacefully and didn't waken until the sun had risen high in the cloudless blue sky.

The first sight that caught her eye in the morning was the statuette of Elvis. In the morning light, the bronze shone innocently, a pale reflection of last night's terror. Had she really been so frightened of this inanimate object?

The features were bland, totally lacking in the dangerous black-leather sensuality she'd come to associate with Elvis. After watching innumerable videotapes of his performances and movies so that she could study the jewelry and paraphernalia associated with his films, Gina had to concede that, although Elvis's taste in dress was not to her liking, he'd been sexy enough to make her toes curl.

And so was Conner.

Hound Dog Hobarth, with the Elvis hips. He'd saved her life. He'd kissed her like . . . Well, it had been a long time since Gina had been so excited about a kiss.

When she threw off the covers and swung her legs out of the bed, her muscles ached. She discovered an assortment of bruises on her legs and arms. But it was nothing she couldn't live with. Wrapped in the velour robe, she went downstairs and found Conner in the kitchen.

He stuck a mug of coffee in her hand. "Are you a good cook, city girl?"

"No." She shook her head. "But I have great taste."

He wore a terry-cloth robe. The front gaped open enough for her to see the dark hair on his chest, and she sighed. Conner looked wonderful in the morning.

"I'll cook," he announced. "That means we're having scrambled eggs and toast."

"What can I do?"

He nodded toward the front room. "This place is heated, but a fire would be nice. We burned all the wood last night."

"Got it," she said. "I should go fell a tree while you're back here cooking. A little mountain role reversal."

His eyes rested lazily on her face, and the warmth in his expression told her that he was thinking about last night, too. Was it possible that his excitement matched her own? That he was wondering, as she was, what it would be like to make love? Gina cleared her throat. "Roger must have a woodbox around here somewhere. I'll go see what I can find."

When Gina started toward the back door, Conner called after her, "You might want to get dressed first."

"I'll just take a look around."

She needed the cold, needed to douse the flame that was drawing her closer to Conner.

In the cloakroom, Gina stuck her feet into the leather boots that she'd discarded here when she was trying her desperate escape on cross-country skis.

When she pushed open the door, Gina stood for a moment and absorbed the beauty of a winter morning. The morning sun glittered on mounds of new-fallen snow. The tree branches, iced with white, looked like a fairy world. The air was crisp and clean. There were never mornings like this in Manhattan. Mornings filled with the pristine silence of nature's renewal.

She glanced around near the door and spied nothing that might be a box for firewood.

Almost covered by the high drifts, she saw a handrail and a short path beside the house. Though she picked her way carefully, her boots sank deep, and the powdery new snow spilled over the edge and tingled against her skin.

Rounding the cabin's corner, she found a sheltered space beneath the overhang of the deck. Roger obviously used this area for storage. There were bikes and a picnic table. And a large wooden box that stood four feet high at the rear and slanted down to a height she could reach into.

This must be where Roger kept firewood, she thought, because there was a path cleared through the other junk that led to the box. She'd gather an armload, haul it inside and start up a blaze to show Conner that she wasn't totally a city girl. There were a lot of things she remembered from her family vacations in Aspen and from basic Girl Scout training. Gina could rough it.

She unfastened the latch and lifted the lid.

The first thing she saw was the blood. His chest had been torn open, and the blood had darkened to an ugly brown. It stained the white jumpsuit he was wearing, an Elvis style jumpsuit with gold studs in the design of a sunburst. She stared down at her uncle Roger.

And she screamed.

Chapter Three

He was dead.

His closed eyelids were sunken deep in the sockets. The flesh, gray and slack, hung from Roger's cheekbones, but his mouth gaped open, frozen in an ironic eternal sneer. His legs and arms were tucked up to fit his large body into the woodbox. One of his hands rested beside his face. The fingers curled as if caught in midwave, and Gina imagined he would grab at her, reach out and pull her into a dark nightmare from which she'd never escape.

She staggered backward. Her hands gripped the edge of a redwood picnic table, and she leaned against it, brushing aside a layer of snow. Ice. Snow. She should have been cold, should have shivered as the chill penetrated her skin. Instead, she felt numb.

She thought she'd stopped screaming, but she wasn't sure. Everything was dead silent.

Conner was beside her. He held her shoulders. His eyes stared into hers, and she saw his lips moving. He must be talking, but she heard nothing but a roaring in her ears. It was white noise, louder than a pounding surf, a tidal wave, an avalanche. In mute silence, she nodded toward the woodbox and watched as he peered inside.

His shoulders stiffened beneath the bathrobe. Slowly, almost reverently, he closed the wooden lid and turned toward her. Beneath his tan, he was pale. "Come on, Gina. Let's go inside."

She heard his words echoing as if he were speaking from the bottom of a well, and she responded. "He's dead."

"Roger's dead. There's nothing we can do for him."

Conner slipped his arm around her, supporting her, and she stumbled along beside him on the narrow path beside the cabin wall. Her knees were weak and she felt dizzy. Gina stopped to draw a breath, squinted her eyes shut and then opened them again. Beyond the morning shadows, the sunlight glittered on fresh, unmarked snow. The tree limbs sagged beneath the burden of last night's blizzard.

Yesterday she'd thought the clues were a joke. She'd mentally cursed her stepuncle for playing a practical joke on her. Her last thoughts of Roger had been that he was a jerk, unworthy of her aunt Lydia, difficult to deal with.

Last night, she and Conner had snuggled on the garish sofa, listening to Elvis and dissecting Roger's character. A sense of guilt mingled with her shock at finding his body. She'd been cruel to Roger. *Don't Be Cruel.*

Even now, she could not think of a kind word for Roger Philo. Her memories of his offensive personality faded before the one final image of his death. Horrible!

"Hurry up," Conner said. "I'm freezing."

Gina stumbled into the kitchen, pulled off her boots and rubbed at her stiff red toes. *Roger was dead.* There was nothing they could do about it.

Conner poured a cup of coffee for her and one for himself. He sat at the kitchen table beside her. His attitude combined a mixture of calm and concern. This seemed so much easier for him, and she remembered that he worked on the mountain rescue team. He was experienced in dealing with sudden, violent tragedy.

She added milk to her coffee and watched the color turn from black to taupe.

"I'm sorry about your uncle."

"So am I," she said, with some surprise.

Though she hadn't been close to Roger, hadn't even liked the man, she felt a dreadful sadness. This would be difficult for her aunt Lydia, and for Roger's stepsons. As soon as possible, Gina needed to talk with them, to offer her support. That was the proper and responsible thing to do. The family thing to do. "I've got to tell Lydia."

"Right after we notify the sheriff."

"The sheriff? Why?"

"Roger was murdered."

"Yes, of course." It was obvious. He'd been murdered. But the very idea seemed impossible. Had anyone in Gina's large extended family ever been murdered before? Probably not. Most of her relatives were professionals who lived safe, sane lives in suburban enclaves. Most of them considered Gina to be incredibly eccentric because she lived and worked in New York City.

Murder? Her mind raced. How would Roger's murder affect his collection of memorabilia? Who would inherit? What would she have to go through to get her hands on the items for auction? Even as these questions flooded her mind, Gina condemned herself as a heartless career woman. Her stepuncle had been killed, and she was counting his assets. It was not a pretty picture.

Conner took a gulp of his coffee and stood up. "I'll get dressed, head over to my place and make the necessary phone calls."

"I'm coming with you."

"I'll make better time by myself," he said. "It's cross-country and uphill."

"Don't leave me here." She remembered Roger's face, the horrible wound in his chest, and the hand that had seemed to be reaching for her. She couldn't bear to stay in his cabin. She balled her hands into tight fists to keep them from trembling. "I'm coming with you."

He rested one hand on her shoulder and gazed deeply into her eyes. "Take it easy, city girl. I'm not going to make you do anything you don't want to do."

"Then you won't leave me here with . . ."

"You're coming with me. We'll take it slow and easy." He pulled her into his arms and patted her shoulders. "God, Gina, I'm so damn sorry. Last night you were scared, and I didn't believe you."

"You don't think we could have saved him, do you? If we'd found him earlier . . ."

"I don't know when he was murdered."

"It had to be before I got here." If she'd arrived earlier, she might have surprised the murderer. She might be dead, too. "That's why there was blood on the statuette."

"But he had a chest wound. I'd say he was shot."

"Oh, my God, Conner." Renewed fear rose up inside her. "Do you think he was killed last night, while we were here? Could we have stopped it from happening?"

"We'll never know. We can't blame ourselves, though." He stroked her hair, and his touch was reassuring. "Every time I find someone up here, every time I confront sudden death, I wonder if I could have prevented it. If I'd been more quick, more alert, would the victim still be alive?"

That was exactly how she felt.

"It's guilt," he said, "because we're alive, and he's dead. Roger is dead. I don't know the right way to feel about it, Gina. But it's better to feel something."

"I'm confused."

"I know."

"Maybe I ought to be crying."

"You can't force it, city girl. Just relax."

She leaned against him. The vee of his terry-cloth robe opened wide, and her cheek nestled in the rough hair of his chest. His flesh was warm. The contours of his body were strong and hard against her more pliant form, and he held her so close that she could hear the steady beating of his heart.

When she wrapped her arms around him, she could tell that he was naked beneath his robe.

She was guiltily ashamed to find herself enjoying the sweet comfort of his embrace. Roger Philo was dead, murdered. He lay in the woodbox below the cabin's overhang, perhaps directly under where they were standing. Gina should have been thinking of Roger, but she was aware of nothing but Conner. His strength. His virility. His arousal. She ought to be mourning.

But when she looked up into Conner's azure eyes, her lips formed a brazen demand. "I want you to kiss me."

Without hesitation, he complied.

Gina's heart beat faster. Her eyes closed, and her mind went blank. There was nothing but Conner. No fear. No guilt. Though grisly death was their companion, Gina reveled in the sensations of life, snatching a moment of pleasure, sensing that there would be little time for enjoyment in her immediate future.

His lips parted as he deepened their kiss. His hands glided inside her velour robe, cupping her breast.

Then, suddenly, he pulled away from her. "We've got company."

"What?" she murmured. "Who?"

"Somebody at the door. Didn't you hear the bell?"

He gave her a quick hug. As he strode from the kitchen through the wide front room, Conner straightened the tie on his robe. He glanced through the picture window and saw Norman Garrett, a deputy with the Pitkin County Sheriff's Department. How had Norm known to come here?

Though Conner had no reason to feel guilty, he was apprehensive, guarded. Last night, Gina had warned him of danger, and he had dismissed her fears. Conner would not make that mistake again. He unlocked the front door.

"Hey, Conner." Norm marched inside without stamping the snow from his boots. He left puddles with each step. Norm Garrett was a notorious slob. Whenever the press demanded that city officials "clean up" the Pitkin County sheriff's office, Norm would find the headline on his desk, accompanied by a whisk broom or a comb or a small box of laundry detergent. He pulled off his knit cap and his thick, sandy hair stuck out in a mass of unruly cowlicks. He squinted at Conner, twitched his mustache and asked, "What are you doing here, man?"

"I got a call last night about skiers in this area, with the blizzard coming and avalanche warnings. I headed over here to take a look and got snowed in for the night."

"Yeah, we got the same call last night, and it wasn't cleared by this morning. So? Is everybody okay?"

"I didn't locate any skiers." Conner hesitated before telling Norm about Roger's murder. Explanations would be complicated. "I think the call was bogus, Norm."

"Yeah? Why?"

Gina chose that moment to appear from the kitchen. Her long red hair was tousled, and her complexion was a blush. Though the velour robe covered her body, the askew collar and tangled sash hinted at what had been going on before Deputy Garrett arrived.

Conner made the introductions and Gina went to get coffee for Norm. The deputy poked his tongue into the inside of his cheek. Under his breath, he said, "So, Conner, I guess I don't need to ask if you've been enjoying yourself."

Conner winced. This wasn't going the way it ought to. This wasn't the right time for casual gibes. "We've got a serious situation here."

"Yeah? You want I should hit the road?"

Conner felt tongue-tied. In rescue situations, he was usually the one in control. His trademark was cool preparedness. He'd dealt with shock, hysteria, trauma and hypothermia. And death. But right now, talking to Norm, he felt as if he had violated accepted procedure. Never before had he been caught with his pants down. Literally. He blurted, "There's been a death. A murder. It's Roger."

"What do you mean, a murder? What happened? When?"

"I don't know when he was killed. We just found the body, maybe a half-hour ago."

"You and—" Norm looked toward the kitchen, where Gina had appeared carrying a steaming mug of coffee. "You and her?"

"His niece," Conner said. "Gina is Roger's niece."

"From Lydia's side of the family," Norm deduced. "Nobody who looks like her could be a blood relation to Roger. And you say he's dead?"

"Let me get dressed and I'll show you."

Norm accepted the coffee mug from Gina and immediately dribbled a mouthful down his shirtfront. "So, Gina, didn't I see you with Roger night before last? At the tavern?"

"I'm afraid so."

The deputy frowned at Conner. "And you, too. If I remember correctly, I saw the two of you dancing together."

Norm's remarks were beginning to sound like an accusation to Conner. True, there had been times when he wanted to kill Roger Philo, but last night hadn't been one of them.

Gina sank down on the sofa. "I argued with Roger at the tavern. Now I wish it had never happened. I feel terrible about our...disagreement."

"You decked him," Norm said.

"Well, yes, I guess I did."

"You want to tell me about it?"

Though Conner had no reason to be worried about Gina talking to Norm, he hustled into the bathroom and dressed. It seemed important to put the right parameters around Norm Garrett's impending investigation...assuming that the sheriff would trust Norm to handle a homicide.

When Conner returned to the living room, Gina was gesturing emphatically and talking a mile a minute about Elvis and getting caught in the snow and about the place she worked. Just like a city girl, he thought fondly. Not even a murder would slow her down. She wanted things done. Now.

And so did Conner. He wanted to pass this investigation on to the police. He stepped up beside them. "Okay, Norm. I'm ready. Let's get this taken care of."

The deputy aimed his mug for a coaster Gina had placed in front of him, but still managed to spill coffee on the table. He followed Conner through the kitchen and out the side door. Outside, he said, "Your friend Gina was telling me a real interesting story. A bunch of weird stuff about last night. Did you see this blood-stained Elvis statue?"

"When I saw it, there wasn't blood. Maybe Forensics can find traces."

"Forensics." The deputy sneered. "We'd be better off with less forensic evidence and more common sense. Those guys are always giving me a hard time about touching stuff.

Always got to follow procedure. Which reminds me, how come you didn't call in this morning about the skiers and the body?"

"The phone's out."

He nodded. "After you show me whatever it is that you're going to show me, I'll go down to my car and radio the station."

Conner pointed to the far end of the overhang. "Down there. In the woodbox. He's in there."

Before proceeding, Norm looked around the perimeter of the overhang. "No footprints in the snow, except going up to the house. I guess this happened before the blizzard."

"Guess so."

"And you two were in the house all night?"

"In separate bedrooms."

"Hey, Conner, she's a good-looking lady. It doesn't matter to me where you slept."

"It matters to me." Norm's assumption annoyed him enough that he added, "I didn't have sex with Gina."

"Whoa! Are you protecting her honor or something?"

"That's right."

Norm bumped his way through the junk that was stored beneath the overhang and opened the lid of the woodbox. He stared for a moment, and then the lid slipped through his fingers and banged shut. When he turned back toward Conner, his entire face had become a frown. He rubbed at his eyes with the back of his hand and blinked.

He pivoted and moved away from the woodbox. Beneath his mustache, Norm's mouth twitched into a smirk.

"Damn it, Conner." Norm snickered. "He's wearing an Elvis suit. I mean, Roger Philo is lying there, dead, with a hole in his chest. And he's wearing a white jumpsuit with gold sparkly things and a fancy belt. And bell-bottoms, for crying out loud. So much for dying with dignity, huh?"

"I don't know, Norm. Is there a tasteful way to be murdered?"

Norm's eyes popped wide open. "Hey, you don't think that Roger Philo was really *him,* do you? Elvis?"

"I kind of doubt that."

"But it makes sense. If Elvis isn't dead, why would he hang out at gas stations and hamburger stands. He could afford to live here. In Aspen. I mean, what if Roger was—" Apparently common sense caught up with Norm because he stopped short, grinned sheepishly and shook his head. "Naw, forget I said that."

"Be glad to."

"He was wearing an Elvis suit." Lydia Philo frowned at Gina and Conner, then lightly touched the corner of her eye with a lace-edged handkerchief.

Gina leaned toward her, but didn't presume to comfort her with hugs or pats on the hand. Her aunt's poise had always been a bit intimidating. Though her behavior showed the strain of facing her husband's death, Lydia fought to keep herself under control. And Gina's heart ached in sympathy. "Lydia, is there anything I can do?"

Lydia shook her head. Her beautifully coiffed silver-blond hair tossed dramatically and fell back into place. She wore a skirt and sweater of soft gray wool, with matching leather boots, and she sat very still on the creamy leather sofa in her Starwood home. Only her hands betrayed tension as she fingered the strand of pearls at her neck.

"Somehow I always knew he would die before I did. He lived so..." She hesitated. Lydia always chose her words carefully. "He lived so furiously. With such energy. I knew he couldn't go on at the pace he kept. I offered to teach him meditation. But it's too late for that now, isn't it?"

Not knowing what else to do, Gina nodded. It was too late for everything.

Lydia continued, "I never imagined he would be... murdered. When I got the call from Deputy Garrett, I couldn't believe it." Her dark eyes sought Conner's face. "Tell me, Conner. Did you...see him?"

"Yes," he said.

"And he was wearing a white jumpsuit? That wasn't a cruel joke invented by Deputy Garrett, was it?"

"I'm afraid not."

"And his face? Was Roger disfigured?"

"Not at all."

Gina suppressed her memory of Roger's body, his claw-like hand, his gray skin. Wasn't death the ultimate disfigurement?

"Well, then..." Lydia said. "I'll plan for an open-casket funeral. Or perhaps I should wait and talk it over with Alex."

"Will Alex be here soon?" Conner asked.

"Yes, right after he identifies the...the body. I suppose that really was my responsibility, but Alex said he could handle it more efficiently, since he is one of the assistant district attorneys." Her eyes brightened as she spoke of her eldest son, and her hands fluttered like autumn leaves before a wind. "Alex is a good son. And he is...brilliant. He could have had a lucrative legal career in Denver, but after his marriage ended, he wanted to be here. Near family."

Gina wished she could share her aunt's pride, but her cousin Alex had always irritated her. Family rumors hinted that the reasons Alex had left the Denver law firm had had more to do with incompetence than with his divorce. Still, she tried to smile at Lydia. "And what about Dean? When will he get here?"

"Alex said he would try to reach him by telephone. Dean had a—what does he call it?—a gig. He had a gig in Vail this evening."

"Dean seems to be doing well, too."

"For a piano player." Lydia's hands came together in a fidget and she picked at her cuticles. "It's such a silly profession, really. And Roger encouraged him. I did not. Oh, dear..."

"What is it, Lydia?"

"Dean will be heartbroken. The only father he's ever really known was Roger. We were married when Dean was only seven years old. Alex was twelve."

"I remember," Gina said. She had also been twelve, and the wedding and vacation in Aspen had been quite an event for the Robinson family. Roger had used his contacts as a booking agent to provide spectacular live entertainment. The guest list had included a number of stars and other famous people.

"Almost sixteen years," Lydia said. "Roger and I were married for almost sixteen years. No one thought it would last, but I stayed with him until the very end."

A tint of bitterness colored her voice, and Gina wondered if her aunt's poise masked something more than grief. Had she loved Roger or hated him? "Lydia, is there anyone else I should call? Would you like for me to help with arrangements?"

"You've done quite enough, thank you." Suddenly her tone was vehement. Her fingers were laced so tightly that her knuckles were white. "I know why he was wearing an Elvis suit. I know, Gina. You two were playing some sort of game, weren't you?"

"Game?"

"Don't deny it. I know what went on in that little cabin. That was where Roger did his private entertaining. Oh, yes,

I knew all about it. We had an agreement, and he promised to be discreet. Now they've found him dead in an Elvis suit."

Gina eyed her cautiously, unsure whether Lydia was more angered by the possibility of her late husband having an affair with his stepniece or by his having died in an Elvis costume. Consciously Gina avoided judging her aunt, while trying to set her mind at ease. "Aunt Lydia, there was nothing going on between Roger and me. I went to the cabin for business reasons. He was going to show me his collection of Elvis memorabilia."

"My dear, that is an absurd excuse."

"I needed to decide which items could be used for the auction at Berryhill's."

"And did you see these items?"

"No," Gina admitted. "When I got there—"

"Please don't insult me by trying to spare my feelings. I'm not blind or deaf, Gina. I heard about your tiff with Roger at the tavern."

Conner spoke up. "Gina was alone when I got to the cabin. We didn't see Roger until this morning."

"Oh, I see. The two of you spent the night together?"

"Not the way you think," Gina explained. "We both spent the night in the house. There was a blizzard. The phone was out and the Jeep wouldn't start."

"My Jeep? The Jeep you borrowed from me?"

"I'll have it repaired. Before we left the cabin, Conner took a quick look at it. We think the battery must have gone dead."

They turned in unison toward the sound of the front door opening and closing in the marble-tiled foyer that opened onto the front room. "Mother? I'm back."

A smile flickered across Lydia's lips as she called out, "We're in here, Alex!"

Alex Philo strode into the room, adjusting the lapels of his three-piece suit. He had already divested himself of his overcoat and hat. He wore street shoes without boots and his trouser cuffs were wet with snow. He acknowledged Conner and Gina with a quick nod of his head, but his concern was for his mother. He sat beside her, taking both her hands in his own. "Are you all right, Mom? Would you like to lie down?"

"Yes, dear. I believe I would." She rose majestically and glared down at Gina. "The battery in my Jeep is brand-new."

Alex stood at her elbow. "Should I help you up the stairs?"

"No, sweetheart. I can make it on my own." When she touched his arm, her hands were calm at last. "Give me a few moments to change into my nightgown. Then I would very much like for you to bring me tea. And please take care of the phone calls, Alex. The message machine is full."

As she made a grand, brave exit up the stairs toward her room, Gina marveled at the transformation in her aunt. The moment her son arrived, Lydia had visibly relaxed. His presence sedated her. Now that Alex was here, Gina hoped Lydia would allow her feelings to surface. It couldn't be healthy to squelch all that rage and sorrow. Not to mention the bitterness that had caused her to lash out at Gina.

She was about to compliment Alex and offer her help when he turned on her. "You've got a hell of a nerve, Gina! Why did you come here?"

"I wanted to help."

"Keep your voice down."

Alex brushed at the cuffs of his trousers. He had always been too proud of his appearance, even as a child. Gina remembered teasing him about his matching outfits. She and the other cousins had called him a "mama's boy" until the summer when the family gathered for her grandfather's funeral. That summer, Alex had been seventeen. He'd become a man, with an outdoorsy tan, platinum-blond hair and broad shoulders. Half the female cousins had swooned at how gorgeous he'd become. The other half, including Gina, had thought he was too conceited to merit a second glance. It hadn't surprised her when he decided to become a lawyer. When Alex thought he was right, he would brook no opposition. His stepfather's philandering ways must have infuriated him.

He fired a self-righteous scowl in her direction. "I think you should leave now."

"What's the problem, Alex?"

"I won't have you upsetting my mother."

Conner stood beside Gina. "Murder is kind of an upsetting business, Alex. Maybe your mother would like to have the rest of her family around."

"I don't need advice from a ski bum."

Conner reacted on pure instinct, taking a step forward. His muscles tensed, ready for a fight. Then he backed off. It took a major exertion of willpower for him not to pop Alex Philo right in the center of his straight unbroken nose, but the guy had just lost his stepfather. He was entitled to be a little obnoxious. But just a little.

"I want both of you out of here," Alex said.

"I could call relatives," Gina offered. "A lot of the family will want to come and pay their respects."

"To Roger? My stepfather wasn't well loved."

"To your mother," Gina said. "Everyone in the family admires and loves Lydia. They'll want to offer their condolences."

"I'll take care of it without your help." He turned away from her, averting his gaze. "You're in trouble, Gina. And I don't want you to bring the trouble here."

"What trouble?" Gina demanded.

"I'm not going to say anything that would help your case, but—"

"My case?" Gina yelped.

"Be quiet." He glanced toward the upstairs, where his mother should be resting. "Don't look to me for help. I'm not the one who's going to bail you out."

"Bail me out? Alex, what are you saying?"

Conner knew. It didn't take a legal genius to deduce that Gina would be a suspect in the murder of Roger Philo. She had been at the scene of the crime. She had opportunity and motive. The night before last, she had threatened Roger in a public place. The situation could get ugly. He hooked his arm through hers. "We should go."

When she looked up at him, her gaze held a striking mixture of anger and confusion. But she went along with him. They pulled on their coats and caps and mittens while Alex yanked open the heavy carved-oak door. As Gina stepped outside, onto the porch, Conner turned toward Alex. "This isn't advice. It's fact. If you hurt Gina, I'll have to hurt you. Real bad."

The door slammed in his face.

Conner looked up at the pure blue of the sky. "I know he's your cousin, Gina, but Alex Philo is a bigger jerk than his stepfather. At least Roger didn't pretend to be superior."

"What did Alex mean when he said I was in trouble?"

"We've got a long drive back to Roger's cabin to get the Jeep." He directed her into the newly plowed driveway and opened the passenger door of his truck. "Plenty of time to talk."

But not enough time to reassure her. On the way to buy a new battery, Gina drew the conclusion that Alex had hinted at. "The district attorney thinks I murdered Roger Philo."

"'Fraid so."

"That's the most ridiculous thing I've ever heard. It's so typical of small-town thinking. When the locals start looking for someone to blame, they look at the outsider. Me."

"Gina, this isn't exactly Hicksville, U.S.A. You can see movie stars at the supermarket and millionaires at lunch."

"Are there any good lawyers?"

"Yeah." He grinned. "But you can't afford them."

"I make a good salary," she protested.

"These are the superstars of law, the guys who handle high-profile cases. You don't need one of them. Besides, you didn't do anything wrong. Why don't we stop by the police station, talk to Norm and get this cleared up?"

"Fine."

With her arms folded across her chest and her brown eyes flashing, she looked like a redheaded time bomb about to explode. Though Conner sympathized with her anger, it wasn't going to do Gina any good to blow up at anybody. As he drove along the quaint streets of the village, he tried to defuse her. "Hey, look over there. It's Jack Nicholson."

"Where?" She scanned the streets.

"Gotcha."

"I knew that." She slouched back. "And right now I wouldn't care if you spotted Elvis in full concert regalia, twanging a gold guitar and singing about a hound dog. This is so unfair. How could the DA suspect me?"

"Take a look at the facts."

"Such as?"

"You had a fight with Roger at the bar. I believe you said you could just kill him."

"People say things like that all the time."

"Maybe so, but in spite of your anger at him, you still went to his cabin to see an Elvis collection that wasn't there."

"But somebody else was there," she said. "Don't you remember? I told you about the statue with blood on it. It had been wiped clean while I was gone. And the records were shifted around on the jukebox."

"The facts," he repeated. "This morning, when Norm and I were outside, there were no footprints leading away from the cabin."

"There was a blizzard," she said. "And the phone was out. If I killed Roger, why would I disconnect the phone?"

"So he couldn't call for help."

She leaned back in her seat. "I see. And I suppose that's evidence that can be used against me."

"Could be. Norm and I checked out the phone line, by the way. It had been knocked down by a tree branch."

"There," she said. "A simple explanation. That couldn't possibly incriminate me."

"But the branch was piled over with drifted snow. Which means it probably fell before the storm."

"And that's just what I said. When I got there, the phone was out."

"Why?" Conner took a right and pulled into the small parking lot beside the police station. "Why would a branch fall unless it was weighted down by snow? It's more likely that somebody knocked down that branch and put the phone out of commission."

"Me?" She bristled. "You think I whacked down a tree branch? Gee, Conner, maybe I arranged the blizzard, too."

"I don't like to give advice," he said. "But I seem to be doing a lot of that today."

"What?"

"Your attitude might be perfect for dealing with the NYPD, but you're in Colorado now. I work with these guys in the sheriff's office, and they're not going to be impressed by how tough and streetwise you can be."

"What are you saying? Should I act dumb? Should I be sweet and helpless?"

"Just keep a civil tongue in your head, okay? You haven't been charged with anything yet. If you play it cool, maybe we can avoid that."

Inside, they found Deputy Norm Garrett sitting behind the desk in Sheriff Brady's office. Conner waved a greeting. "Have you been promoted, Norm?"

"The sheriff is on vacation in Africa. One of those photo-safari things. We're still trying to get hold of him. Until we hear otherwise, I'm in charge." He kicked his feet up on the desk, knocking off a stack of file folders. "Glad you two stopped by. I got a couple of questions for you."

A bad development, Conner thought. With the sheriff out of town, Norm had his chance to prove himself, to be a big shot. He'd be looking for the fastest solution to Roger's murder. He ushered Gina into a straight-backed chair and sat beside her. "Okay, Norm. Shoot."

"The money," he said. "There was a packet of cash there, and your name was on it, Gina. What was that for?"

"I have no idea."

"You went to the cabin to see some Elvis stuff. Right?"

"Right. But there were only a few things there. I went to the cabin expecting to meet with Roger and Wendell Otis. Have you spoken to him?"

"Not yet. But I talked to a secretary in his Los Angeles office. She said he left Aspen early because he heard about the blizzard and needed to be back for some business today." He stirred a pencil through his already tangled hair. "I'd have thought Roger would tell you Wendell canceled."

"He never told me." A thought occurred to her. "Maybe he intended to call from the cabin, got there and found the phone was out."

"Maybe," Norm conceded.

Conner asked, "Does the coroner have a time of death?"

"That's going to be hard to pinpoint. He was pretty well frozen in that woodbox, and that's where he died. From loss of blood. The way the coroner figures, Roger was knocked unconscious, dumped in the woodbox and then shot."

"Dumped in the woodbox?" Gina questioned. "Somebody carried him there?"

"Or else he was out gathering wood." Norm covered his mouth with his hand, but Gina could still see the deputy's amused grin beneath his mustache. "Out gathering wood in an Elvis jumpsuit."

"I might be able to explain the jumpsuit," Gina said. "Though I didn't take a close look, it might be an authentic costume, one that was worn by Elvis himself. If so, it's a valuable item. Roger told me he had a surprise at the cabin, something that would make me believe that Elvis was still alive."

Both Conner and Norm stared blankly at her, so she elaborated. "He was talking about himself. He planned to dress up like Elvis and impress me."

"That fits with what I've been thinking," Norm said.

"What's your theory?" Conner asked.

"Common sense. Roger had a crush on Gina here. He's got her name written in his appointment book, with a doodle of a heart next to it. Same thing on the envelope of cash." He lowered his feet from the desk. "Did he make you some kind of indecent proposal, Gina? Offer you cash for—"

"No," she said firmly.

"Did I mention that the forensics guys found traces of blood on the Elvis statue?" Deputy Norman Garrett folded his hands atop the desk. When he stared at Gina, there was no trace of clumsiness in his manner. His eyes were dead serious as he said, "There were fingerprints on the statue, too. Your fingerprints, Gina."

Chapter Four

Unfortunately, Gina wasn't the only one with a temper. Conner slapped his flat palm on the top of the desk. "Dammit, Norm. There's no way Gina could have killed her uncle."

"I'd like to think you're right." Flush with his new responsibilities as acting sheriff, Norm frowned self-importantly. "We might be friends, Conner, but I've got to look at the facts."

"One set of prints, Norm. That's all you've got in the way of facts. And Gina admitted to you that she picked up the statue."

"What about the fight the night before last? In front of all those witnesses?"

"There must be twenty people who have fought with Roger in the past six months. He wasn't an easy-to-get-along-with kind of guy."

"And the envelope," Norm said, "with the doodle."

All his arguments were a load of doodle as far as Conner was concerned, but he didn't have a chance to tell him so because just then the phone on the desk buzzed and Norm lifted the receiver.

When Conner heard Norm address the mayor of Aspen, he could guess at the topic. This was a tourist town. Murders needed to be expedited so that the visitors would rest assured that there was no apparent danger to themselves.

Though Norm's smug expression when he hung up the phone didn't boost Conner's confidence, he tried to explain logically. "From the way you've outlined the murder, Gina couldn't have done it. Take a look at her. She's not big enough. Even if Roger was halfway into the woodbox when he got knocked out, Gina isn't big enough to flip him in, turn him over and shoot him."

"It doesn't take any muscle to pull a trigger."

"You know what I mean." He didn't want to yell, but Norm was being flat-out unreasonable. "A woman wouldn't have the physical strength to do this."

"I beg your pardon," Gina put in. "Many women can lift a man's weight. And there are pulleys and hoists and stuff like that. So, if I had really wanted to move—"

"Whoa, city girl." She didn't get it. He was trying to erase her name from the major-suspect list, and she just didn't get it. "Gina, now is not the time to be a feminist. I'm trying to prove—"

"I know what you're doing, Conner." Her big brown eyes narrowed dangerously. "But this isn't a matter of proof. Is it, Norm?"

A scribble of worry lines tattooed his forehead and he tilted back in his chair, trying to get as far away from her as possible. "I don't know what you mean, Gina."

"Alex put you up to this, didn't he?"

"Alex Philo?"

"No, Alexander Graham Bell," she snapped.

Conner should have been calming her down, but his anger was simmering on high. "Wait a minute, Norm. Alex hasn't been assigned to this case, has he?"

"Well, of course not. But he is taking an interest. Roger was his stepfather."

"In my book," Conner said, "that makes him a suspect, too. Does he have an alibi for yesterday?"

"Matter of fact, he was in court all day."

"All day?" he questioned.

"Except for recesses. And he spent some time in his office." Norm leaned forward in a shot, bracing his elbows on the desk. "Forget about Alex. He didn't do it."

Conner stared into his eyes, daring Norm to look away. "How can you be so damn sure?"

"Because I feel it in my gut."

Conner remembered Norm's distaste for forensics, his belief that most cases could be solved with common sense. Counting the prospect of career advancement—which meant staying on the good side of the district attorney's office and the mayor and every other damned city official—Norm had some compelling reasons to hope Gina committed the crime. She was the most obvious suspect, and the deputy wasn't going to look seriously at anyone else until he was presented with some solid evidence.

Those were the boundaries Conner had to work within, and it wasn't going to do any good to rant and rave against the brick wall of Norm's gut feeling. Calm, Conner told himself. He needed to be calm and rational. "Do me a favor, Norm."

"What?"

"Tell me how you think Gina moved the body."

"It took two people to move him."

"You're saying she showed up at the cabin. Roger did his Elvis impression, offered her money, got clunked, shot and dumped in the woodbox by Gina and a friend who left before I showed."

"I didn't say any of that."

"Good. Because that's nuts! She was alone when I pulled her out of the snowfield. Nobody else was at the cabin, and I was there from dusk until morning."

"Exactly." Norm sighed, blowing papers around the desk. His voice held heavy regret as he added, "You were the only other person there. If she needed help..."

"What?"

"Hey, Conner, everybody knows you hated Roger. There was that stuff with the commercials after you did the Olympics. You should have made a fortune, but Roger mismanaged the whole thing. Hey, Conner, I'm sorry. We're friends, but I got to look at the facts. This is a homicide."

Norm's accusation snapped like the last strand on a frayed rope, and Conner plummeted to the end of his self-control. He bolted from the hardbacked chair. "Are you saying that you think I killed Roger?"

"Didn't say that."

"I *save* lives, Norm. That's my lifework."

The deputy rose to face him. "What if it is your job? You might be some kind of local hero, but you're still a suspect. Nobody's above the law, Conner. Not even you."

"Are you going to arrest me? Read me my rights?"

"Not yet, Conner. Not quite yet."

Conner pivoted and stormed through the door of the sheriff's office. From behind him, he heard Norm call out, "Neither one of you leave town for a couple of days. Hear me?"

Outside, Conner strode across the parking lot and slammed into his truck. He was surprised when he looked over and saw Gina hop into the passenger seat. "Way to go," she said. "That little display certainly smoothed relations with the local cops."

"There are two things that drive me crazy." He fired the ignition and pulled away from the snowbanked curb. "I hate when people are careless and stupid."

"What else?"

"When I'm the one who's being a dunce. God, I hate that." He aimed the truck for the back roads leading to Roger's cabin. "How could I have missed that one? Of course they'd think we were working together. In cahoots. When Norm arrived this morning, we looked as if we'd spent the night together."

"But we hadn't—not *that* way."

"I'm aware of that." His voice ricocheted in the cab of the truck. "We didn't make love. And we didn't kill Roger."

He braked too hard at a stop sign and his truck fishtailed before he brought it under control. *Slow down,* Conner reminded himself. *When you go too fast and don't consider all the hazards, you make mistakes.* That was what happened with climbers who didn't bring enough rope. When cross-country skiers took off into rough terrain with no idea where they could find shelter, they were looking for trouble.

Conner had more smarts than that. He would not allow unpreparedness to lead him into a murder accusation. He was a survival expert. "I need to get the lay of the land."

"That's easy. It's Aspen."

"Aspen. That's one of the reasons it's complicated."

As he waited at the stop sign, three cars rolled past. A beat-up Volkswagen. A Land Rover. And a sleek black Porsche.

He watched the miniparade that represented the evolution of Aspen. From Volkswagen to Porsche. Conner had lived here all his life, and he still didn't understand this place. Because tourism kept Aspen thriving, the locals took care not to offend the visitors or the people like Roger and

Lydia who were wealthy enough to live in Starwood. When they demanded special privileges, they were heard. Still, there were times when the locals dug in their heels and made restrictions—like the law that had been passed a couple of years ago banning fur coats within city limits.

Conner could count on that stubborn streak. The people here knew him. Even if Norm was shooting for a promotion and a quick solution, he'd catch on. He'd know that Conner Hobarth wouldn't kill anybody. Suspicion of Gina was another matter. With her mass of fire-engine-red hair, she looked flashy. And she acted like a smart-aleck city girl—the type who would irritate the locals. They couldn't know her the way he did.

Last night, she'd been hurt and vulnerable. But he'd seen the core of inner strength that made her more of a woman than anyone he'd met in a long time. He liked her bravado, her sense of humor in the face of disaster. A lot of people would have crumbled under the pressure of the accusations leveled at her today. But Gina's chin was still up.

"What do you think we should do next?" she asked.

"Gotta think. I've got to figure this out." For him, that meant going to the source, to nature. He always did his best thinking outdoors. "First, we fix Lydia's Jeep. Then, I'm going skiing."

Gina stared through the windshield at the glistening white aftermath of last night's blizzard. They were heading west on state highway 82, following the icy rush of the Roaring Fork River. Dotting the terraced hillsides were the fabulous homes of Starwood. The sheer magnificence of Aspen and the Rockies should have been enough to cleanse her mind.

But she felt unsafe, insecure. It was as if she could see the cracks beneath the snow, the beginnings of disaster. How could he possibly think of skiing? "In case you missed it,

Conner, you've been accused of being an accessory to murder.''

"I didn't miss it."

"But you're ignoring the accusation. When the going gets tough, the tough go skiing, is that it?"

"It'll all sort itself out."

"What if it sorts out wrong? What if you and I are arrested?" She felt the need to do something—anything. "So far today, I've talked to three people. Lydia, Alex and Deputy Norm. All of them think I killed my uncle."

"Not Lydia."

"That's right. My aunt only thinks I was having an illicit affair with her husband. Oh, yes, indeed—she's in my corner."

"Calm down, Gina."

"You're a fine one to talk about calm. After the way you blew up at Deputy Norm."

"I was mad," he admitted. "But I'm over it."

"Well, excuse me all to bits, but I'm not so forgiving about murder accusations. And I don't like being framed."

Framed for murder. As soon as the words left her lips, Gina knew she'd spoken the truth. Someone had taken the trouble of arranging the circumstances of Roger's death to make it look as if she'd killed him. Why? Softly, she repeated the words. "I was framed."

Conner nodded. "That's one of the reasons we need to fix the Jeep. It looks like a dead battery, but it's possible that somebody deliberately disabled your aunt's car so you couldn't leave. After the calls about cross-country skiers in the area, somebody was sure to come to the cabin and find you."

"Somebody did. You, Conner."

And now he was suspected of helping her. She felt really terrible about that circumstance. It wasn't fair. Though

Roger had been Gina's stepuncle, and she was saddened by his death, Conner had more to lose than she did. He lived here. Aspen was his home. He must be hurt that his friend Norm had accused him of murder. "I'm sorry about all this, Conner."

"Not your fault. It's bad luck, bad timing."

"What do you mean?"

"Nobody in Aspen has a reason to frame you, right?"

"I don't think so. Nobody really knows me."

"So, the murderer saw your name in Roger's appointment book and took advantage of the timing. You were set to show up at the wrong place at the wrong time."

Gina hoped that was the answer. Simply a matter of timing. It frightened her to think someone had framed her because he had a personal vendetta against her.

"Same thing with me," he said. "I *happened* to find you. The blizzard *happened* to hit. And I *happened* to spend the night. All coincidence."

"You make this sound like a minor inconvenience."

"Of course not. I take death seriously. And murder? To tell you the truth, I've never been close to a murder before. But I don't feel lighthearted about it."

"So, what do you think we should do?"

"I told you, Gina. I'm going skiing."

"Will you have time? It'll be almost dark when you get back from Roger's." Nightfall came quickly in the mountains, when the sun slipped behind the towering peaks. "The lifts will probably be closed."

"I've got connections. They'll open for me." He glanced over at her. "You want to come along?"

"I haven't even rented skis yet. But thanks for asking."

"How about tomorrow? Eight o'clock. Meet me at lift one."

She hesitated. Roger's death was a family tragedy and it didn't seem right to be making ski plans.

"Come on, Gina. What else are you going to do? Your aunt Lydia and Alex made it pretty clear that they didn't want you hanging around the house."

"Yes, they did."

He eyed her skeptically. "Promise me, Gina, that you won't try to investigate this by yourself."

"I might. I'm not confident of Norm's abilities."

"Don't," he said. "It's dangerous. We're dealing with a murderer."

She almost snapped a retort before she recognized the validity of his warning. There was the threat of peril. If she got too close to the killer, she might be the next victim—which was much worse than being a suspect. "But I have to do something."

"Maybe not. Could be that Norm will settle down and realize that you and I are victims of circumstance."

"Do you really think so?"

"No. In a perfect world, that's exactly what would happen. But human reasoning isn't perfect."

"What is?"

"Nature." He stretched his arm across the cab of his truck and squeezed her shoulder. "Mother Nature is unpredictable, but perfect. Blizzards and avalanches in the mountains. Blistering heat in the desert. It's all for a reason."

Maybe this trip to Aspen had been for a reason, Gina thought as she caught his hand and held it on the seat between them. She might be here, accused of murder and searching for Elvis artifacts, for some huge, life-changing reason.

She studied Conner's handsome profile as he drove steadily along the highway. Her gaze dropped to their joined hands. In spite of everything, it felt right to be here with him. Maybe the natural reason that she was here in Aspen was simple. Maybe it was Conner. "I'll meet you tomorrow morning at lift one. But I warn you, I haven't skied for two years, and I'm rusty."

"It's a date," he said. "Oh, yeah, and I want to invite you to a party. Saturday."

"A party?" She wasn't sure that partygoing would be appropriate. She ought to at least make an effort to behave with solemn decorum.

"This is an annual thing at the Hotel Jerome. A Pisces party, to celebrate February. It's formal. A showplace for the rich and famous. You'll like it."

"Are you assuming I'd like it because I'm a shallow city girl who is impressed by celebrities?"

"I'm assuming you'll go because I'm asking."

"Arrogance becomes you, Conner. If I'm here on Saturday, I'll be delighted to come to the party and be thrilled by all the beautiful people."

At Roger's cabin, Conner parked nose-to-nose with Lydia's Jeep so that he could jump-start the battery if necessary. They had tried jumper cables earlier, using Norm's vehicle, but the Jeep had failed to respond.

While Conner popped the hood on the Jeep, Gina positioned herself in the afternoon sun and stared up at the amazing blue sky. The natural beauty hypnotized her, almost made her forget that she was here to disprove an accusation of murder. How had it happened? When had Roger been killed? She needed to think. Maybe there was a clue she'd forgotten. She forced herself to turn around and look at Roger's cabin, at the top of the long path and staircase. She remembered how she'd fled the cabin after finding the Elvis statue, how the blood on her hand had marked the handrail. That trace had been obliterated by the blizzard. So many possible clues had been erased by the storm and the wind. Footprints and tire tracks. None of those markings would be here now.

She saw movement—a shadow passing across the angle of the deck that was visible from where she stood. "Conner, someone's up there."

He peered out from under the hood. "What?"

A voice echoed from the cabin. "Hey, Gina! Is that you?"

"Dean?"

The tall form of her younger cousin appeared at the top of the path. He waved and started down the hillside. To Conner, Gina said, "Why would he be here?"

Her aunt Lydia had assumed that Dean would be deeply affected by Roger's death. Maybe he had come here to mourn, but as he approached down the path he seemed as energetic as a puppy. He came up beside her and gave her a hug. When she gazed up into his brown eyes, a dark brown that was similar to her own, she saw the evidence of tears. "I'm sorry, Dean."

"Me too. I'll miss him."

Conner came around the Jeep and stuck out his hand. "How are you doing, Dean?"

"I don't know." He shook Conner's hand and stuck his own unmittened fingers in the pockets of his parka. "Guess it hasn't really hit me yet that he's dead. That's why I came up here. I kind of wanted to say goodbye in my own way. To give Roger a send-off on his next journey."

"His journey?" Gina questioned.

"You know, the great adventure. Death."

"Oh." She might have expected that Dean, the rebel in the Philo family, would mourn in his own eclectic manner.

Dean looked around the opened hood. "What's wrong with the Jeep?"

"Won't start," Conner informed him.

"That's weird. It's a new battery."

"Do you know anything about fixing cars?" Conner asked.

"No way, man."

As if to emphasize his ignorance, Dean turned away from the Jeep and gazed out beyond the trees.

His sharp-nosed profile contrasted with the smooth, tanned skin of his face and the thick brown hair that hung straight to his shoulders. Gina suspected that Dean was aiming for a rugged-mountain-man style, but he was still too boyish to look craggy. He was handsomer than his brother, in Gina's opinion, though Dean's features lacked the perfect symmetry of Alex's.

"Have you seen your mother?" she asked.

"Not yet. I figure Alex has that stuff under control. He's good with her." Dean pulled his hand out of his pocket and held it out, palm flat. "Do you get any vibes from this rock?"

It looked like a plain gray pebble to her. The edges appeared to be honed to sharpness, like an arrowhead's. "Vibes?"

"Guess not." He turned the stone over in his hand and rubbed his thumb over the surface. "I came up here, searching for a sign, you know."

"A sign?"

"Like an indication that Roger was okay with being dead."

Gina gritted her teeth to keep from speaking. If there was one thing that annoyed her more than bad taste, it was New Age philosophy.

Dean continued. "I kind of wanted something that would remind me of Roger. I wanted to go in the house, but it's all closed off with yellow police tape, and I didn't want to mess up the investigation or anything. So, I was walking around. Thinking. And I saw this rock. It was stuck on the edge of the stump where Roger chopped wood for the fireplace.''

"Why did that remind you of Roger?"

"Back when we had the pine-beetle disease and had to take down a bunch of diseased trees, I used to chop wood for Roger. We'd sit out back with a couple of beers and do guy stuff."

Father-and-son stuff, Gina thought sympathetically.

"Wow," Dean said. "Do you know how weird this is?"

She watched him turn the rock over and over in his hand. The edges appeared to be very sharp, and when Dean closed his fingers tightly around the small bit of gray stone, he winced, as if he had suddenly cut himself.

"It's weird. You can ask Conner. Usually these little rocks are buried by snow and they don't come out until spring thaw. But there it was. So, I figured it was a sign. I'm going to carry it with me all the time. So I always have a little piece of Roger."

A sweet sentiment. Maybe Roger would finally have someone who truly regretted his death. "You were close to your stepfather, weren't you?"

"Huh? Nope, not really."

"Your mother said—"

"I get it. Mom likes to think Roger was some kind of great father to me, because we're both into music and stuff. But I have a father, a real father. He lives in Chicago, and he's a decent guy. Paid for my college while I was going to school." Dean grinned. "And he hates my hair."

"So do I," Conner said as he came around the front of the Jeep. "I think I've found the problem. I should have noticed this before, when Norm was here, but I wanted to get away from this place. We probably didn't need the new battery."

"What is it?"

"A loose coil wire. The engine wasn't getting any juice from the battery. I hooked it tight. So, let's jump it and see if the Jeep starts." He asked Dean, "Did Lydia have problems with this car?"

"I think so. That's why she got the new battery."

Conner glanced up and down the hillside. "I don't see your car, Dean. How'd you get up here?"

He returned the rock to his pocket and pulled out a garage opener. Aiming the device like a laser pistol, he fired at the low two-car garage, which was about ten yards up the road from where Gina had parked. The door shuddered, squawked and opened. Within were two vehicles. A van, painted on the side with a scrawl that read Philo-maniacs. And a BMW station wagon.

"A garage," Gina said. "I never knew it was there."

"Kind of a big building to overlook," Dean said.

"Well, I saw it, of course. But I didn't think it went with the house."

She groaned. "If I'd known, I could have avoided all this. I could have taken Roger's car."

"Well, you couldn't," Dean said. "It's not like he left the keys in the Beamer."

Seeing the garage brought up several other issues: Could the murderer have hidden in the garage? Had Roger's car been there all night? Where were his car keys? Gina wanted to prowl, to investigate, to dispel all the suspicions that pointed toward her as the murderer.

With the jumper cables hooked up, Conner waved for her to get into the car. On the third try, the Jeep chugged to life. While she gunned the engine, Conner left his truck and came up to her window.

"I'm going to return the Jeep to Lydia's," she said.

"Do you want me to follow you?"

Gina hedged. Distances were such a problem in this part of the world. And, of course, there was nothing even vaguely resembling public transportation, except in town, where there were trolleys and buses and a horse-drawn stagecoach. "Well, I'll have to get back to my hotel, and I hate to bother Alex."

"No problem," Dean put in. "I'll follow you to Mom's place and take you back to your hotel."

"I really can't ask you to do that," Gina said. "I'm sure you have a lot of other things—"

"Hey, I'm always ready, willing and able to help out my cute little redheaded cuz. I'll meet you at Mom's."

He loped toward the garage, and she looked up at Conner. "Dean doesn't seem anxious to spend time with Alex and Lydia."

"Can't say as I blame him."

"Well, what do you think, Conner? Was the Jeep sabotaged?"

"Maybe. The wire was loose. It might have jolted loose. Or somebody might have pulled it."

"No proof, huh?"

"Wouldn't make much of a difference. If Norm and Alex want to prove a case against us, they can say that you screwed up the car yourself." He pulled off his glove, reached through the open window and touched her cheek, tilting her head toward him. His lips curved in a smile. The irises of his blue eyes sparkled with reflected light from the snow. "Don't investigate, Gina. Promise?"

"I don't know, Conner. It seems as if I should."

His mouth descended to hers for a light, tantalizing kiss. "Maybe tomorrow. After we go skiing."

A trembling heat melted her impulse to play detective. When he touched her, she was complacent, gentle and amenable. She struggled past those soft feelings. "This is more unfair to you than to me. It hardly seems right to meet you, have you rescue me from certain death by freezing, get you accused of murder and then ... just ignore this mess."

"Not right at all." He traced the outline of her lips.

"Conner, we have to look into Roger's murder. Deputy Norm is in over his head, and I'm afraid—"

"We can poke around. Later. Tomorrow."

"I'm afraid of what Alex might do. He's never liked me."

As Dean drove past them with a honk and a wave, Conner gave him a thumbs-up sign. "He's not a bad kid."

"Hardly a kid," she said. "He's twenty-three."

"Seems younger. It's probably the hair." He stood and took a step away from the Jeep. "Go to your hotel. Get some rest. When the going gets tough..." He left the thought dangling.

"Not skiing," she said. "Conner, we need to think about this. I have lots of ideas. We should definitely contact Wendell Otis and find out when he left and why."

"Sure, Gina. Definitely."

"Not to mention that he does have an Elvis collection, and I might be able to find something for the auction."

"Oh yeah." His tone was sardonic. "I'm sure you're not thinking at all about your career. See you tomorrow."

She watched him return to his truck and pull back so that she could turn around on the narrow road. Gina suspected that he was patronizing her and had no intention of sleuthing. If any other male had casually dismissed her plans with an invitation to ski, she would've pivoted, slam-dunked his ego and walked away fast. Why was she cutting him so much slack?

Using the four-wheel drive to maneuver, she managed to get herself turned in the downhill direction. It was a long drive back to Lydia's, and she spent the entire time reminding herself that there was no way that she and Conner could ever have anything more than a quickie vacation romance.

Meeting him had not been part of her program. When she came here from New York looking for Elvis memorabilia, she hadn't expected to find a handsome, masculine man who stirred her heart. Not that her attraction to him meant anything. Gina had been alone for so long that she could hardly imagine living any other way. She'd been resigned to a pleasant solitude, with her career as the most important thing in her life. And, of course, that hadn't changed. Even if she and Conner became involved, she would be leaving Aspen very soon. Unless, of course, she was detained in the Pitkin County Jail on suspicion of murder.

Gina shoved that unpleasant aspect from her mind and returned to her musings about Conner. Never could she form a serious attachment to a small-town guy who was rooted in Aspen. He would not transplant well to New York, and she had no intention of dumping her career and coming to live in a town where she'd been framed for murder.

The specter of imminent arrest raised itself again. "Dammit."

She hadn't done anything wrong. How could these allegations be serious? Still, Deputy Norm had said not to leave town. And Alex had hinted that he had some deep, dark evidence at the DA's office. She needed to accept the possibility that she'd actually be accused.

She parked the red Jeep in the drive at Lydia's and went to Dean's van. He was sitting in the driver's seat, bobbing his head and singing along with a tape. "Dean? Do you want to go inside?"

"Nope."

In fact, he sped away from his mother's house as soon as Gina closed the passenger-side door. She stuck the car keys and house key in an inside pocket of her parka. Later they'd be an excuse to return and make her peace with Lydia. She turned toward Dean. With the extra-loud music from his tape deck, it was barely possible to think, much less carry on a conversation.

Dean glanced at her and turned the volume down. "Sorry."

"Why do you play it that loud?" she asked. "As a musician, don't you have to protect your ears or something?"

"It's not like I'm a concert pianist," he said.

"But you're good. When I saw you at the tavern, you were really good."

"Yeah? Thanks."

"Was that your group?" She recalled the name on the side of the van. "The Philo-maniacs?"

"The Maniacs were three years ago. Me and four other guys. And Roger was our agent. He came up with the name. I don't know why, but it always makes people think of stamp collectors."

"Philatelists," she said, suppressing a grin. Dean really was cute. "How did you like Roger as an agent?"

"At first it was cool. He took a real interest. Told me that if I stuck with him I'd be bigger than Elvis."

He started to laugh, but choked up. Gina knew he was more upset than he was letting on.

"He used to take me up to the cabin," Dean continued, "and show me all his Elvis junk, you know. The statues. Signed pictures. The jumpsuit. He even had a couple of Elvis's handguns. And he'd tell me about Colonel Tom Parker, the guy who was Elvis's manager. Without Colonel Tom, Elvis would have been nothing, and Roger was going to be my Colonel Tom."

"Oh, my gosh, Dean. You've actually seen Roger's collection of Presleyana?"

"Presleyana? If you mean Elvis toys, yeah." He tossed his head, flipping his hair off his face. "Are you a fan?"

Surely he remembered why she was here. When she arrived in Aspen, Gina had talked with Dean and Lydia and Alex. He couldn't have tuned out the whole conversation. "The Elvis memorabilia," she said. "That's why I came out here. To take some of those items back to New York for auction. Do you know where Roger kept it?"

"Some of it at the cabin. But mostly in LA."

"Why?" And why hadn't he told her that his collection wasn't even here in Aspen?

"Don't know," Dean said. "I guess he kept his collection at the offices he used to share with Wendell Otis. Oh, man, that Otis is one weird dude. He eats his weight in vitamin pills every day."

"Can you tell me about Roger's collection?" she repeated. "Is there any particular item you remember?"

"Some really amazing sunglasses," he said. "Gold frames. Real gold. And Roger had one of those pins that Elvis used to give to his special friends. They said TCB, with a lightning bolt at the bottom. Did you know TCB means Taking Care of Business?"

"Yes, I did."

TCB had been Elvis's motto, but it apparently wasn't Dean's. He tapped his fingers on the steering wheel, turned the volume a bit higher. Apparently he was finished talking, and Gina didn't push. Settling back in the passenger seat, she listened to the driving beat of the music and tried to decipher the rapper's words, which seemed to have something to do with "being on the run" or "looking for a gun."

When they pulled up in front of her hotel, Gina thanked him nicely and hurried into the lobby of the Taos Lodge, where the southwestern-style decor provided an adobe-and-turquoise backdrop for stunning guests. The cosmopolitan clientele chatted in French, Japanese and Texan while they sipped après-ski Grand Marnier in the lounge beside the entry.

Gina hurried across the tiled floor to the elevators and went to her room. Behind the locked door of her third-floor room she was alone. Sanctuary! Finally!

The beige-and-gray Navaho-patterned bedspread beckoned to her, and she stretched out on top of it. She was tired. Her inclination was to slide between the cool, clean sheets and cover her face until this storm had passed; but hiding never solved anything. She'd been accused of murder. Framed. She couldn't lie here and wait for Deputy Norm to come and slap on the handcuffs.

But there was something else to consider. There was Conner. In the midst of this Elvis-inspired business trip, it seemed impossible that she was experiencing this juvenile hormonal attraction. And yet she whispered his name with a sigh. "Conner Hobarth. Hound Dog Hobarth."

He could have hated her for dragging him into a terrible situation; most men would have felt that way. Most of the men Gina had dated were eager to pile on the blame. If it rained on their first date, if they didn't get a good table at a restaurant, if the sushi wasn't to their liking, they whined. At her. At the maître d'. At cabdrivers. At everybody.

But Conner was different. He reminded her what a man, a real man, should be like. He was strong. His job was to rescue people. He was noble. A regular hero...

She closed her eyes. Though she hadn't planned to, Gina slept.

When the ringing of the bedside telephone wakened her, night had fallen. The caller was Dean, and he told her she had a problem.

"What problem?"

"I shouldn't tell you this, but Alex has some kind of a note or letter... regarding you."

"What does it say?"

"I'm not supposed to talk to you about any of this, but I figured you ought to know what's happening."

"Dean, would you please tell me?"

"It's in Roger's handwriting, and it says something about how he wants you to be his, uh, his girlfriend."

"So what? He never gave me this note."

"Okay, forget it." Dean sounded miffed. "Just trying to help you out."

"Sorry, Dean. I'm a little on edge."

"Yeah, well, you're going to be more on edge, cuz. The DA is going to bring you in for questioning. Maybe even charge you with murder."

Gina was dumbstruck. What had she ever done to cause Alex to hate her so much?

AFTER MIDNIGHT, he lay in his bed and stared at the ceiling. It was late, but adrenaline kept him awake. He'd taken chances, but it looked as if he'd pulled it off; no one suspected him of Roger's murder.

There was only one redheaded loose end: Gina. With all her poking around, she might find something, might direct the suspicion in his direction.

When he had waited around at the cabin and seen her skiing off into the blizzard, he'd been pleased. She should have died in the storm, and it would have looked as if she'd murdered Roger, then tried to flee the scene.

Now, however, she was a problem, and she needed to be erased. A convenient accident would be nice, he thought. Something subtle. Or maybe he could make it look as if Gina were overwhelmed by guilt and committed suicide.

In any case, he couldn't allow her to run around free and easy, causing trouble. He had to make sure that redheaded fox was caught in a steel trap.

Damn the bitch. He kicked off his sheets and climbed out of bed to pace. Damn her.

She was like all of them, all the women who had ever rejected him and mistreated him. Starting with his mother.

Chapter Five

"The best justice system in the world," Conner said. From atop Aspen Mountain he surveyed the panorama of jagged, snowy peaks and breathed the pure air. He and Gina were among the first skiers of the morning, and the powdery terrain that lay before them was virtually unmarked. "Up here, no one can lie."

On the slopes, everyone was equal. The rich, the powerful and everybody else skied side by side. All humanity was leveled by the harsh majesty of the Rocky Mountains. Nature was queen, and no one could buy protection from her winds. No one could conquer her. Conner always felt smarter, braver and more powerful when he was up here, skiing.

Today, he'd chosen an intermediate slope, in deference to Gina's abilities. After they dismounted from the lift, he waited for her to ski up beside him before announcing his thoughts on justice, lying and the mountains. "Well, Gina, what do you think?"

"I think this is a beautiful day. Frankly, Conner, I don't want to worry about liars."

"Or murder charges?"

A shiver danced across her shoulders, and Gina shrugged to dismiss her rising fear and tension. "I thought about it last night and decided there's nothing I can do."

"Then you don't want to solve the case?"

"Well, of course I do. But how? I'm an appraiser, an art historian. I can tell the difference between Ming, Tang and Sung dynasties. But I'm not a detective or an attorney."

"Ah, sanity..." He heaved a sigh. "I came to basically the same conclusion."

She gripped her ski poles and regarded the trail before them. "The best plan is to ski and not waste this weather."

"You're right. It's warm for February."

"Warm? I wouldn't say eight degrees above zero is warm." She beamed up at him, determined to have a good time and not to think about the murder of Roger Philo. "Listen, Conner. I used to be a better-than-average skier, but I haven't been out for over two years. If you want to go faster, you don't have to wait for me."

"I don't mind going at your pace."

"No, really," she protested. "You told me that you wouldn't dare to lie, and I know you'll be bored if I hold you back."

"Exactly how slow are you planning to ski?"

"Slow enough that I won't break my neck." She was well aware that the Aspen Mountain area of this sprawling resort had expert, advanced and intermediate slopes. No beginner trails. "And I'd really rather not do the famous Aspen-extreme thing, with daredevil vertical drops."

"Sure." He pointed with his pole. "Follow that trail."

"Okay. You first." Gina would rather not have him observing her progress. Conner Hobarth had been a professional skier, and she was not anxious to make a fool of herself in front of him. "I insist."

Without further question, he schussed away from her, kicking up sparkling clouds of snow as he swiveled his hips like Elvis and charged the moguls on the far right of the trail. His movements reflected the effortless yet exuberant grace of a man who was completely at ease with a pair of extremely long skis stuck to his feet.

Gina pushed away more tentatively, traversing the smoother side of the steep trail. Her competent initial performance encouraged speed, and she couldn't resist. Soon, she was flying, soaring. With the wind swirling past her, she reached the exhilarating edge of control and swept to a stop downslope from Conner.

"You look good," he told her.

Her heart was beating fast. Her thigh muscles trembled, unaccustomed to this exertion. "It's like riding a bike. Once you've learned, you never forget."

"You look great."

"That must be the truth," she said. "Because you said you could never tell a lie up here."

He dug in his pole tips and swooped forward. Like a giant bird, he made a quick turn in midair and landed directly in front of her.

"Conner, what are you doing?"

"Getting closer." Facing her, his skis separated in a wide parallel position, he eased forward, coming to a precise stop with each of his skis outside hers and his body against hers. When he pulled her even closer and kissed her, his mouth was hot. Their mingled body heat penetrated through layers of turtlenecks, sweaters and parkas.

When their kiss ended, he looked down at her. "That wasn't a lie, either."

Before she could wonder what he meant, Conner had skied backward, away from her, and was off again. He was magnificent! A master skier! Gina was totally captivated. For the next ten minutes, she skied an inspired route.

Then, when they were resting again, Conner's walkie-talkie made a shrill beep. He pressed the button and answered. "What is it, Tommy?"

"Conner, we need you down here in the rescue shack, right away."

"Give me fifteen." He hooked the walkie-talkie back on his belt and turned to Gina. "I'm sorry, but—"

"You go ahead." She hoped there was no mountain rescue disaster. "I'll catch up with you later."

"Keep following this trail. There's nothing from here on down that'll be too hard for you. I'll meet you at the bottom, near the lift."

His progress down the slope was incredibly fast, yet safe and purposeful, as he weaved his way among other skiers and disappeared behind a wall of conifers. A sense of pride made Gina stand a little straighter. Conner was her man— at least her date. He skied like an Olympic champion as he whooshed off to rescue people. He was a hero. Like Mighty Mouse. Like Elvis?

Gina smiled self-consciously at her own train of thought. What did that make her—Priscilla Presley? Gina tossed her head. Maybe neither. Just because she was hanging out with a hero, she didn't have to become a swooning heroine. After all, Gina prided herself on being a modern, independent career woman.

Her career. And how long would that last? When she called in to Berryhill's this morning at seven o'clock her time and nine o'clock their time, her immediate supervisor had grumbled about the fact that Gina would be staying in Aspen for the weekend. The rock-and-roll auction was in less than a month, and Gina had not provided the Elvis inventory she'd promised.

Her supervisor had expressed disapproval. This was not the way they did business at Berryhill's. Their reputation, polished over fifty successful years, did not allow for errors in judgment. And Gina had better not come back empty-handed.

Gina decided not to tell her supervisor that she was a suspect in a murder investigation.

She made a brief traverse of the slope, slipping twice on patches of ice beneath the powdery snow. It was kind of a relief not to have Conner watching, like being able to let out your stomach after holding it in for hours.

She crossed the slope again, more confidently, but at a slow, contemplative speed that allowed her to think about more than the direction her skies were pointing. From the corner of her eye, she sighted a man in a black ski mask who seemed to be observing her.

On her third pass across the hill, she picked up a little speed. She sensed movement behind her and turned in time to see the man in the black ski mask bearing down on her. It seemed as if he was aiming directly for her. Before she could shout, the tips of her skis crossed and she landed in a heap by a thick copse of trees bordering the slope.

The man in the black mask skied on by—not even offering to help. What a creep!

Gina pulled herself up, dusted off the powder and stamped her skis. One tumble on her first ski run in two years was nothing to be ashamed of.

Gliding again, she came over a ridge. And she saw him. The man in the mask. He seemed to be waiting for her, probably to apologize. She waved with her ski pole to show him she was all right, but he did not acknowledge her gesture. He stood at the edge of a tree line, like a thick black shadow.

In a moment, she was below him, coming onto another wide field of snow that was bumpy with moguls. Gina practiced her technique on the center area before seeking the edge, where the snow was smoother.

In her peripheral vision, she saw the man in the black mask, coming toward her again. She slowed to avoid a collision, but he was still coming. There was nowhere to turn except into the trees. Gina fell again. Her arms and legs tangled, and she slid for three yards, coming to a stop just short of a thick evergreen trunk.

"Hey!" she yelled. "Watch it!"

He skied away from her, disappeared in the trees. It almost seemed as if he were purposely trying to run her down. That was exactly what he was doing. She knew it! There were five or six other skiers within her immediate frame of vision. But they were all in motion. She needed to cry for help, to flag down someone. This mystery skier wasn't playing a prank. He wasn't some teenager who was having some fun with her.

His assault was too purposeful. He meant to attack her, to frighten her. Somehow it struck her that he was the man who had murdered Roger Philo. And now he was coming after her.

Fortunately, she'd fallen on the groomed slope and didn't have to fight her way through a couple of feet of unpacked snow to gather her skis. She had to get away from him. Jamming her boots into the bindings, she grabbed her hat and took off. Powdery snow clung to the backside of her ski pants, and the cold seeped through to her thermal underwear. The tip of her nose felt as though an icicle were hanging from it. But there wasn't time to lament the weather.

She concentrated on getting downhill. Across a narrower slope, she saw him. In his black outfit, he was almost invisible against the trees.

Purposefully she pointed away from him. There was a path through the trees directly in front of her and she entered it too fast. The snow beneath her skis was icy. No way to stop. She flew at top speed.

She heard someone behind her. It was him. It had to be him. Her fear made her bold as she tucked into a crouch. She couldn't fall, couldn't allow the stalker to catch up to her. She prayed for balance. Only a little bit farther. The icy air whizzed past, stinging her cheeks. Her legs ached. She emerged from the dark tunnel of trees and burst into the sunlight.

Gina was unfamiliar with the terrain, and here she was, skiing too fast on expert slopes. Instantly she banked uphill, trying to slow down, struggling to gain control. Directly in front of her was a vertical drop, an extreme challenge. She had to stop. If she flew over this edge, she could fall and break her neck.

The man in the black mask came so close that he skied over the backs of her skis. She felt his hand at her back, shoving, and Gina tumbled, her arms and legs flailing. She landed facedown in the snow.

She imagined him standing over her. She was helpless. He could draw back his ski pole and plunge the sharp end between her shoulder blades. He hadn't been teasing her. His chase had not been a game. Gina was sure that this man meant to harm her.

"Are you all right?" The voice was female, thank goodness. "Young woman, are you all right?"

"I think so," Gina said.

Tentatively she moved her arms and legs. There didn't seem to be any broken bones or severe injuries. But there would be bruises tomorrow and a deep scar across the face of her confidence. This sudden rush of terror was more intense than anything she'd felt at Roger's cabin, because this time she'd seen her attacker.

"Did you see him?" Gina asked. She looked into the leathery-tanned face of a woman. "The man in the black ski mask who pushed me. Did you see him?"

"Oh, my, you took quite a fall, didn't you?" Through the woman's rose-colored goggles, Gina could see disbelief in her eyes as she offered, "Let me help you up."

"I'm not lying." Gina remembered Conner's words. No one could tell a lie up here, so close to nature. "Why don't you believe me?"

"I didn't see him. Didn't see anyone. I came around those trees and there you were. All in a heap. You're a regular yard sale, with all your equipment scattered."

"But he was here."

"Well, then, you be sure to report him to the ski patrol." She offered Gina a friendly smile. "But really, honey, it's no shame to fall down every once in a while. Everybody does."

"I didn't."

"But you must have. Here in Aspen, we don't tolerate rude behavior on the slopes." She stuck out her hand. "My name's Mary Garrett."

Garrett? As in Deputy Norm Garrett? Gina noted that her parka was buttoned wrong. Though all of her gear was practical, her colors clashed loudly. "Are you related to Norm?"

"My son, the cop. He could have been a lawyer, you know. But no! Norman failed the bar twice and gave up."

Mary busily gathered up Gina's equipment. Without further discussion, she helped Gina pull herself together. "Should I ski with you?"

"I'm fine. Thank you for stopping."

"Good karma for me to help you. Someday I'll need help." She stared hard at Gina. "How do you know Norm?"

He suspects me of murder. "We've just met briefly."

"He'd make a good husband," said Norm's mother. "Bye now. Try not to hurt yourself."

Mary swiveled into a turn and zipped away. In contrast, Gina proceeded slowly, fearfully. But she didn't see the man in the black mask again.

At the bottom of the slope, she rested her skis and poles in a rack and staggered toward the base lodge. Coffee. She needed coffee, and time to think.

"Gina!" Conner caught her at the steps leading up to the entrance. "I was watching for you. Which way did you come down?"

She turned and pointed.

"Why? I told you to stay on the other slope. That's the place the freestylers use to practice. Expert."

"Well, excuse me all to bits, but there was this guy who kept trying to run into me, and I had to get away from him."

"A guy?"

"It was the murderer, Conner. I know it was."

"Okay."

His eyes slid away from hers, and she knew he didn't believe her any more than Norm's mother had. This was Aspen! Murderers and deviants simply were not allowed! "I should probably forget about it, huh? No investigating. No making waves."

"Tell me what happened."

"He was wearing a black ski mask. Which, unfortunately, is not a particularly odd costume in Aspen. Who knows how many convicted felons are walking the streets right now, with ski masks hiding their identities." Her voice raised. "In New York, the criminal element at least has the courtesy to look the part. I hate this place."

Conner took her arm. "Are you all right?"

"I'm just dandy." Her ski boots made loud clunks as she climbed the stair. "I want some hot coffee, and—"

"There isn't time for that." He tugged at her arm, but Gina was rooted as firmly as an evergreen. "Come on, Gina. Don't be stubborn."

She allowed him to direct her away from the lodge. "Did you take care of your emergency?"

"That's what I'm doing right now. You and I, Gina. We are the emergency." He shepherded her toward the Village where his truck was parked. "The call on my walkie-talkie came from Tommy Kuhara at the rescue shack. Our presence is requested at the DA's office in the courthouse."

"Why?"

"Tommy's been talking to the cops and there's more evidence on Roger's murder."

"A note," she said.

"How did you know?"

"I got a weird call from Dean last night, warning me."

Gina shivered. The morning chill had sunk to the marrow of her bones. It wasn't even ten o'clock, and she'd already been menaced by a masked skier and faced once again with the murder allegation. More evidence? How could there be so much evidence? She was so clearly being framed, but no one would believe her. "When I first started at Berryhill's, we did an auction of eighth-century Chinese brasses and sculptures. One of the pieces was a jade dragon with three heads that had been used by a bandit warlord to guard his treasure. The dragon was supposed to be invincible, bringing bad luck to all who challenged it. According to legend, each time one of the heads was silenced, another would rear and strike. Unless the owner deserved the dragon sculpture, he would be cursed with terrible misfortunes."

"Superstition," Conner said.

"Perhaps. But the woman who unpacked the piece slipped and broke her arm. During the bidding, one of the bidders keeled over with a heart attack, right there on the floor. I was told that the man who took the dragon home with him was either a hired assassin or a ranking agent in the British secret service."

Conner regarded her with a confused expression. "And?"

"When I was working around those sculptures, there seemed to be a bad aura surrounding that jade dragon. It sounds silly, but it scared me. And I feel the same way now—as if there's a three-headed dragon attacking me."

They stopped beside Conner's truck and she looked up at him. "Why won't anyone believe I'm innocent?"

"I believe you." He held open the door and helped her inside. "When we get to the courthouse, we can clear up all this circumstantial evidence. We'll talk with Norm and convince him to look in another direction."

But Gina wasn't so sure. When Conner slammed her door and went around to the driver's side, she remembered Mary Garrett, a woman who was trusting enough to believe in karma but thought Gina had invented an attacker to cover up her own clumsiness.

"I met Norm's mother on the slopes."

"Mary? She is the pushiest woman I've ever seen. She's always fixing poor Norm up with dates."

"No wonder he's so thrilled to be in charge of this investigation. It's probably the first time he's had any power."

"You might be right about that." Conner merged into the tourist traffic wending its way through the Village. "Most people don't take Norm seriously because he's such a klutz."

"But you do?"

"He's worked with me on rescue jobs. Norm's a brave man. I've seen him cross avalanche chutes to reach a victim. I respect him. And I thought he respected me enough to know I wouldn't be involved in a murder."

The seriousness of his tone worried her. "Doesn't he? Conner, how bad is the situation?"

"Pretty bad."

"Tell me."

"Here's what Tommy Kuhara has heard. There's nothing to indicate that anyone, other than you and me, was at the cabin yesterday afternoon. The phone was taken out in a somewhat suspicious manner. There was the Elvis statuette with your fingerprints and blood. We never reported finding the body. There was an envelope with money."

She nodded. "The envelope with forty thousand dollars that I found on Roger's desk."

"Well, according to what Tommy has heard, the latest police theory is that you were going to use that money to pay me off."

"Why? Does this theory have a motive for me to murder Roger?"

"More money. According to the theory, you conned Roger out of a small fortune. My share, my payoff, was forty thou."

"What about the Jeep?" she questioned. "Somebody must have pulled that coil wire and purposely stranded me up there."

"Or it could have jolted loose and that's why you didn't make a clean getaway."

She nodded her head. "It does sound pretty bad."

"I owe you an apology, Gina. I wasn't ready to play detective because I trusted these people, my friends and co-workers. I thought they'd take extra pains to clear me from suspicion. But I was wrong. They want a conviction, and they want it fast.''

At the courthouse, they waited a good half hour, sequestered in a small conference room. It was the same room where Ted Bundy had been held, the room he'd escaped from before coming to trial for the brutal murders of young women.

Though Gina had been served coffee, she was still cold. Only her feet, encased in rental ski boots, had begun to sweat.

When Deputy Norm Garrett and Assistant District Attorney Alex Philo joined them, she tried to summon up some grace under pressure, but Alex's hate-filled glare unnerved her. She didn't know how to act in the presence of such hostility.

"I understand you have new evidence," Conner said.

"That's right." Norm sat opposite them and fumbled through his pockets, trying to find a pencil. "I wanted to ask you a few questions."

Alex remained standing, looking down from a superior height. "I don't agree with this informal questioning. You should both be charged. Your statements should be recorded by a stenographer."

"Then we're even," Conner said. "I don't agree with you being in charge. Looks like a conflict of interest."

"I'm taking an interest," Alex admitted. "The DA okayed it."

He placed a cassette recorder on the table, pressed the record button and recited the date, the time and the names of the individuals present. Then he turned to Gina. "State your name, for the record, then tell us what happened three nights ago at the tavern."

Dutifully she repeated the story of how Roger had patted her bottom and she'd slapped him. Alex interrupted, asking, "And what did you say to him?"

"'Roger, I could just kill you.'"

"Speak up."

"'Roger, I could just kill you.'"

"Are you in the habit of making death threats?"

"It wasn't a threat, Alex."

"So, you actually intended to—"

"Of course not. I was angry. That's all."

"Because Roger Philo propositioned you."

"Roger never actually came right out and propositioned me. You can talk to Wendell Otis about this. He was there the whole time. Have you talked to Otis?"

"Yes," he said, curtly. "Are you saying that Roger never asked you to go to bed with him?"

Her exhaustion slaked as her temper rose. "We were related by marriage. Roger was making jokes, little innuendos."

"Sexual innuendos." Alex pursed his lips puritanically. "Apparently, his comments and harassment angered you enough that you assaulted him."

"I slapped him."

Under the table, she felt Conner take her hand. Gina knew that Alex was baiting her, trying to make her explode so that he could use her hot temper against her. "If I murdered every man who made a lewd comment to me, I'd make Bundy look like a piker."

"Comparing yourself to Ted Bundy? Do you admire the late Mr. Bundy?"

"Would you please stop twisting this around, Alex? I didn't kill Uncle Roger. I was annoyed with him, but I still agreed to meet him at the cabin to see the Elvis memorabilia."

"Let's talk about that," Norm said. "The crime scene."

Gina described the cabin, the records, the money and her sense that someone else was there. "I tried to escape by—"

"Escape?" Alex questioned. "Fleeing the scene?"

"I was caught in the blizzard," she continued. "If Conner hadn't come along when he did, it's possible that I would have died on the mountainside."

"So Conner saved your life and brought you back to the cabin, where he warmed you up. Did he help you bathe? Did he hold your hand to restore circulation? Did you—" he paused, sounding exactly like his mother "—share bodily warmth."

"Oh, please. Now you're the one making innuendos, Alex."

Norm put in his two cents' worth. "When I showed up in the morning, you two looked like you were getting along pretty well."

"We were," Conner readily admitted. "I like Gina."

"Let's talk about the money," Alex said. "Forty thousand dollars in cash. It was found in a large padded envelope with Gina's name written upon it. Where did it come from?"

"I don't know." She offered an explanation of her own. "Maybe there was something Roger had to buy with cash."

"But here's the weird part," Norm said. "We can't figure out where Roger got it. We've been checking his accounts, and there weren't any large withdrawals."

Alex cut him off. "That will be enough. We're not here to discuss Roger Philo's business practices."

"But it's important," Norm said. "We can't—"

"I think we can all agree that Roger wasn't the most ethical person in the world, especially when it came to money. That's moot. All we need to know is if he planned to present the money to Gina."

"I can't imagine why," she said. "I was here to obtain items from him for auction."

"What items?" Alex leaned across the table and got right in her face. "Where are they?"

"I wish I knew," she snapped. "Dean told me that Roger kept most of his Presley collection in LA, in the offices he shared with Wendell Otis."

"Ridiculous! Why would Roger do that? He and Otis barely got along."

"Maybe they had an agreement. Maybe Otis had something of Roger's in exchange."

"Such as?"

"I don't know, Alex."

Alex clicked off the tape recorder. "This time you've gone too far, Gina. You've always been the cute, smart family favorite. But you're not going to get away with murder."

"Whoa there..." Norm said, rising to his feet. "You're out of line, Alex. Gina and Conner are witnesses, nothing more. And I won't have you intimidating them."

"You bumbling donkey! The sheriff will be back within the week and you'll be off the case. I hope you don't screw things up too badly before then."

"Within the week?" Gina asked in dismay. "I have to leave before then. I need to get back to work."

"Oh, let's not forget your very important job," Alex said scornfully. "Gina Robinson, the art snob. That's a damn hobby, not a profession. Nobody makes a living in art. But you did. Everything falls into place for you, doesn't it?"

"What's your problem, Alex?" Gina flared.

"Settle down," Norm commanded. "This questioning is over, Alex. Right now."

"Don't presume to tell me what to do. I'm an assistant district attorney."

"And I'm going to insist that your boss be here the next time you question either one of these witnesses."

Alex snatched his tape recorder, stalked to the door and slammed it behind him.

"Sorry," Norm muttered. "I don't know what's gotten into Alex. He sure doesn't like you, Gina. Conner, I'm real sorry."

"It's okay," Conner said. "I wanted to ask you about this new piece of evidence. A note."

"How did you find out about that? Have I got a leak in the department?"

"Get real, Norm. I work with you guys all the time. Of course I'm going to hear about stuff from my friends."

"Aw, hell, I feel the same way. You're a good man, Conner, and I can't believe this mess." He inhaled a deep breath, almost popping one of the buttons on his shirt. "I'm going to tell you a couple of things that maybe I shouldn't. But I bet you can explain them to me."

"Thanks," Conner said.

"We found a note in Roger's handwriting. It said, 'Gina, I have a lot to offer, but you'll have to give me a chance.'"

Gina nodded. "Makes perfect sense. He was referring to the items he had for sale. That note might even work in my favor—as an explanation of why so few of the Elvis pieces were at the cabin."

"Alex sees it as a sex thing that goes along with the money. He figures that Roger invited you up to the cabin, intending to seduce you with money, this note and that god-awful Elvis costume. Between you and me, I think Alex is more upset about Roger's messing around with women and embarrassing his mom than anything else."

Gina agreed wholeheartedly. She leaned forward, giving Norm her full attention. "Then what does Alex think happened?"

"He's guessing that when you got to the cabin, you didn't want to play along. And we've all seen evidence of your hot temper, Gina."

"Roger wasn't there when I got to the cabin," she repeated, for what seemed like the ten-thousandth time.

"Let me finish," Norm said. "We're assuming that Roger was sitting in the kitchen when he got whacked over the head. We found traces of blood between the tiles. Maybe he was coming on to you, Gina. And you bashed him with the Elvis statue. In self-defense."

When he turned his gaze upon her, his expression was as canny as a fox's, and Gina knew this was the point he'd been leading toward. Norm was offering her a self-defense plea. She suspected that the whole business to which she'd been subjected was a variation of the good-cop-bad-cop routine. Did he really think she was so stupid? With wide-eyed sweetness, she said, "Gosh, Norm, I wish I could confess for you, but Roger wasn't—"

"That's where we figure Conner came into the picture."

"How so?" Conner questioned.

"When Roger keeled over, Gina was scared. She tried to run and almost got swallowed whole by the blizzard. Then you come along and save her life. Now, Conner, we all know that you were never buddies with Roger..."

"I didn't like Roger," Conner agreed. "But I didn't hate him enough to kill him."

"But it wasn't like you went after him or anything. You were only helping out Gina by hauling the body to the woodbox."

"Then I shoot him in the chest?"

Norm hedged. "That's the part that doesn't fit."

"Guess not," Conner said. "I'm fairly good with first aid. I would have known that Roger wasn't dead and could be revived—thereby getting Gina out of trouble without killing her uncle.''

"But the blizzard was coming." Norm tapped his pencil on the table, so vigorously that he broke the lead point. "You knew you couldn't get an ambulance or a rescue helicopter. Maybe it looked like Roger was going to die from the head injury anyway. Maybe he made some kind of threat or something. I'm not sure."

There were many parts to this farfetched scenario that Norm seemed unsure about. Conner could tell that the deputy was between a ledge and a landslide. And walking on shaky ground. "You know, Norm, none of this makes any sense."

"Self-defense, Conner." Norm made his appeal. "You could get a reduced sentence on those charges. Easy. A jury might let you off with probation and a slap on the wrist."

Or else . . . he'd go to jail. For the first time, Conner accepted that possibility, and it scared him. Jail? Might as well put a bullet through his head. Conner couldn't live without the mountains, skies, forests, slopes. He couldn't wake up in a cell, not knowing if it was spring or winter, not hearing the wind. That wouldn't be living. "Let me ask you something, Norm. One question."

"Shoot."

"I don't want you to answer too fast. Because this means a lot to me." It meant a hell of a lot. "And I don't want you to think of me as the suspect that Alex and the mayor and the DA want to accuse."

"Hey, Conner, nobody's trying to railroad you. You're a local hero."

"Not anymore." Conner was clear about his local identity as a small-town boy who had once made good. But there weren't any more Olympics in his future. Most of the people around here—the people like Alex—considered him to be nothing more than another Aspen ski bum. "I'm not a celebrity. And I'm not going to expect special treatment."

Norm started to object, then went still. He looked down at the table, at the pencil in his hands.

"I'm just a guy you've skied with, Norm. A guy you've known since high school. A guy who works with the sheriff's department on mountain rescues. We've shared some good times."

"And some bad," Norm said.

"There have been a lot of theories floating around here. And I know you're under pressure to make an arrest. But I want to know what you really believe."

"About what?"

"I want you to look me in the eye and tell me if you really believe I was involved in the murder of Roger Philo."

When Norm finally dragged his gaze from the tabletop and confronted Conner, eye-to-eye, there was nothing clumsy about his manner, nothing folksy about his speech. "Until I notify you otherwise, both you and Gina are under suspicion of the murder of Roger Philo. If you attempt to leave town, I will arrest you."

Chapter Six

While she and Conner drove through the picturesque Village of Aspen, through streets where the people were all robust and happy, Gina fumed. The quaint charm of the ski town annoyed her. The beautiful, crisp weather affronted her. How could Deputy Norm Garrett make such unfounded accusations? And her cousin Alex—what had she ever done to offend him so deeply?

Gina searched her memories of the family experiences that she had shared with Alex and she couldn't remember anything remarkable. As cousins, they were fairly typical. Not close, but not hating each other. "I don't know why Alex is so mad at me."

"Could be that he's protecting his mom," Conner said. "Alex is one of those straight-arrow kind of guys. He must have hated the way Roger played around."

"So did I," she said.

"But Alex doesn't know that. All he knows is that you came out here to see Roger. You talked to him on the phone, made the dates with him."

"It was business."

"From what Alex said in that interrogation, he doesn't consider your job to be a real profession."

Immediately she bristled. But she acknowledged the truth in Conner's suggestion. "He doesn't. He doesn't see beyond his own lawyer's nose."

"Alex might think you and Roger had something else going on."

"Like what?"

"Sex or money. Or both. Take your pick."

Gina shuddered. What an awful choice! But if Alex believed she'd been after Roger's wallet, and willing to sleep with him to get it, he would want to protect Lydia.

When Conner parked outside the Taos Lodge and came around to the passenger side to help her out, she said, "Alex is just being cruel."

"Don't be cruel," he said.

"What?" When her feet touched the hard-packed snow in the parking lot, she winced. Though she rented the very best Technica ski boots, they were rentals and not meant for stomping away from courthouses. "What did you say?"

"A quote. 'Don't Be Cruel.'"

"You're quoting an Elvis song title? Is that supposed to cheer me up?"

"At least it's not 'Jailhouse Rock.' Not yet, anyway."

He took her arm and guided her through the lobby and past the lounge, where morning skiers had gathered for late breakfast or early lunch. Their tanned, smiling faces and hearty laughter contrasted with her anger. Gina had half a mind to storm into the lounge and lecture them all on the problems of the world in general, and her own problem in particular, but her feet and ankles throbbed so painfully that she couldn't think of anything else until they were in her room.

She kicked off the ski boots, flopped across the bed and stared up at the wood beams across the ceiling. She sighed. Relieving the intense pain in her feet made her aware of other aches and probable bruises—the result of her collisions with the man in the black ski mask.

Her rage had almost played its course, leaving her with dark feelings of frustration and confusion. "Do you think we'll look back on this and laugh someday?"

"I won't." He went to the window and opened the floor-to-ceiling curtains, revealing a view of blue sky and distant snow-capped peaks. Then he pulled over a chair and sat with his feet propped at the end of the bed. "We've got to face it, Gina. If Norm doesn't find another suspect, he'll arrest us. Don't let his bumbling around fool you."

"I wasn't fooled at all by their good-cop-bad-cop routine. I feel as though I was in the middle of a television program."

"What do you mean?"

"First Alex screams and yells and tries to be intimidating to throw us off-balance..."

"You think that was an act?"

"Some of it. And some of it was Alex being his naturally rude self," she said. "Then good old Norm holds out the olive branch and offers that absurd self-defense theory, hoping we'll spill our guts in a confession."

"Spill our guts, huh? They do that on television?"

"Sure. But the actors on TV cop shows are lots more effective than Norm and Alex. Haven't you ever seen that?"

"I don't have a TV set."

She rolled over on the bed, discovering a particularly painful spot on her lower hip. "No TV? No VCR?"

"I don't get good reception at my cabin. If I want to watch the Bronco games on Sundays, I'll come into town."

She stared at him in fascination. His life-style was so different from her own. "What do you do for mindless entertainment?"

"I do have an excellent CD player."

"What kind of music do you like?"

"A little bit of everything. Classical. Jazz. Kenny Loggins. Billy Joel. Elvis Presley."

When he leaned back in the chair and smiled, Gina knew she was in the presence of a truly unusual creature—a man who was content with his life. Not ambitious, not hard-driving. Conner had achieved a certain calm assurance. And strength. He had nothing to prove. She imagined him on a winter's night, sitting before the fireplace and reading a book while a CD played softly. In the summer, he would sit on his porch and survey the natural surroundings he loved so well.

All that quiet! She'd never been quiet in her whole life. "Conner, what are we going to do?"

"We have to solve this murder. And we have to start now."

Gina resisted the temptation to say, "I told you so." "Where do we start?"

"Wendell Otis."

"I have his office phone number. Should we call him now?"

"First, let's get organized." Conner turned his head to look out the window. Watching Gina was much too distracting, and he needed to concentrate. His mind raced through alternative plans for investigating. In some ways, they had the advantage, because they were not only the main suspects, but the main witnesses, as well. "We need to remember everything, Gina. I keep thinking there's something we overlooked. Some major clue."

"I'm sure there is. That's why the guy in the black ski mask tried to run me down on the ski slope." Fear struck a resonating chord within her. "He kept waiting for me. He'd ski ahead and hover at the edge of the slope until I was in sight, then he'd swoop down. He was stalking me."

"And you think he was the murderer?"

"I'm sure of it."

"Slow down, Gina. Let's get logical. If this guy set up the perfect frame, he wouldn't want to hurt you, because you're the person who's going to take the rap."

Conner thought for a minute, tried to put himself into the mind of the murderer. He'd killed Roger. And he'd set a trap for Gina, knowing from Roger's appointment book that she was going to show up at the right time. Why would he come after her now?

Though Conner wasn't a hunter, he knew a lot of guys who were. They'd tell him that it didn't do any good to set a trap in the forest if the quarry didn't take the bait. "He's coming after you because you won't lie back and accept your fate," he said. "You won't take the bait."

"How could I? How could I give up without a fight?"

"Most people would. Most people would hire an attorney and let the system do its thing." He caught her gaze and held it. "That would be the safest course, Gina."

"I can't do that."

"Are you sure? If we keep on looking for the murderer, he's going to feel threatened. He'll come after you."

"I'm not a quitter. God help me, I've never been passive."

"Okay." He wasn't comfortable with the idea. He didn't like to think about a murderer coming after Gina. But he couldn't change her. And his own freedom was at stake, too. "Let's talk about the guy in the ski mask. What did he look like? Can you describe him?"

"Black ski mask. Black parka. Black pants."

"What about his skis? Did you notice his ski equipment?"

Gina closed her eyes and tried to remember. Her visual sense of memory was excellent, honed by her job, in which recalling each and every detail of an artwork was essential to verifying authenticity. She recalled the cerulean Aspen sky, and the glittering white of the slope, marked by dark morning shadows as the sun slanted through the treetops. In her peripheral vision, she had seen the silhouette of a masked man. He'd stayed at a distance, blending with the shadows until he raced toward her. "I wasn't close enough to see his skis until he was on top of me."

"I don't like this," Conner said. "You're in danger. We have to—"

"What? Report it to the police?" Her voice was sharp. "You know they wouldn't believe me."

"We should get out of town," he said. "You can't stand around and wait for him to strike."

"Marvelous idea, Conner." Her eyes snapped open. "If we leave town, Norm promised to arrest us."

And he'd meant it, Conner knew. Norm was willing to sacrifice his friendship for the sake of a conviction. It was a cold world when friends would betray each other for the sake of a reward. In Norm's case, it was career advancement. He would please the DA and the mayor. Probably the sheriff, too.

"We've got to think," he said. "Think, Gina. There must have been something at Roger's cabin, something that might betray the killer's identity."

"But what?"

Conner couldn't think of a single significant clue. When he searched the cabin with Gina, there had been no indication of who had been there. They'd seen everything . . . and nothing. There was a frustrating lack of solid physical evidence.

"Maybe," Gina said, "it's something that *wasn't* there? Like the murder weapon?"

"Roger was shot. We didn't see a gun."

"When I was talking to Dean, he mentioned that Roger had a couple of Elvis's guns, and those weren't at the cabin." She shook her head. "But he also said there were sunglasses and jewelry."

Her voice was subdued. When he glanced at her, he saw a glimmer of fear in her wide brown eyes. She looked so small and vulnerable that he wanted to pull her into the shelter of his arms and promise her that nothing or no one would ever hurt her. But that would be a lie. He couldn't guarantee protection.

The irony was Conner's job. Mountain rescue. In the past three seasons, he'd tracked down dozens of skiers stranded by avalanches. He'd climbed down sheer rock pinnacles to aid climbers who had fallen or been trapped by their own carelessness. He'd found a lost little boy with curly blond hair who had wandered away from his parents. If there was one thing he'd learned, it was hope. No matter how impossible the situation, there was always hope for survival.

But he never forgot the failures. He remembered interminable tense hours, searching for avalanche victims and finding them suffocated and broken beneath snow that had set like cement. Buried alive.

Gina dragged herself to a sitting posture on the blue-and-gray patterned bedspread. "I need to change clothes and take a hot shower. I've got bruises on top of bruises."

"Cold is better," he said. "Keeps the swelling down."

"A cold shower? I'd rather swell! I'd rather puff up like a balloon in the Macy's Thanksgiving parade!"

With exaggerated moans and groans, she limped stiffly toward the bathroom. Though she was making light of her injuries, Conner could feel her pain, and it hurt him, too. How the hell was he going to protect her when he didn't know who the enemy was?

He heard her laugh. "Hey, Conner, take a look at this."

In the bathroom on the counter lay a copy of a tabloid newspaper. The bold headline screamed Elvis Visits Truck Stop—Orders Banana Cream Pie.

"The chambermaid must have left it here," she said. "Or else I'm being haunted by Elvis."

She flipped to the classified advertising. "We placed an ad here. See? I objected, of course. Berryhill's is a prestigious house. We don't need to support this rag. But everyone in my office is caught up in the spirit of totally tacky rock and roll."

Conner read the small notice that announced the auction and promised Elvis memorabilia, among several other items.

"This type of ad is why I have to produce," Gina explained. "This is why I put up with so much obnoxious behavior from Roger. He told me that he had a ton of stuff we could auction. And I believed him."

"People actually pay good money for this stuff?"

"The beat-up guitar Elvis played in *Viva Las Vegas* sold for twenty-two thousand dollars." She exhaled a deep sigh and sat on the edge of the bathtub. "If I come back with nothing, I could lose my job."

Unemployment seemed like the least of her problems to Conner. She could be physically assaulted by this madman. She could be arrested and jailed for the murder of Roger Philo. He hunkered down beside her in the cramped hotel bathroom and placed his hand on her knee. "We'll take care of it, Gina. We'll find this guy and turn him in. Then you can get on with your life."

"Really?"

"I promise."

Her wide brown eyes searched his face, penetrating deep into his steady gaze, seeking hope. And she must have found something that soothed her, because she smiled and visibly relaxed. "I trust you."

"Good." Amazingly good, he thought. Her words made him feel ten feet tall and invincible. "I won't let you down."

He left her to shower and went into the bedroom to pace. He had to find a way to protect Gina and to solve the murder. They needed answers. How the hell was he going to figure this out? *Think, Conner, think.*

There were obvious steps to be taken: Review the scene at Roger's cabin. Write it all down. Study all the possibilities. Remember everything. Contact Wendell Otis in California.

And what about motive? Who would have wanted Roger dead, and why?

Though Lydia might be able to help, Conner remembered the nasty scene yesterday morning and decided that interviewing the Philo family was the last resort. There had to be someone else; Aspen wasn't that big.

Because Conner had generally avoided contact with Roger, he wasn't familiar with his circle of friends ... and enemies. But it was safe to assume that Roger associated with the upper strata of Aspen society, a clique that was impossible to infiltrate without a Ferrari and a listing in the *Fortune* 500. Still, Conner had a couple of friends, skiers, in that group.

A plan began to formulate in his mind. He reached for the telephone.

Moments later, Gina stepped out of the bathroom, dressed in a cream-colored turtleneck and forest green Levi's, looking fresh-scrubbed, with a pink glow highlighting the sprinkling of freckles on her cheeks. Her hair was wet.

"Hurry up, Gina. I thought of somebody who might be able to help with figuring out the motive."

"Who?"

"His name is Jerry Sage."

Her jaw dropped. "Jerome Sage? The Broadway composer who's had consecutive hit shows for the past twelve years?"

"Yeah, I think so."

"You think so? Conner, the man is a living legend. And he's so reclusive that I've only read one interview with him."

"He's a damn good skier, too. Anyway, I just talked to him on the phone and I think he can help us. He knows a lot of people, and he and Roger were in the same business."

She scoffed. "Saying that Jerome Sage and Roger Philo were in the same line of work is like comparing Picasso to a housepainter."

"Whatever. Can you hurry?"

Wheeling around, Gina returned to the bathroom, where she kept up a steady line of patter about Jerome Sage and her own favorite Broadway musicals. At the same time, she blow-dried her red hair and applied a dash of makeup.

As he observed the process, Conner enjoyed each step in her grooming process. Women were such strange, wonderful creatures, he thought. Her hair fascinated him. It was the color of molten lava and the texture of silk. He wanted to tangle his fingers in those strands, to feel the softness against his cheek, to see those long red curls spread across his pillow.

"Conner? Have you heard a word I've been saying?"

"Huh?"

"Men!" She gave him a mock scowl. "I'll never understand the gender!"

His hand reached toward her, and his fingers disappeared in the mass of her red hair as he held her head and tasted her soft lips. She responded to his touch, gliding her body against his. Her arms slipped around his torso.

He increased the pressure of his kiss. His arms drew her closer. An aching passion built inside him. My God, he wanted to make love to this woman, to kiss her breasts and hear her moan his name. He wanted to enter her, to stake his claim to her body.

When he gazed down and studied the perfection of her features, her eyes seemed unfocused and glazed. Her voice was breathy. "Now look what you've done. I'm all messed up."

"I like the way you look."

"Isn't your friend waiting?"

"He'll understand."

"No, Conner." She leaned away from him. "We'll have time for this later."

He swallowed hard and nodded his head. Later? That sounded like a promise to him. "I can wait."

But not for too much longer.

WHEN SHE MET Jerome Sage at the door of his Starwood home, Gina tried not to embarrass Conner by gushing. But she truly did admire this musical composer, who had achieved his first renown about fourteen years ago, with a brilliant and stirring score for an otherwise forgettable movie. Jerome Sage had won an Oscar for it. After that, he'd begun working on Broadway, producing one hit after another.

Though she had seen photographs of this man, with his dramatic mane of pure white hair, the pictures were always heavily shadowed. He seldom made public appearances in Manhattan or Los Angeles, but the man Conner introduced as "Jerry" seemed far less guarded about his privacy while in Aspen.

In person, he was handsome, probably in his mid-fifties, with classic features. A strong Roman nose. Full lips. And deep-set blue eyes, heavily lidded. There was something familiar about him, and when he opened his mouth and spoke with a warm southern accent, Gina knew what it was.

If his hair was midnight black instead of white, Jerry Sage would very much resemble Elvis Presley.

After he'd served them cappuccino, made with an elaborate brass-plated machine in the bar, he served himself a Pepsi.

Elvis's favorite beverage, Gina knew from her research.

He ushered them into a living room with a wall of cantilevered windows. The room was so spacious that the white baby grand piano did not dominate the decor, which was otherwise unremarkable and un-Elvis-like. Disappointed, Gina said, "This is attractive."

"Thank you very much. I'll tell my designer you like it."

"You didn't design it yourself?" If he had, would it look like Graceland? Would there be splashy orange and mirrored ceilings and ebony?

"I don't have real good taste." His upper lip curled in a vaguely familiar way. "Now, what can I do for you? Conner, you sounded mighty upset on the phone."

"Have you heard about Roger Philo's murder?"

"Yes, sir, I have. Seems like I've heard nothing else for the past day and a half."

"Norm Garrett suspects Gina and me. And so does Alex Philo. You've heard that, too. Haven't you, Jerry?"

He nodded. "You and Roger had your share of fights. After he got you mixed up in that advertising fiasco, I wouldn't have blamed you much if you'd punched his lights out. You could have made a lot of money with the right manager, Conner."

"Yeah, if I'd been willing to dress up like a clown and prance around."

Jerry chuckled. "Wasn't exactly a clown suit they wanted y'all to wear."

Gina's interest perked up. She'd heard a lot about these commercials and how Conner and Roger had disagreed about them. "What did they want you to wear?"

"His undies," Jerry said.

"Those were the well-dressed ads," Conner put in. "Roger wasn't exactly interested in marketing my ability as a skier when he could make more money getting me naked. There were underwear ads, a soap company that wanted me in a shower and something where I was skiing in a skimpy bathing suit."

"But why? People knew you as a skier."

"I believe Roger's exact words were, 'You didn't win gold. You're a loser. Now strip.'" He shrugged. "That was when we parted company."

"And rightly so," Jerry said. "You should have gone with another agent."

"Didn't want to," Conner said. "I'm not a celebrity. I'm a skier. Anyway, Jerry, that's not why we're here. I'll make this long story short. Gina and I are trying to figure out who killed Roger so the police will get off our backs."

"Why come to me?"

"I'm looking for motives, and you know everybody around here, especially the artsy crowd. Can you think of anyone who might have wanted Roger dead?"

He laughed. "Start with the *A*s in the local phone book. Roger wasn't real popular."

"What about money?" Conner said, thinking of the forty-thousand dollars in a plain brown envelope with Gina's name in the corner. "Did Roger owe anybody money?"

"I might've heard some gossip about how he wasn't raking in the big bucks like he used to. But Roger was pretty well set. And Lydia does real fine with her real estate business."

"Lydia is my aunt," Gina said.

"A fine woman," Jerry said.

"I know. She seemed okay with her marriage, but I don't know why. Roger was always flirting, and..."

Words failed her. She felt disloyal accusing Roger of infidelity in front of Jerome Sage. Worse, Gina thought, she hated to cast her aunt in a poor light.

Conner had no such reservations. "Roger was playing around with other women. That might have led to a motive."

"For Lydia?" Jerry questioned.

"Oh, no," Gina said. "I would never want to imply that my aunt would even think of murder. She's not capable of thinking that way. Never in a million years."

"I'm sorry," Conner said. "But Lydia has to be considered. She probably stands to gain financially by her husband's murder. And, as you pointed out, Roger wasn't winning awards as the world's greatest husband."

"No," Gina protested. "Remember the way the murder was committed, Conner. The body was lifted and carried some distance. A woman couldn't have done it."

"Unless she had help," he said.

She sucked in a ragged breath and glanced toward Jerry. "We're being very indiscreet. I hope you understand that we're only speculating."

"I do understand," Jerry said. "If it helps any, I can tell you that I've never heard divorce rumblings from your aunt, Gina. Whatever arrangement Lydia and Roger had suited them. They attended all the social events together and looked to be having a good time. I just saw them together a couple of months ago, at the Christmas Ball." He leaned back, spreading his arms on the back of the sofa. "Conner, I didn't see you at the ball."

"No date."

"How come? Don't you tell me that a hotshot skier like you is afraid to ask a woman out."

"Not scared. Just not interested in anybody."

"What about the Pisces party this weekend? You coming?"

"Sure." Conner nodded toward Gina. "I'll be there, if my date is still in town."

"I'll be here." She was curt, still a bit steamed about Conner's having mentioned Lydia as a suspect. "I've been ordered not to leave town. Remember? I'll be happy to be your date, Conner. If I'm not in jail."

"Hey, there," Jerry said. "That ain't exactly the way to build a man's ego—telling him that he's one step up from the hoosegow."

"Did it sound like that?"

"Yes, ma'am. It did. You're probably a feminist, right?"

"Probably."

He rolled his heavy-lidded eyes as he looked toward Conner. "Oh, my boy, you're in for a rough ride."

"I know," he muttered. "But I like a challenge. The best rides come from the horses that are hardest to break."

"Conner, dear . . ." Her voice was like a silken cloak concealing a dagger. "Are you comparing me to a horse?"

"Now, Gina," Jerry said, "don't get your back up."

"Like a cat? Now you're comparing me to a cat?"

Jerry hooted with laughter. "I like you, Gina, and I'm sure you're one-hundred-percent human female. I hope you stick it out with Conner. He could use some fire in his life."

To Gina, this situation was bizarre. No one would believe that she had spent time in the Starwood home of Jerome Sage, world-renowned composer. And he was playing matchmaker for her.

"Wish I could promise you a good time on Saturday." Jerry frowned. "Roger put together the entertainment for this year's Pisces party. He was talking about Michael Penrose, but he's just a lounge singer in Vegas who has a group and plays trumpet. Can't imagine him carrying the whole affair on his skinny shoulders." He glanced at Conner. "Do you know Penrose?"

"Can't say that I do."

"I would've been just as happy with somebody local, like Dean Philo, but Roger said Penrose would do it for free—just to take advantage of contacts, you know. And the party is supposed to be raising money for a homeless shelter."

"In Aspen?" Gina questioned. "Is there a homeless problem in Aspen?"

"Hell, no. We'd have to import them. This money is going to a shelter in Denver."

For someone who was supposed to be a recluse, Jerry Sage seemed to be a very social creature. Personable, charming, and charismatic as Elvis himself. "You're different than I expected," she blurted.

"That so? Well, the media makes me sound like Howard Hughes, with twelve-inch-long fingernails, because I refuse point-blank to do interviews. But I'm not a hermit."

"I guessed that," she said.

"I don't like to be bothered when I'm working. I need quiet." He cleared his throat. "And you two need more help on motives. Anything else I can tell you?"

"What about Wendell Otis?" Conner said. "He was supposed to be at the meeting with Gina but didn't show. Do you know anything about him and his relationship to Roger?"

"Not much. I met Otis once and he lectured me about my cholesterol count. Never wanted to know the man better." Jerry brightened. "Now, I think he'd be a fine suspect. I can just see him suffocating somebody with a block of tofu."

"We still need to call him. Gina, do you have his phone number?"

"Right here." She pointed to her purse. "When we get back to the hotel, we can talk to him."

Jerry offered the use of his phone. Though Gina politely insisted that they would wait, he suggested that the weight of his name might help in getting past a receptionist to Wendell Otis himself.

"Why would I have a problem?"

"You might not. But the man is a talent agent. And I just happen to be in the position of always looking for talent."

Gina stood at the windows beside the piano and talked in the direction of a sophisticated speaker phone. After charging the call to her phone card, she reached a receptionist who took her name and said she would check and see if Mr. Otis was available.

He was not.

"Perhaps Mr. Otis would be able to talk with my friend," Gina said smoothly. "His name is Jerome Sage."

"The composer?"

"The very one." Gina smiled at Jerry, who had taken a seat at the piano bench.

"Oh, really?" The receptionist's voice was frosty. "And how do I know this is really Jerome Sage?"

"I can let you speak to him."

"I've got a better idea," Jerry said. His long fingers descended to the piano keys, and he ran through a brilliant one-minute medley of his hit tunes before saying, "This is Jerome Sage in Aspen. You put Mr. Otis on the line, hear?"

"Oh, Mr. Sage, I'm so very sorry. But Mr. Otis really and truly is not in his office. I can page him. Can he call you back?"

Gina left the number and within five minutes they heard the slightly nasal voice of Wendell Otis. "Jerome? How are you? Hope you're not still eating bacon."

"Extra-crisp bacon. Grits. And biscuits with gravy. I'm from the South, Otis. It's in my blood. Here's Gina Robinson. She wants to talk to you."

"Mr. Otis. I suppose you've heard about my uncle."

"Yes, and I'm sorry. Terribly sorry. I've spoken to Lydia and I will arrange to be at the funeral. Have they chosen a time and date yet?"

"Not as far as I know," Gina said truthfully. "Listen, Mr. Otis, I wanted to ask you about the meeting at Roger's cabin. I understand you left before that."

"The weather was turning bad. I went to the airport. But we didn't actually get cleared for takeoff until dawn the next day."

Gina raised her eyebrows. So, Otis had been in town at the time Roger was murdered. "I don't suppose you made it to the cabin before you left. If you had been there, you surely would have left a copy of the inventory list for me."

"I wouldn't have left a paper clip with Roger."

"That hardly seems fair. I was led to believe that Roger left most of his valuable Elvis memorabilia in your care."

"You might say that."

His silky tone rang with falsity, but Gina wasn't sure if they were talking about murder or about Elvis. Her own motivations were equally unclear. If Otis had a good collection of Elvis memorabilia, she wanted it. "I need to see your collection. When will you be coming back here?"

"Listen, Gina, I can't be bothered with your auction right now. When I return to Aspen, all my time and effort will be devoted to Lydia. She's going to need my support in this difficult time."

Gina made a sudden, impetuous decision. "If I came out to California tomorrow morning, could we talk?"

There was silence on the line, and then Jerome said, "I sure would appreciate if you'd help out my friend Gina. Within the next two months, I'm going to be casting for my next Broadway production."

Otis said, "I'll be delighted to meet with you, Gina."

She got his office address, home address and private home phone number before disconnecting. She turned to Jerry and grinned. "Thank you. I never would have gotten past that snotty receptionist without your help."

Conner stood close beside her but she avoided looking at him.

"Gina," he said patiently, "Norm told you not to leave town."

"But Otis obviously knows so much. He's close to Lydia. He was Roger's former partner. And he does have that Elvis memorabilia. I could take care of my Berryhill's business with him and be back here before Norm notices that I'm gone." She was determined. She was going to California. "Listen, Conner. I'll understand if you don't want to come with me...."

But, somehow, she knew that he would.

Chapter Seven

He'd never meant to be a murderer. He hadn't killed Roger for fun. But now, when he thought about it, about the instant he'd pulled the trigger, he felt a guilty sense of pleasure. That was the best kind.

When he was a kid, the candy he stole from the drugstore had tasted sweeter. Getting away with cheating was more important than the test score. A hooker was more satisfying than a lover or a wife. Guilty pleasures.

Going after Gina was the same way. At first, he hadn't planned to frame her. Circumstances had guided him. Logic had dictated that he choose a victim, and Gina had presented herself.

She was proving herself to be a worthy adversary. She wouldn't quit, kept fighting back. He wished he could compliment her, then tell her how clever he'd been.

Of course, he wouldn't take that chance. He couldn't say a word. Not ever. He must remain silent and allow the seeds of evidence he had planted to grow and flourish like giant brambles that would imprison Gina. And Conner, too.

He stood at the door of his rental car, the vehicle he'd rented so that no one would notice him. Gina and Conner had outsmarted themselves. Getting on a plane disobeyed a direct police order. Now she would pay. She'd be tracked down like a fugitive.

She would pay for her lack of respect.

He'd make it his business to see her pay.

"NORM WILL NEVER KNOW," Gina said.

She stretched out her legs in the passenger seat of the rental car and inhaled the salty air that meant they were near the ocean. Though Wendell Otis lived very close to the Beverly Hills zip code, she and Conner had decided to stay at the beach tonight.

The breeze through her half-opened car window blew a cool caress across her cheeks and through her hair, but the southern California evening was balmy compared with the winter cold of the high Rockies. The fabric of her cloth jacket, when compared with parkas and thermal underwear, seemed marvelously unrestricting.

"This is paradise," she said. "Tall, waving palms and blooming flowers and oranges you can pick right off the tree. I wish we could stay here for a week, basking in the sun and sipping rum drinks with little umbrellas."

"It's not quite that warm, Gina. Not many people sunbathe in February."

"That's because they haven't been freezing half to death in Aspen. This feels fantastic."

"I hope we won't regret it."

"I keep telling you, Conner. Nobody will know. I didn't check out of my hotel room in Aspen. And all you told Tommy Kuhara at the mountain rescue shack was that you were taking tonight and tomorrow off." Their stories made perfect sense to her. If they timed it right, they'd be gone for only a little over twenty-four hours. "They'll all assume— as they've been assuming, anyway—that we've sneaked off for an illicit night of passion."

The thought of such a night had most certainly occurred to her. Every time Conner touched her, she came alive in a way that was both exhilarating and frightening. Indeed, the temptation to fall into bed with him was strong, especially here in California, with her body temperature rising to meet the weather. But the timing was all wrong. She had a murder accusation hanging over her head. She needed to be reasonable and sane and calm. Not passionate!

In a businesslike tone, she concluded, "Our appointment with Otis is for eight in the morning, then we'll catch the first plane and be back in Aspen before anyone knows we're gone."

"It ought to work."

In theory, Conner agreed with her. However, unlike Gina, he did not underestimate the seriousness of the charges against them, or the power of the Pitkin County law-enforcement officials. If Norm found out that he and Gina had skipped town, he would arrest them. Though the purpose of their trip to California was to investigate, Norm—and Alex, too—would see it as an attempt to escape, ergo, an admission of guilt.

Conner hated even to think of being arrested. His idea of hell was confinement. Being locked in a cell without windows? Breathing stale air? In all of his life, he couldn't think of one single day when he hadn't gone outdoors. Even when he was sick as a child, he'd sneak to the window and open it wide. No way could he stand being in jail. No way in hell.

But he couldn't have let Gina come out here alone. What if Otis was the murderer? He couldn't take that chance.

As the rental car crested a hill and the Pacific came into view, Conner's mind cleared. On the distant horizon, he saw the flicker from boat lights. Moonlight reflections danced across the dark, rippling surface of the waves. The sea was a sultry temptress, promising warmth on sandy shores, beckoning with dreams of travel to faraway lands.

He took the first turn toward a long pier. Where were they? Malibu? Newport Beach? It didn't matter. In the morning, they would find their way back to Beverly Hills. For right now, Conner wanted to be close to those waters, to wade, to wash away the frustrations of the past few days.

He parked the car in a shoreside lot. Though the long pier was well lit and busy, he saw few people on the beach now, after sundown. And that was where he wanted to be. Apparently Gina did, too. By the time he unfastened his seat belt and got out of the car, she'd already crossed the asphalt lot and stood at the edge of a long stretch of beach, where she peeled off her socks and shoes.

"Have you ever lived by the ocean?" she asked.

"Never. You?"

"New York, of course. But it's not like this. The Atlantic reminds me of an Andrew Wyeth painting, with a harsh, rocky coast. The Pacific is Gauguin." She cocked her head to look up at him. "Are you familiar with Gauguin?"

"He paints brown women with bare breasts." He grinned. "Pretty smart for a ski bum, huh?"

"Sorry, I didn't mean to sound like—"

"An artsy city girl?"

"A snob," she said.

"You're smart and cultured, and I like who you are," he said. "You don't have to apologize to me."

When Conner inhaled, the tang of salt air tickled his nostrils. His gaze feasted on the white froth of the breakers rushing to meet the hard-packed sand. He listened to a symphony of waves and squawking gulls.

He stood with Gina at the edge of the tide. When the icy water nipped at their toes, she gave a little yelp, rolled her slacks above her knees and crept forward to meet the next wave. Laughing and invigorated by the delightful contrast between freezing-cold water and warmed air, she splashed and dodged. Her hair cascaded around her shoulders. Her eyes were bright, and it occurred to Conner that he'd never seen her when she wasn't under pressure.

She urged him closer to the waves. "Come on, Conner. The water's wonderful."

"I'm fine right here." He rolled up the cuffs of his Levi's a couple of turns. "I'm not in the mood for bodysurfing."

"Don't be an old man," she teased, catching hold of his hand and pulling him. "Let's enjoy this while we can. We won't have time tomorrow."

He took one step forward, then planted himself firmly on the sand, with the cold water barely reaching to the tops of his feet. She kept pulling, teasing, laughing.

With one strong yank, he dragged her to him and captured her in his arms. With her head thrown back and her hair tumbling free, she looked like a water nymph or a mermaid. He felt as if he'd caught a beam of moonlight in his arms as he kissed her.

Her arms wrapped tight, and her slender torso flattened against him. Her firm breasts crushed against his chest. The wavelets coursed around their ankles as their feet made deep imprints in the sand.

When she moved in his arms, he felt himself growing hard, wanting her. He kissed her forehead, her eyelids, her throat. When she gasped, the small sound of her pleasure fueled his need. Gently, he parted her legs with his thigh and lifted her ever so slightly. Her supple body molded against him. God, he wanted her. If he didn't stop now, Conner wasn't sure if he could. Holding her buttocks so that her hips stayed joined with his, he looked into her eyes. "Hungry?"

Her full lips stuttered before saying, "A little."

His thigh pressed harder between her legs, and she responded with a delicious wriggle. This was a woman who enjoyed sensual pleasure, and he was eager to please her, to set loose the fire within her.

Slowly his hands ascended the arch of her back, savoring each womanly curve. "We could find a hotel and call room service."

"No, Conner." Her dark eyes flamed, but her words denied their mutual need. "No room service. Separate bedrooms."

His fingers splayed at the small of her back. "Why?"

"It has to be that way."

When she left his embrace, they stood a distance apart. Both of them were breathing hard. Desire swirled around them like the ocean breeze and the liquid kiss of the incoming tide.

"We can't make love," she said.

"Why not?"

Her fingers delicately pushed tendrils of hair off her face. "We need to concentrate on solving this."

It sounded like a poor excuse to him. "But there's nothing we can investigate tonight. It's just you and me, Gina." He nodded toward the lapping surf. "Here in paradise, with the waves and the palm trees and the gulls."

"Please, Conner. Try to understand." Her voice was low, husky, almost sad. "You and I live in different worlds. As you keep telling me, I'm a city girl. And you're a man who thrives in the mountains, in solitude."

He walked slowly, parallel to the receding tide line and below the seaweed and flotsam that had washed up on shore. "I've heard it said that opposites attract."

"Maybe in physics." She fell into step beside him.

"Maybe in life, too. People who are different can fit together real tight."

"For how long? There's no possibility of a relationship for us. We only have time for a quick little winter romance, and I want more than that."

"From me?"

"From life." She tried to smile. "I'm twenty-eight years old. I want commitments. Oh, Conner, we could never, ever have a future together. You love your mountains, and I love my work."

"I get it now." The salt air tasted suddenly bitter, and the sea looked murky and dark. "This is all about your precious career."

"What do you mean?"

"You say that we're here in California to investigate. But the main reason you wanted to make this trip was to check out Wendell Otis's collection of Elvis souvenirs."

"Well, of course I'll do that. As long as we're here."

He bent down and picked up a waterlogged chunk of driftwood that felt slimy and old. He cocked his arm and flung it as far as he could back out to sea. "You know, Gina, I'd sure as hell hate to think I was risking my freedom for the sake of Elvis."

"Of course you're not. But I need to see this memorabilia for my work, so that I can evaluate it for the auction. It's not as if I have any personal stake in Elvis."

"Might be easier to take if you were some kind of wild Elvis fan. At least you'd be driven by passion." He picked a shell off the beach and flipped it over in his palm. "I could understand a fanaticism better than this calculated plan."

"I don't get it."

"You conned me."

"I didn't."

Gazing down at her face in the moonlight, it was hard to believe that a woman who was this vibrant could have a heart so cold. Deliberately he looked away from her, picking a few more shells from the sand. "I came out here to protect you, Gina. And because I believed we were working together."

"We are!"

"Not right now. This trip is for you, for your career. You want to get your hands on Otis's memorabilia, and that's why we're taking this risk."

"Fine. If you don't want to be here, run back to Aspen."

"Too late for that now."

"You can manage. Catch the next flight, and before you know it, you'll be home. You can snuggle up with your buddies, Norm and Alex. And all you good old boys can figure out some way to blame the wicked city girl for your local murder."

"I'm not blaming you, Gina."

"No? That's what it sounds like. And I'm sick and tired of playing Eve to your Adam. I didn't tempt you to take the wrong path. I didn't give you this apple, Conner. You decided of your own free will to come along with me."

"You're right. I did. I'll take the consequences for what I've done."

"Just like a man." She kicked a fine spray of salt water at him. "You'll deal with the facts and ignore your emotions until you're furious and you accuse me of conning you."

"You did con me," he pointed out.

"Hey, I didn't ask you to come along and be my protector. Besides, you don't seriously suspect Otis, do you?"

"I don't know enough about him to suspect him or not."

"Well, he couldn't have been the guy in the black ski mask who attacked me on the slopes yesterday. He was in LA."

"Maybe he's working with somebody else. Norm seems to believe a two-person theory."

"But Norm is a fool."

And what am I? Conner couldn't believe this. She'd brought him to paradise, then told him he couldn't touch her. Were they here to solve a crime? Or to save her job?

He turned his face away from her and gazed out to the dark unfathomable depths of the Pacific. He didn't understand her. Moreover, he didn't know why it seemed so damn important that he should comprehend the mental processes of this small, redheaded female who was so impulsive and so full of fire.

Conner looked down at the shells he'd picked from the beach. Rapid-fire, he threw them back in the sea. They were too small to make a splash.

"Conner? I'm sorry."

"I accept your apology."

But forgiveness was another matter, he thought. If this jaunt to California resulted in jail time, he would never be able to forgive and forget.

In silence, they returned to the rental car and drove along the shore until they found a motel. In separate rooms, they spent a long and restless night.

THE HOME of Wendell Otis nestled in the Hollywood Hills. Gina and Conner found the place with no problem, and they arrived a bit early. Since it was before eight in the morning, they decided to wait, watching the last rays of sunrise spread across the dormant winter landscape. A row of short, fat palms stood like sentinels, guarding the southern end of the house. It was an interesting structure, a rather stark design, featuring monolith slabs and a glass-pyramid entryway.

"Very I. M. Pei," Gina commented, referring to the famous architect. "Otis must be doing well as an agent."

"From what I've heard, he was always more successful than Roger. He's a better businessman."

She pushed open her car door. "Let's ask our questions and get back to Aspen."

"Right."

Gina was rather surprised that Otis answered his own door. Given the size and pretension of the house, she'd expected a butler. And she was even more surprised by his clothing. Otis wore silky black jogging shorts and nothing else. When she saw him before, in Aspen, he'd been dressed for the cold. Now, he looked smaller of stature. But his arms and legs were muscular. The hair on his well-tanned chest was curly and gray.

"Would you like herbal tea?" he offered as he ushered them inside. "I have berry flavors. And sassafras. And chamomile."

"How about coffee?" Conner asked.

"I have a tea that tastes just like coffee. Without the caffeine, of course."

"Fine."

Beyond the foyer and the front room was a gleaming white kitchen. One wall was windows, with a lovely view, but Gina was more impressed by a vast counter space that appeared to be completely filled. As far as she could tell, Otis was equipped with every small appliance known to modern man.

As she stared, mesmerized by the gleam of white enamel and chrome, Otis came up beside her. He was only slightly taller than Gina, and he spoke directly into her ear. "I don't suppose you remember me at the wedding."

"Wedding?"

"When Lydia and Roger were married. You were just a kid."

"I'm sorry," Gina said. "But I don't recall."

"I was hugely obese." Proudly he gestured to his kitchen equipment. "Now, food is my life. I have complete control over each and every morsel that goes into my mouth. And look at me."

She looked. "You certainly are skinny."

"I'm in shape. Exceptional shape. I run five miles every morning, before the sun comes up, and—most important—I monitor every function of my body with precision."

Before he could offer a detailed explanation of that process, Gina changed the topic. "You're quite a collector, aren't you?"

"Are you talking about my appliances?"

"I'm talking about you, Mr. Otis." When she met with him in Aspen, with Roger dominating the conversation, she had noticed that Otis wore three different pairs of sunglasses at different times. They'd had identical frames but different colored lenses. "When you find something you like, you need to own every variation."

"I suppose that's true."

"I'm familiar with that way of thinking." Gina tried to turn her observation into a compliment. "At the auction house, I've come in contact with some of the world's greatest art collectors. These people will go to the ends of the earth and will spare no expense in finding exactly the right piece."

"That sounds obsessive." Otis busied himself with the preparations of the tea that tasted like coffee. "I'm not like that."

"But it's a wonderful trait. A talent."

"Really?"

"I'll bet you have a really good memory," she said.

When she glanced over at him, she realized that Otis was staring at her with a strange intensity. His dark eyes shone hard as obsidian in his gaunt face. Instinctively she moved closer to Conner, who had settled on a stool at a white counter.

He shook himself and refocused his attention back to the tea. "I didn't notice before, Gina, but you resemble Lydia. Your coloring is different, but the bone structure..." He turned his back to them before asking, "How is Lydia taking Roger's death?"

"Alex is handling the details. Lydia seems to be okay."

"Dignified," he concluded. "She has class."

"That she does," Conner put in. "I always wondered how a woman like Lydia could put up with a dork like Roger."

"Class and beauty," Otis said wistfully. "I loved her once. Perhaps I still do."

Behind his back, Gina and Conner exchanged a glance. Otis had been in love with Lydia? Was that a motive to murder Roger?

He placed the steaming tea on the counter in front of them. "At one time, I loved her so deeply I thought my heart would explode. I loved her enough to kill for her."

Chapter Eight

Wendell Otis expelled a deep sigh. As the breath went out of his lungs, his skinny chest fell. His rib cage made a sharp outline against his leathery tan. He looked older and tired. Without spirit or strength. He looked tragic, Gina thought. And she almost felt sorry for this small man who professed unrequited love for his former partner's wife.

He reached out with skeletal fingers and pressed a button on a gleaming white blender. The whir of the machine churned the air, forcing life back into the sterile white kitchen. Otis recovered his poise as he explained, "This is my special morning health drink. I was putting it together when you arrived. Hope I haven't left it sitting too long."

"What's in it?" Gina politely inquired.

He shot a bitter glance at her, then at Conner. "Why would you care? You two, you're both young. You have your whole lives in front of you, and you don't yet realize that someday you'll be old, you'll have to watch your body age and slowly, pathetically disintegrate. You're not aware of your mortality yet. You never think of death."

"Not true," Conner said. "Gina and I have been thinking of death a lot lately. Roger's death."

"His murder, you mean." Otis poured the greenish liquid into a tall crystal glass, which he lifted in salute. "Here's a toast. To Roger Philo. May the old cock rest in peace."

"How much did you hate him?" Conner asked.

"Hate?" Otis paused with the drink halfway to his lips. "I don't know if *hate* is the right word. Roger offended me. He was sleazy. A pig. He disgusted me. His bluster and boom hurt my ears. But I believe in paying credit where it's due, and I owed Roger a debt of gratitude. He got me started in the agenting business. I was an accountant before, and Roger talked me into joining him as a full partner."

"He was good at that," Conner said. "Talking people into things."

"Very, very good." Otis turned to Gina and asked, "Did he ever get you into the sack?"

"Certainly not."

"He would have," Otis predicted. "He could talk anybody into anything, which is why I greatly relished every opportunity to get the best of him. Gina, would you like to see the results of my dealings with Roger?"

"If you're referring to your Elvis memorabilia, I would."

Otis downed his blended green drink in one extended gulp, then set the glass on the counter, made a face and shuddered. If it tasted that bad, Gina wondered why he'd drink it. There was a masochistic streak in Wendell Otis that made him less sympathetic as a tragic victim of unrequited love. Gina wondered what he would have done if Lydia had responded to him.

Otis strode to the wall of windows, and his scrawny silhouette was framed against the morning sunlight. What a strange little man! Why wouldn't he put on his shirt? He must be cold, Gina thought. Was this nakedness another way of punishing himself?

Abruptly he turned to his left. "Come with me. Both of you."

They followed him down a staircase at the edge of the windows. The effect of stepping into an enclosed space after being in the brightness of daylight disoriented Gina, and she grasped Conner's arm for balance. He didn't flinch or pull away, though they had not touched since last night, when they had kissed on the beach.

They hadn't discussed the argument, and Gina wasn't sure she could have talked about it without crying. Her anger had dissipated, and now there was only sadness and deep regret. Conner mistrusted her. He thought she was using him to further her career.

And maybe, on some unconscious level, she was. That was the worst realization. When had she become so selfish? When had she decided to place her career needs above everything else?

In the dark, narrow stairway, she blinked up at him. She wanted him to hold her, to care about her, to forgive her. And, yes, she wanted him to make love to her.

But all she could say was "Excuse me."

He leaned close to her ear and whispered, "You do most of the talking. I'll stay out of the way."

"Why?"

"He's taken with you. It's this Lydia connection." He added, "I think Otis did it. He killed Roger."

"But he's too small," she whispered back. "He couldn't have carried Roger's body to the woodbox."

"Don't forget the two-person theory," Conner said. "And I think he's stronger than he looks."

"Hurry up!" Otis shouted. "I haven't got all day!"

Conner called down the stairs, "You're in good shape, Otis. Do you do weight training?"

"Indeed. I have a personal trainer."

"What do you lift?"

"Three hundred and twenty in jerks. Bench-press at three hundred and eighty."

Gina nodded. Okay, so Otis could have hefted Roger's body without breaking a sweat. But she still didn't think he'd killed his former partner. There was something else going on in Otis's mind. Something a little twisted.

They joined him in front of a large white double doorway. A likeness of the gates in front of Graceland was painted in black on the white doors. With a sense of ceremony, Otis unlocked the doors and flung them wide. He stepped inside the room and flipped a switch.

The lights went on and music blared forth. The first dramatic notes from the soundtrack of *2001: A Space Odyssey* echoed through the basement area.

"Quite an effect," Gina said as the drumbeats faded like distant rolling thunder.

Otis giggled, and his laughter sounded a discordant, almost demented note. Perhaps she should be scared. This man might be seriously disturbed, even psychotic.

"As I'm sure you know," he intoned, "Elvis usually started his concerts with that majestic theme."

"And ended them with the announcement 'Elvis has left the building,'" Gina said. "Yes, Mr. Otis, I've done my homework. I've watched all the concert movies."

"Have you?"

"I take my work as an appraiser seriously," she said. "With all the film footage, Elvis left a marvelous record of his possessions, which I can use to verify authenticity."

"How?"

"Memory. Of course, I check sources and compile data on whether or not I'm looking at an original or a copy. But, if I'm familiar with the subject, my first impressions are generally correct."

"You don't sound like a fan," Otis commented.

"I'm not. My only interest in Elvis is gathering items for the auction."

"Perfect," he said. "And I'll tell you a little secret, Gina. I never saw Elvis perform. I'm not a fan, either."

He waved them inside. Entering the large basement area was like stepping into a hall of mirrors where every surface reflected Elvis. Framed Elvis posters from his movies alternated with paintings of Elvis on black velvet along the walls. There were statuettes and decanters and jewelry cases containing rings, gold necklaces and heavy chain bracelets. A huge bookcase was packed with volumes about Elvis.

"Amazing," Gina said. She felt a bit as if she'd entered King Tut's tomb. "Which of these things belonged to Roger?"

"None of it. Why would you think that?"

"Dean said you were keeping some of Roger's collection for him, storing it."

Otis cackled. "No doubt that was the lie Roger used to cover up his own stupidity. Some of these things belonged to Roger. A long time ago. But he sold everything to me. All of it."

Gina's gaze fastened upon two life-size mannequins wearing Elvis jumpsuits. She recalled the cabin, the moment when she'd found Roger's body in the woodbox. She remembered the glitter of the Elvis costume, the golden sunburst surrounding the ghastly wound in his chest.

She stared at the costume before her. It was another white jumpsuit, with a detailed thunderbird design in silver and turquoise. Below it was a photograph of Roger Philo wearing this very costume. He would have liked to be remembered this way.

Lydia would hate the gaudy display.

And Otis? There was a cruelty in him that she could not dismiss. It was as if he'd taken all the marbles from Roger and was hoarding them, even now, when Roger was dead. Her skin prickled with goose bumps as an ominous feeling swept over her.

"The—the suit..." she stammered.

"Yes," Otis said. "Roger was found wearing a suit similar to this one."

Gina nodded and looked around for Conner. He was poring over one of the display cases, completely oblivious of the fear that was building inside her as Otis closed in. "Do you know why he got himself all dressed up? Because of you, my dear."

From across the room, Conner waved a strip of black material. "Do you believe this? It's one of Elvis's karate belts."

Gina kept her attention riveted on Otis. "Because of me?"

"He wanted to seduce you. And you were so interested in his supposed Elvis collection that he guessed you would be impressed if he paraded himself around, dressed like the man he called the King."

"How do you know what Roger was planning to do?"

"He told me."

She couldn't stand to look into his cold, reptilian eyes. "When exactly did you talk to Roger?"

She spoke loudly enough that Conner could overhear, but he wasn't even listening. He was trying on a broad-shouldered sport coat from Elvis's early years. It was yellow-and-black plaid, with a black collar. "It fits," he said. "Hey, Gina. Look at this. It fits." He struck a hip-twitching Elvis pose. "Hound Dog Hobarth. What do you think?"

She thought he was behaving like a lunatic. "Mr. Otis, did you meet with Roger on the day he was murdered?"

"Indeed I did. But I won't be passing that information on to that bothersome deputy from Pitkin County. And if you tell him, I'll deny it." He turned away from her and her gaze traced the rigid line of his backbone. "I don't have time to participate in a murder investigation."

"It's your obligation. If you have information—"

"Spare me the moralistic lesson, Gina. I don't care if Roger's murderer is caught and punished."

"It matters to Lydia," she said.

"But most of all, it matters to you." When he confronted her, Gina had the impression that he was enjoying seeing her squirm. "If I'm not mistaken, you are the number one suspect. You and Hound Dog over there."

"Did you kill him?"

"Why should I? You see, Gina, I've already had my revenge. I'm a hundred times more successful than Roger ever was. I deal with big names for big bucks."

There was a twang from across the room as Conner played a chord on a twelve-string guitar. "Did this belong to Elvis?"

"No, that belonged to Charlie Hodge."

"Wow! Charlie played backup guitar," Conner said. "He was one of the Memphis Mafia. This stuff is amazing. Gina, you've got to come here and look."

"I don't think so," she snapped. Conner had picked a fine time to turn into a blithering Elvis maniac. She turned back to Wendell Otis. "Look here, Mr. Otis, I've had enough. Tell me what you did on the day Roger was murdered."

"I went to the meeting with Roger. At his cabin. But he had apparently given me a time that was an hour and a half before he expected you to arrive."

"Why?"

"Two reasons. He wanted to make me a private offer. And he wanted to get you alone."

"What kind of an offer?" Gina folded her hands together. Her fingertips were freezing cold, and she couldn't imagine how Otis managed to stroll around in this basement, almost naked, without turning blue.

"He wanted to buy back some of my Elvis souvenirs. Roger had been misrepresenting himself for years, saying that he had a superior collection. Undoubtedly that's what he told Dean, as well as you. But it's all mine now."

"I can't imagine why he'd part with these treasures." She thought of the forty thousand dollars in cash. "Was Roger in some kind of financial difficulty?"

"Not really." He opened a display case and took out a huge, diamond-studded Maltese cross on a silver chain. Balancing the glittering piece on his fingers, he held it near Gina's throat. "Would you care to try it on?"

"No." She caught his forearm before he could reach behind her neck and fasten the clasp. His skin felt oily, as if he'd been sweating, and Gina was repulsed. She turned away and found herself once again gazing at the photograph of her stepuncle. "Why did Roger sell these things to you?"

"You have to understand his appetite. Roger wanted to devour everything. Especially people. Shortly after I split off from him, I hinted that I fancied one of these things." He held up the necklace. "This one, in fact. And Roger couldn't resist striking a deal with me. I paid more than twice the market value, and Roger thought he was putting something over on me."

"But you had your own plan in mind."

"Exactly. Before Roger realized what he was doing, he'd sold me half of his legendary collection. And I wouldn't sell it back at any price. Then he pretended that he didn't care, and he sold me more pieces."

"Then your own acquisitiveness kicked in," she concluded. "You wanted the best collection. No matter what the price."

"You're right." He sounded surprised. "One of the reasons I went to Aspen was to purchase a couple of Elvis's handguns. And when Roger said he'd already disposed of them, I was disappointed."

"Collecting can become an addiction," she said.

"Perhaps." He frowned as he discarded the Maltese cross. "Now the joke is on me. Roger's dead and I have an entire room of memorabilia celebrating a man I didn't particularly admire. I don't even like this junk."

"I can take care of that problem," Gina quickly offered. "The auction—"

"Yes, I know. And I'm considering it. But I might keep this room exactly the way it is. As a memorial to Roger."

"He'd like that," Conner said.

"Would he?" Otis said, whirling around to face Conner.

"You bet. Roger would love it."

Gina glared at him. His timing was less than perfect. All the time she'd felt threatened by Otis, Conner had been playing with the Elvis toys. Now, when she almost had the auction deal cinched, he bounced across the room like a big dumb puppy dog—a hound dog—to encourage Otis not to sell. Conner continued, "Yes, sir, if Roger went to heaven and knew he'd have this fine collection dedicated in his memory, he'd look down and smile."

"He's in hell," Otis said with great authority as he stalked from the room. "And I'll sell it all. Gina, arrange to have these things shipped to Berryhill's this very afternoon."

"Yes, Mr. Otis."

Behind his back, she lifted her gaze to heaven and whispered a thank-you. This was great! Better than great! A promotion at Berryhill's was almost guaranteed.

Trailing Otis up the staircase, she fell into step beside Conner, who gave her a big grin and patted her shoulder. "That worked well. You got your memorabilia to auction."

"Are you telling me you gave that little 'looking down from heaven' speech to convince Otis to get rid of that junk?"

"It's not junk," Conner said. "And you're welcome. I'm better at manipulating than I thought I was."

She wasn't sure whether she should thank him or slap him. She'd think about it later. Right now she wanted to do victory dances and celebrate.

Conner lowered his voice as they neared the head of the stairs. "I heard what he said about going to the cabin. Give me a chance to talk to him alone."

"You've got it." She shuddered. "Wendell Otis gives me the creeps. I mean, Roger was a slimeball, but he meant well. Otis is different."

"We need to hurry," he reminded her. "If we push it, we can still get back to Aspen by this afternoon."

In the kitchen, Gina said, "I'll get the paperwork from the car. Can you provide the delivery person with an inventory?"

"I always keep an undated account of my possessions."

"I'll be right back."

As soon as she left the room, Conner turned to Otis. "Mind if I ask a question?"

"Yes, I do." Otis turned on his heel. "If you'll excuse me, I need to get dressed."

He left Conner perched on a stool in the kitchen, trying to think up reasons why Wendell Otis should bother talking to him. This investigating routine would be a hell of a lot easier if he and Gina were operating in an official capacity.

But they weren't. So Conner would have to proceed on instinct alone. He strode down the long hallway to a closed bedroom door and knocked. There was no answer, and when Conner listened carefully, he could hear the shower running. He eased the door open and peeked inside. Sky-lights bathed the spacious bedroom in light. Conner looked around. The decor was mostly white, but there was a splash of color above the dresser, directly opposite the bed. A portrait. It was a four-foot-by-three-foot picture of Lydia Philo.

While Conner stood and stared, he heard the bathroom door open. Otis stepped into the room with a towel wrapped around his waist. "What the hell are you doing in here?"

Conner nodded toward the portrait. "I'd say you're more than fond of the lady."

"I liked the picture. This room needed some character."

On the bedside table, Conner noticed three other pictures. He picked up a heart-shaped frame containing a photo of an attractive woman he didn't recognize. "Who's this?"

"My mother." Otis spoke sharply. "Put it back. Don't touch it."

"Okay." A heart-shaped frame for a picture of Mom? Conner bent down to study the other framed photographs. Both were of Lydia. "More character for the room?"

"She's one of my dearest friends. I'm an old man. My friends are important to me."

"My God, Otis. The way you talk about age, you sound ancient. What are you? Mid-fifties?"

"I'm sixty-eight."

"You're in good shape."

"Takes a lot of work. Now get out of here."

"I need to talk to you. I want to get this figured."

"You?" He sneered. "You intend to figure something out?"

"Is there a problem with that?"

"I simply don't believe that you're capable of reasoning anything more difficult than the decision about which type of wax to use on your skis." He shook his head. "It's amazing that a ski bum like you can be so graceful on the slopes and so clumsy in simple human interaction."

For half a second, Conner considered marching across the plush bedroom carpeting and knocking Wendell Otis flat on his taut little butt. But that would just prove Otis's point, and Conner was damn sick and tired of being characterized as a stupid ski bum.

"You may leave now," Otis said. "Right now."

Conner knew the shortest distance between two points was a straight line, so he cut to the heart of the matter. "I'm not leaving until I get some answers. I think you killed Roger Philo."

"Don't be absurd."

Dismissively Otis strutted into a walk-in closet. Conner was right on his heels. If Wendell Otis was a murderer, he didn't want to let the man out of his sight. Otis might reappear with a gun in his hand.

Conner propped his shoulder against the doorframe. "You told Gina you were at the cabin on the day Roger was murdered."

"He was alive when I left."

"And you've got motive," Conner said. "Lydia. You wanted Roger's wife."

"I suggest you leave before I telephone the police to have you removed." He selected a starched white shirt from his closet and stuck his arms into the sleeves. "I have a low threshold of tolerance for fools."

"What about Lydia? Can you tolerate the thought of her being questioned at the police station, being prosecuted by her own son?"

"You wouldn't dare to drag her into this."

"Here's what I wouldn't do. I wouldn't go to jail to protect her reputation. Or yours, either." Conner blocked the exit from the walk-in closet. "I suggest you cooperate."

Otis regarded him coldly. "If I do, will you leave Lydia out of this?"

"Tell me what happened on the afternoon when Roger was killed."

"She was there when I arrived at the cabin. They were talking about Dean, her younger son. Do you know him?"

"I know Dean."

"He's a talented musician, you know, and not half-bad as a songwriter. I have considered taking him on as a client. In any case, it seemed that Roger had initially booked Dean and some other local talent to play at the Pisces party in Aspen. It really would have been perfect for him, would have given him a showcase in front of some important people."

Though Conner was growing impatient with this sidetrack, he said nothing and allowed Otis to ramble.

"Lydia was annoyed that Roger had dropped Dean from the program and had given the final booking to Michael Penrose, who is best known as a lounge singer in Las Vegas." He finished buttoning his shirt. "I never would have handled it that way. If I promise a booking, I deliver. But Roger's sloppy business practices are the primary reason we ceased to function as a partnership."

"That and Lydia," Conner said. "You hated the way Roger treated her."

"I won't deny it."

"So, what happened at the cabin?"

"Dear Lydia had heard about Roger's altercation with Gina at the tavern the night before. Usually his infidelity didn't bother her, but that incident upset her." He pulled on his trousers and tucked in his shirt. "She begged him not to humiliate her by making a play for his own stepniece in public. And he told her he was only joking, and that his business wasn't anything she should worry about."

He paused to select a necktie. Conner saw a slight tremor in his hands. "Roger could be cruel," Otis said. "A real bastard. Lydia started weeping and went into the bathroom. I talked briefly with Roger—"

"Did you argue?"

"Yes." His voice hissed like steam. "I told him that he'd hurt her for the last time."

To Conner, that statement sounded very much like a threat. "How did Roger respond?"

"Played the buffoon, a role he knew quite well. He guffawed and slapped me on the shoulder. Said Gina was coming up later and he was going to impress her with his Elvis costume. Then he went and put a stack of Elvis records on his stereo."

"What happened to Lydia?"

"He cajoled her, gave her a hug, a little kiss. God, I hated when he touched her. He didn't deserve to be in the same room with her, much less to put his hands on her."

"She was his wife," Conner said.

"A mistake of nature." He lashed the necktie around his scrawny throat. "He assured her that he would be home later that day, unless the snow got too bad. And, of course, we all knew that a blizzard was coming in. That was his plan. To catch Gina in the snowstorm and have her snowed in."

"What about the telephone?" Conner asked. "Was it working then?"

"I don't know. Nobody called."

"Then what happened?"

"I offered to drive her home. She said that she was okay, but I could tell she was shaken. I followed her all the way down the mountain."

Unfortunately, Conner thought, his story sounded plausible and reasonable. Otis had arrived at the cabin in time to witness an altercation between Roger and his wife. Otis had chimed in with his two bits' worth. And they had all gone their separate ways.

But the whole story seemed somehow out of sync. Maybe Otis wasn't directly lying, but maybe he wasn't revealing every important detail, either.

The small man muscled up to him. "If you'll excuse me, I have business with your little friend Gina."

"Did you go back to the cabin?"

"No, the weather was turning bad, and I needed to get out of Aspen before the storm hit."

Again, that sounded rational. But something was missing, some piece of the story had been left out. "What else?"

Otis cocked an eyebrow and studied him. "Maybe, Conner, you aren't as dumb as you look."

"You haven't told me everything."

"Come to think of it, no. I haven't told you one rather important fact." The slight curl of his lips was purely evil. "Michael Penrose, the singer who is booked to sing at the Pisces party, has possible ties with organized crime. You might start looking there for your murderer, Conner."

AFTER DRIVING back to the airport at top speed, returning the rental car and booking flights, they were on a plane headed back to Denver before lunchtime. If the weather was good, they'd arrive in Aspen by midafternoon, and Conner was pleased about that. He hadn't felt right about disobeying a direct order not to leave town. Still, this trip had turned out for the best. After takeoff, he reached over and rested his hand atop Gina's on the arm of the seat.

She turned her hand palm up and twined her fingers through his. "You're not still angry, are you?"

"I don't hold grudges, Gina."

And yet she sensed a distance between them. He was guarded with her, more cautious. Though she'd said that she didn't want a commitment or a relationship, she missed the possibility of having one.

Conner continued, "When we tell Norm about Otis and Lydia being at the cabin, it'll give him a whole new perspective to worry about. At least we'll be off the hook as the *only* suspects."

"Alex won't like that." She couldn't take her eyes off Conner. His shoulders were cramped in his window seat. His long legs bumped up against the seat in front of him. He never looked comfortable indoors, she thought. In a plane, in a car, in a house, he was out of his element. But he was smiling and his calm expression was a relief. "So, what do you think about Wendell Otis? Is he the murderer?"

"I don't know. As Dean would say, he's one weird dude."

"He's evil," she said. "I've never felt anything like it. He's a mean person. Deep down inside, where most people are trying to do the right thing, he's cold and hard. And what was this thing about parading around in his jogging shorts? Is that acceptable southern California behavior, or was he trying to make me uncomfortable?"

"He's proud of his body."

"Why?" She shuddered at the memory of his scrawny leathery chest and the disgusting feel of his skin when she'd touched his arm. "With all that health food and exercise, he ought to be glowing, but Otis is like a creature who lives in a dank cave. He's spent so much of his life wanting revenge against Roger that the hatred has poisoned him."

"On the other hand, that hatred and revenge makes me think Otis didn't kill Roger."

"Did not?" she questioned.

"Murder would be too easy. Otis wanted to destroy Roger, to rip him apart in tiny pieces." He frowned. "And there's something else Otis said that I ought to tell you."

Gina settled back to listen as he filled her in on the details of his private conversation with Wendell Otis. The deep, rich cadence of Conner's voice was so soothing that she didn't catch all the words until he mentioned Michael Penrose and his supposed connections.

"Organized crime?" She sat up straighter in her seat, trying to absorb this new twist. It was crazy! Senseless! Involvement with organized crime was the last thing she'd expected.

When she suggested solving the murder, Gina had expected the clues to present themselves in some kind of orderly fashion, as in a crossword puzzle or a board game. She was good at those exercises. Her memory for details served her well. "This is too confusing. Did Otis suggest that Roger was killed by a hit man?"

"He didn't offer any theory. He wasn't trying to help."

"Well, we're certainly going to have to tell Norm about this. The minute we land in Aspen, we've got to find him."

They didn't have far to search. When their small jet glided to a landing at Aspen Airport, Deputy Norm Garrett was waiting for them at the end of the runway. Two other officers stood beside him. The deputy tugged his cowboy hat down lower on his head and walked slowly toward them.

"Hello, Norm," Gina said. His serious expression spoke volumes. For the first time in her fast-talking life, Gina couldn't think of another word to say.

"Gina Robinson and Conner Hobarth," Norm said, "you're under arrest."

Chapter Nine

A frenzied panic shot through Conner's heart. The sensation was unlike anything he'd experienced before. The blue Aspen sky constricted before his eyes. The clouds congealed, eclipsing the sun behind a thick darkness. He knew the wind was blowing, but he couldn't feel it. His ears heard nothing.

This must be fear.

He was about to lose his freedom, to be confined to a small, dark room. And he was afraid.

"No..." he whispered.

He couldn't allow this to happen. And yet he stood paralyzed, inert, incapable of movement.

Beside him, Gina was talking at top speed, and he tried to register her words.

"...such nonsense, Deputy. We had to make the trip to California to find out what Wendell Otis knew. I had the feeling that he wasn't telling you the whole truth about what happened on the day Roger was killed. And he wasn't. Wait until you hear what we found out. This is going to change everything."

"Save it, Gina." Norm motioned to the two other officers who accompanied him, and they stepped forward.

"These guys are going to read you your rights and book you."

"Please. You've got to listen to me."

"No, I don't." His voice was raised in anger, but she heard a note of frustration, as if he really didn't want to perform his duty. "Dammit, why? What the hell were you thinking?"

"What difference does it make? We found new evidence."

"You can't take the law into your own hands. You have no right to investigate."

"But we did it anyway. You can't throw away the information I'm handing to you on a silver platter."

"You were told not to leave town. You are suspects in an ongoing homicide investigation, and your trip to California looks a whole lot like an admission of guilt."

"But we came back!" she shouted. "If we were guilty, why would we come back?"

She saw Alex leaving the airport terminal building. His long camel-hair overcoat spread like a cape as he strode briskly toward them. His supremely confident attitude was a stark contrast to Norm's reluctance.

He nodded to her, but spoke to Norm. "What's the delay?"

Gina blurted, "He's having an attack of common sense."

Alex cocked his head to one side and studied her. "You might be wise to do the same. Really, Gina, it's time to quit behaving like a spoiled little girl. If you can't be serious about the death of your own uncle—"

"Stepuncle," she said. "I hardly knew Roger. Only saw him five or six times in my whole life, and he was one of the adults, while I was only a kid."

"This isn't a family matter. I can't indulge you, Gina. There are procedures I need to follow."

"At least listen to me." Her voice cracked with the strain, but her tension was nothing compared to Conner's mood. He hadn't twitched a muscle. He'd hardly breathed since Norm had confronted them. "Please, Alex."

"I will listen, Gina. However, you've put us all in a difficult situation."

"And what is that, Alex? Forcing you to find the real murderer? Forcing you to investigate?"

"I want to find the killer," he said. "I need proof. If you actually learned something from Mr. Otis, I can't use your information in a court of law."

"Why not?"

"It's hearsay. Anything Wendell Otis told you is useless as proof." He stepped up beside her and wrapped his arm around her shoulder. "Your judgment in this situation was poor. You should have left the investigating to Norm and the DA's office."

"You can call me as a witness. That's evidence."

"Let me explain."

He pulled her away from the others. When she looked up at him, the years fell away. She saw the smug teenager who'd thought he was better than everybody else. A golden boy. Simply winning the game wouldn't be enough to appease his ego. He had to defeat, to destroy, to humiliate his opponent. He was so close that she could smell his expensive after-shave. "If you were called as a witness, Gina, you could say what you saw. You could repeat conversations. However, in this case you wouldn't be credible. You would say anything to save your own skin. You shouldn't have left town."

She shook her head. To Norm and the others, it must look as if her cousin Alex were comforting her. "If you've got some kind of vendetta against me, we'll fight it out in court. But don't drag Conner into this."

"This isn't personal."

"Come on, Alex. You know it is."

"Okay, I'm angry about how you screwed up. You don't have the smarts to play with the big boys. Otis knew that. He's a wise old bird, and he knew that he could tell you any damn thing he wanted to. He could have confessed, and it wouldn't matter, because it's not proof."

His logic pained her. Why hadn't she thought that far ahead?

"Now, Gina . . . If you do as I say, I might be able to help you. But you must . . . cooperate. Really."

Her temper flared, and she pushed away from him. "What about the truth?"

"What about it?"

"Doesn't it matter to you? Don't you want to catch the right person?"

"Of course we do." He was patronizing to the core. "And the Pitkin County District Attorney's Office wants to *convict* the right person." He nodded to Norm. "Deputy?"

Norm shuffled his feet, clearly reluctant.

"I want you to take these two people into custody."

"What are the charges?" Gina flared. "You can't do this to me, Alex!"

"That's where you're wrong." He turned away from her and spoke to Norm. "If they're in a jail cell, they won't be tempted to flit across the continent and botch up your investigation."

"Guess you're right." Norm doffed his cowboy hat. "Gina, Conner. I've said this before. You're under arrest."

"No!" Gina took a step away from them. "Alex, this isn't right and you know it. Lydia wouldn't want for you to arrest me. She didn't raise you to be a bully."

She saw his back stiffen but he didn't turn around to face her. In a clear voice, he issued an instruction to the two officers who'd accompanied Norm. "You'd better cuff her."

"That won't be necessary," Conner said. "We'll come with you. We'll cooperate."

"I'll decide what's needed." He snapped at the deputies, "Do it!"

She saw the gleam of winter sunlight on steel handcuffs. Gina would have bolted if Conner hadn't caught her arm and held her. When she looked into his eyes, she saw the painful depth of his despair. A cry escaped her. "No..."

His voice was calm but dark. "Do what they say, Gina. It's only going to be a minute."

She yanked away from him. Her feet were planted firmly on the tarmac. There was nothing she could do. No escape.

She tossed her hair from her face and held her arms in front of her. Though the deputies fastened the cuffs gently on her bare wrists, above her mittens, she felt brutalized. Gina trembled so violently that she could barely move when one of the deputies took her arm and recited her rights as he led her to his official vehicle.

Before he helped her inside, she glanced back at Alex. His eyes shone with a cold, opaque light, utterly without expression.

ON THE RIDE to the police station, Conner's brain kicked into high gear. There wasn't any point in struggle or protest. Alex and Norm had all the damn cards stacked in their favor. They were the authorities, the law. Conner knew his only chance for escape was to use his wits.

He leaned forward to talk with the two cops in the front seat. "Leon, Chas, what's going on?"

"Man, you're in deep trouble." Chas was the driver. "Everybody wants your butt in jail. The DA's going to treat you like a couple of damned dangerous criminals."

Leon was older and spoke with more authority. "If the sheriff was here, this wouldn't have happened. Not like this. The sheriff wouldn't let Alex Philo tell him what to do."

"When's he getting back?"

"Don't know. They still haven't been able to get ahold of him. He's out in Africa, somewhere in the bush country, taking pictures of gorillas or something."

Leon turned toward Conner. "Just for the record, son, I know you didn't kill anybody. Not even Roger Philo."

"Thanks, Leon."

"I don't like this," he said. "You're being railroaded and Norm Garrett is in way over his head."

"You're right," Conner said. "That's why Gina and I took off for California to talk to Wendell Otis. We've almost got this murder figured out."

"I knew it," Chas said. He glanced away from the road, toward his partner. "Didn't I tell you?"

"I'm going to need your help, guys." He looked directly into Leon's eyes, willing him to remember all those times when they'd worked together as part of a team. They had skied together, gone on rescue missions together. They'd celebrated when they'd arrived in time to save lives, and they'd gotten drunk together when they'd failed. "You have to trust me."

Leon turned away. The line of his jaw was sharp as flint. He was a hard man to read. A man who followed orders, but wanted to do the right thing. Quietly he said, "Conner, do you remember that time, must have been six or seven years ago, when I apprehended a housebreaker? And I left him in a holding room at the courthouse before I took him next door to the jail to get booked."

"I don't remember that," Chas said.

"Before your time, son." Leon continued. "There was something about that holding room. I'll be damned if the guy didn't make a run for it. Got clean away."

"I remember." It was the window, Conner thought. The housebreaker Leon had arrested had made an escape through the window, and Leon had taken a whole lot of ribbing about his mistake. Conner repeated the standard joke at the time. "That's when you got the reputation for being a cop who doesn't do windows."

"I think you catch my drift."

Leon was offering him the chance to escape. Now it was up to Conner to decide whether or not he would take the chance. If he escaped, he'd be a fugitive, a hunted man. But if he stayed, he'd have to trust that Norm and Alex would solve the murder. And that didn't seem too damn likely.

"You know, Leon, I think those cuffs on Gina are too tight."

Leon grinned as he reached into his pocket. "Well, I can't disobey a direct order and take off the cuffs. It's my sworn duty to protect the citizens of Aspen from dangerous people like that little redhead." He held up the key so that Conner could see it, then let it fall to the floor in the back seat. "Oops, I seem to have dropped something. Conner, would you hand it to me?"

He took the key and bent over Gina's hands to unfasten the cuffs. In a low voice, he murmured, "Everything is going to be all right. Just do what I say."

When he looked into her wide brown eyes, he saw the brimming tears that had streaked her reddened cheeks. Her lips quivered and she pressed them tightly together. He wanted to kiss her, to hold her and protect her. "Don't worry, Gina. This will all work out. We'll be fine."

"Are we going to escape?" she whispered.

He shushed her. Conner handed the key back to Leon.
"Here you go. I think you dropped this."

He accepted the key without looking back. "I'm giving
you a head start, Conner. But we are going to have to come
after you."

"I understand."

They parked by the Pitkin County Courthouse. Built in
the 1890s, the Italianate building, with its central tower, was
still handsome, but it was not well secured. Inside, Leon and
Chas made good on their word. They escorted Conner and
Gina to a small holding area. Before he closed the door,
Leon said, "Good luck, son."

The moment they were alone, Conner checked the window nearest the door. The glass slid up and the heavy metal
screen pushed away from the outer wall easily. He mounted
the sill, preparing for a drop of about ten feet on the other
side.

"Conner, what are we doing?"

"I'm taking off." Over his shoulder, he tossed a warning. "You can stay here. Do what they say. You haven't
broken any laws, Gina. Not yet."

"I'm coming with you."

He wasn't sure he agreed with her. Being on the run might
be dangerous. But he understood her need to be free, and
there wasn't time to argue. Conner swung over the ledge and
dropped to the hard-packed snow below.

Gina plopped down beside him. She sprang to her feet.
"Now what?"

Conner clasped her hand. "You've got to do everything
I say, city girl. No hassles."

She nodded silently.

Hand in hand, they fled into a nearby thicket of pine.
They were on the run.

GINA WALKED BRISKLY along the Aspen Mall, where the quaint Victorian buildings were iced with fresh snow and the streetlamps were twined with garlands of fragrant evergreen. Many of the pedestrians were skiers. All of them seemed healthy and happy. It was a beautiful place, picturesque and charming. And she was terrified.

Gathering every shred of her poise, she stepped into a trendy little boutique and stared blankly at racks of ready-to-wear clothing. Conner had instructed her to go here. He'd said the best place to hide was in plain sight. The police wouldn't expect to find her in a boutique. He'd advised her to slip into one of the changing stalls until he came for her. *If he came back.*

She felt horribly dependent, as if she wanted to cling helplessly to him and trust that he would know what to do, that he could make everything better. She hadn't wanted them to be separated, but he'd explained that he had to find a car and skis and provisions. He had a lot to do, and she'd be in the way. Her bright red hair was a beacon to the officers who must be searching for them by now. *Would he come back?*

"May I help you?"

Gina fairly jumped at the words. "No, I'm fine. Just looking."

The salesperson, a slender brunette with a skier's tan and a singsong voice, reached toward her and plucked a twig from Gina's hair. "Like, did you take a spill on the slopes?"

"That's right." Her mouth felt dry, her lips parched. "I decided to shop instead of ski."

"Good move, way good move." There were only two other women in the shop. "So, you go ahead and browse. Feel free."

Feel free? Gina only wished that she could.

She pivoted and pretended to study the nearest rack. Silk turtlenecks in a rainbow array. She peeled off her gloves and touched the fabric. Her mauve fingernail polish contrasted with the bloodless white of her hands as she allowed the smooth texture of the silk to slip through her fingers.

Within ten minutes of aimless wandering, Gina had seen everything in the store. The sporty outfits, the lingerie and the jewelry accessories. In the portion of her mind that was still attached to a reality where she could shop like any other law-abiding citizen, she noted that the selection of dressy clothing was excellent. Designer names. Very modern. High quality. The styles matched the background music—avant-garde jazz.

Though this was exactly the sort of shop she preferred, Gina couldn't stand being here. She should have gone with Conner, should be moving forward—not standing here, counting every second.

This situation was ludicrous, she thought. How could she pretend to be a carefree shopper when her purse, cash and credit cards were impounded at the police station? How could she browse when she'd just escaped from the court-house? A reckless smile curved her lips; perhaps she should ask the salesperson how to accessorize prison stripes....

Where was Conner? Had he been caught? She shifted her weight from one foot to the other and strolled toward the turtlenecks near the door. From here, she could look past a couple of angular mannequins and see out the front window to the street—which also meant that other people could see in. Prudently Gina worked her way farther back among the displays. She was the only customer in the shop.

The tinkle of a bell on the door signaled someone else coming into the store, and Gina looked up, daring to hope. It wasn't Conner. But it wasn't a policeman, either.

A young woman with a long braid bounced through the aisles of clothing and squealed a greeting at the brunette salesperson. From their high-pitched chatter, Gina deduced that they were friends. But they were also witnesses. She needed to hide. The fewer people who saw her, the better.

Gina pulled three outfits from among the better clothes and headed toward the dressing rooms in the back.

"Excuse me." The brunette interrupted her conversation with her friend to pop up beside Gina. "Did you, like, want to try those on?"

"Yes."

"They're really cool. That blue one ought to be totally great with your hair." She smiled so wide that her eyes blinked. "So, is this for a special event?"

"The Pisces party," Gina said. "I've never been before. Are these appropriate?"

"Oh, wow, these are really, really perfect."

"Really," Gina said sardonically.

Behind the woven curtain of the dressing room closest to the rear of the store, Gina hung up the clothes and collapsed onto a bentwood chair. The weight of her escape closed around her like steam in a pressure cooker. She was a fugitive. Until a few minutes ago, she hadn't done anything illegal. But now she was guilty. What would be the charge? Alex would know. He would smugly quote chapter and verse before throwing the book at her. Resisting arrest? That must be it. Oh, God, how had this happened to her? What had she ever done to deserve this?

Gina stared at her face in the mirror. Though her color was high, there was an unhealthy cast to her skin. Her tension showed in the tautness of her expression, as if the flesh were pulled too tightly across her cheekbones and jaw. The whites of her eyes were red from the tears she'd wept on the way to jail.

When she stood, every muscle in her body seemed to ache. Gina pulled off her parka and slipped her sweater over her head. If only she could change her identity as easily as she tried on new clothes. She slipped a dark blue satin jumpsuit with white lace trim off its hanger and held it in front of her.

"Oh, ma'am?" the salesperson called to her.

"Yes."

"I've got to go outside for just a minute. My friend has something in her car. Are you going to be, like, okay?"

"I'll be fine." Gina smiled to herself and wondered if the salesclerk would be so ready to leave if she knew that the woman in the changing rooms was a fugitive from justice.

The bell above the front door tinkled merrily as the two young women skipped out. And there was a stillness in the boutique. The background music played a low, mournful, bluesy song with saxophones. And Gina gave up the pretense of shopping. She sank down on the chair in the dressing room and tried not to look at her cowering, undressed body in the mirror. Her pale skin contrasted with her black bra and bikini panties.

She heard the bell at the door. Someone had entered the shop. It couldn't be the clerk, because she would have announced her return. Another customer? Or was it Conner? She almost poked her head out for a look before she remembered that it might also be the police.

Straining to listen, she heard footfalls on the wood floor of the boutique. A heavy tread. The step of a man. He seemed to stride quickly through the shop. She heard the floorboards groan just outside the short hallway with the three dressing rooms along one side. Why would a man come back here?

Silently Gina pulled her feet up on the chair so that they could not be seen under the woven curtain. There was another step, and then a rattle as the curtain of the first dressing room was yanked back on its metal rod. Gina held her hand over her mouth, holding back her instinctive gasp of fear.

There were only three dressing rooms, and Gina was in the farthest one back. Another rattle of the curtain along the rod. Her dressing room was the next.

She huddled on the chair in her bra and panties. He must be standing outside her dressing room. Any second now, he would tear back the curtain. As she waited, her nerves were pushed to the breaking point. She heard a low whisper. "You looking for trouble?"

The Elvis song! That song had been on the stereo at Roger's house. The man who stood outside her dressing room was the murderer. Her dread mingled with fascination. Finally, she would see his face. Finally, she would know the name of the man who had first framed her and now stalked her.

Why? Why wouldn't he leave her alone? It was enough to be suspected of murder, to have the police after her. Why was he stalking her? What did she know?

She saw the curtain move. He was grasping the fabric in both hands, preparing to tear it down. He meant to kill her. He wouldn't reveal himself unless he intended to kill her.

The bell at the door rang out and she heard the cheerful voices of the two young women.

The fabric of the curtain fell straight again. The heavy footfalls echoed toward the back of the store. The rear door opened and a breath of winter air swept across Gina's flesh.

"Ma'am?" The salesclerk was outside Gina's dressing room. "Do you, like, need any help in there?"

She wanted to scream, *Yes! I need a weapon! I need a safe place to hide! I need Conner! I need his strong arms to protect me!* "No, I'm fine."

"So, how's that blue outfit?"

Gina looked at the satiny jumpsuit that she had clutched in her hands. Though she hadn't torn the fabric, it was dreadfully wrinkled. "It's lovely."

She dressed quickly in her own clothes, her winter clothes. She had to get out of there before the murderer came back. *Where was Conner? Why was he taking so long?*

As she slipped her arms into her parka, she heard the bell, immediately followed by Conner's warm voice, talking to the salesclerk and her friend. "Hi, ladies. I'm looking for my friend. She's about this tall. Has red hair."

"Oh, she's trying on clothes in the back."

Gina hurried from the dressing room. Never in her life had she been so happy to see someone.

He smiled. His pose was casual, unhurried. "Did you find anything?"

The clerk put in, "The blue outfit. Like, am I right?"

"We'll take it," Conner said. He'd managed to hang on to his wallet in the police station. He pulled it from his pocket, handed over a charge card and turned to Gina. "Are you feeling better?"

"I'll be okay." Straightening her shoulders, she pulled herself together and matched his bravado. Now that he was here, she felt immeasurably better. At least she wasn't alone. "Did you get everything taken care of?"

"Absolutely." He signed the charge slip.

"Thanks." The clerk handed him a bag. "Have a really, really nice day."

"It's already been . . . eventful," Conner said.

Outside, the sun had begun to set; dusk came early in the mountains. Conner took her arm and led her around the corner to a small yellow Volkswagen with two pairs of cross-country skis on a rear-mounted rack.

She climbed into the passenger seat. "Where did you get this car? Did you steal it?"

"No, I didn't." He rolled his eyes. "I'm not an experienced criminal, Gina. I borrowed the car from Tommy Kuhara's cousin, who's out of town." He reached over and touched her arm. "You look scared to death. Are you all right?"

In a small, frightened voice, she said, "He was there. In the boutique. The murderer was there."

He reached across the bucket seats and pulled her as close as the gearshift would allow. "Tell me."

Her words came haltingly at first, then tumbled out as she described him coming closer and closer and whispering the words to the Elvis song. "He had his hands on the curtain, Conner. He was going to pull it back and—"

A violent shudder interrupted her, and she gasped, crying without tears.

"He took a hell of a risk," Conner said. "Why? Why would he plot the perfect crime with Roger's murder and then come after you in a public place?"

"He would have killed me."

"We've got to get out of town." He stroked her hair, patted her on the back. "Listen, Gina, you've got to pull yourself together. We'll figure this out."

She pulled away from him, wiped her dry eyes with trembling hands. "Okay."

"We're going to make it. I've got provisions. Now, put on that cap. The cops will be checking for a redhead."

She pulled a black knit hat down low on her brow and tucked her hair up into it. It wasn't much of a disguise, and Gina was apprehensive about the drive through town. Though Conner avoided the main roads, she kept a careful watch. "A Volkswagen," she muttered. "What are we going to do if we get into a high-speed chase?"

"Fasten your seat belt," he said.

"Why?" Her eyes widened. "Oh, Conner, we aren't being followed, are we?"

"No. There's no one after us. But I'll keep watching."

He concentrated on getting them out of town. Conner knew these mountains as well as a ship's captain knows the sea, and he navigated a roundabout course to make sure they weren't being followed before heading east on the highway. This would be the worst part, he thought. If the police had set up roadblocks, this was where they'd be stopped. There was, basically, only one main route through Aspen. Detours would slow them down tremendously.

He pulled up the collar on his parka and advised Gina to sit low in the seat. Practically every car up here had a ski rack on top. In the rearview mirror, they all looked like police cars. He took care not to speed.

It wasn't until they were ten miles out of Aspen that he turned, taking a side road that curved toward Smuggler's Mountain. Conner breathed a little more easily. "We're past the worst part, Gina. We've got a chance of making it."

The little car chugged up steep roads and cornered nicely on the hairpin turns. He was satisfied that they would be safe. For tonight, anyway.

Gina was uncharacteristically quiet, he thought. But that wasn't an altogether bad thing. They both needed time to think, to reflect. Becoming a fugitive was not a step to be taken lightly. Becoming a fugitive who was stalked by a murderer was even worse. Why had the killer come after Gina?

And how were they going to catch him? They needed something tangible, they needed irrefutable evidence. "The gun," he said.

"What?" Gina stared at him.

"We need to find Elvis's gun. That would be evidence."

"How do we know Roger was killed with Elvis's gun?"

"Maybe we don't. But we know Roger had a couple of guns that once belonged to Elvis. Dean mentioned them. And so did Otis. He even admitted that he came out here to buy the guns from Roger."

"So?"

"On that first night at the cabin, we made a pretty thorough search. We didn't find any guns."

"Slow down, Conner. Do you really think the murderer is foolish enough to hang on to these guns?"

"I sure as hell hope so."

When Conner finally parked the car at the end of a road that was little more than a path, it was almost dark. He jumped out. "Hurry up, Gina. I'd like to settle in before nightfall."

He'd already stashed their provisions in huge backpacks. He waited until Gina changed into heavier boots, helped her fasten her cross-country skis, and gave her the smaller of the backpacks. He donned his own outfit quickly, and tried to explain the situation in a way that wouldn't frighten her.

"We're skiing in. The place we're going is a warming shack. It's important we make the approach quietly."

"Because someone else might be there?"

"No." He peered at her through the dusky light and said just one word. "Avalanche."

Gina nodded, didn't argue a bit. And he was glad for that. The area they were crossing was primed for disaster, and he would be hard-pressed to explain why he'd decided to take this risk. Skiing into known peril went against everything Conner believed in. He respected the mountains. He wasn't a thrill-seeker.

No one who knew him would ever imagine that Conner Hobarth would take it upon himself to challenge the power of nature. And that was exactly why he'd chosen to come here. They would never think to look for him in one of the many warming shacks and abandoned cabins along these backwoods trails.

Keeping a slow but steady pace, Conner led the way through the trees and across small clearings. In places, the snow beneath his pole sounded hollow, and he knew that the danger of having the crust break away beneath their feet was high.

They'd gone about a mile when he stopped at the edge of a wide field—probably a hundred yards to another thicket of trees, then another two hundred yards of open field. To ski the safest route, up over the ridge that loomed above them, would take another hour. And it was already dark. Their only illumination was clouded moonlight, and the temperature was falling.

He decided to take the direct route.

The first person crossing a potential avalanche chute had the best chance of making it, but Gina had no idea where they were headed. "Follow me," he whispered. "Stay about twenty yards back. If you hear a loud cracking noise, if the snow starts to break, ski like hell to the other side."

She looked down at her Black Diamond cross-country skis, unwilling to show him the terror in her eyes. *Avalanche.* The very word conjured up horrible images of a churning, boiling wall of snow, unleashed with suffocating fury. She'd learned that in an avalanche the snow froze solid around you, like a concrete prison. But few people lived long enough to be buried alive. The weight of the snow shattered their bones and crushed their skulls. Few people survived the first impact.

She watched Conner start across the field and forced herself to glide into step behind him. Her ears were attuned to the smallest sound, the creaking of tree branches, the night breeze. In the far distance, she heard the mournful roar of a cougar.

Her ski caught an edge and she was off-balance for a moment, disoriented in the dim, flat light, clumsy with the weight of the pack against her shoulders. What if she fell? Would her tumble trigger the quaking snow that seemed to move beneath her feet as she skied?

Conner skied through the first line of trees, but Gina could go no farther. She stopped. Though the slender trunks of pine would be no protection against an avalanche, they were still shelter. She was afraid to move. Holding back a sob, she clung to the rough bark like a shipwrecked sailor hanging on to a piece of driftwood.

Forty yards away, she saw Conner stop. He turned and motioned for her to come ahead. As she watched, she realized that her fear had put him at greater risk. Instead of proceeding smoothly, he was coming back for her. And then what? Would he have to carry her? No, she decided. She'd have to make it herself.

She pushed away from the trees. Her heart was pumping in double-time. Her vision was shaky as she forced herself to go on. One slow push after another.

Until, finally, she'd reached the opposite side of the field. They followed a narrow path through the trees, their progress easier now. The more distance they put between themselves and the field, the better.

At a tiny cabin, he slipped off his skis, shucked off the pack and came to her. "We're here, Gina. We made it. Home free."

But home would be a place of safety, a haven against the multitude of threats they had encountered. Gina wasn't sure she'd ever feel safe again.

Chapter Ten

With a couple of logs blazing in the fireplace of rough-hewn stone, the one-room cabin had warmed to a bearable temperature. Gina wished she could relax, wished she could become comfortable. But tension was strung tight within her. "Conner, does anybody know about this place?"

"Yeah, I'm sure they do."

"Then we shouldn't have a fire, should we?"

"This isn't the first place anyone would search," he said. "This isn't part of the hut-to-hut Nordic touring system. It's just an old abandoned cabin."

"About the fire . . ."

"We'll chance it for tonight. I don't want to freeze."

It might have been cozy, Gina thought. But no amount of heat could mask the dank smell of old ashes and dust. It was obvious that no one had lived here for many years.

"Besides," Conner pointed out, "nobody would cross that snowfield unless they had to. This route is a disaster about to happen."

"That sounds like our lives," she said.

They'd found four cots against the walls and taken the mattresses from three of them to spread in front of the fire. Atop the mattresses they'd placed two sleeping bags that Conner had brought along in the backpacks. He pointed to the nest they'd made. "Why don't you get inside one of the bags? Try to get comfortable."

She did, snuggling deep. "Did you pack any food?"

"Nothing gourmet. I didn't have time to shop, so I just grabbed whatever Tommy had in his cabinets." He rummaged in the pack. "Peanut butter. A loaf of bread. Honey. Aha—granola bars."

He tossed her one, which she immediately unwrapped and bit into. The grainy bar tasted dry in her mouth. "Anything else?"

"Instant coffee, of course. A couple of packages of soup."

They'd found a metal coffeepot in the cabin, along with a few utensils, and Conner had filled it with fresh snow to melt for hot water. He pulled out the rest of the things he'd packed. Matches, a small hatchet, a knife and rope.

"That space in the pack could have been filled by food," Gina said. "But I suppose we need all those things."

"Survival equipment does come in handy."

"But I want a steak. A big, juicy T-bone."

"Sorry, Tommy's a vegetarian."

She wriggled inside the sleeping bag until she was on her back. "I guess this is a fugitive's diet, huh?"

"I wouldn't know. I've never been on the run before." He laid out the food on metal plates and set it on the floor beside Gina's mattress. Then he unsnapped his parka, pulled off his boots and sat on the mattress beside hers. "Here you are, madame. Elegant dining."

She poked at the food. Though her stomach was growling, the granola bar had settled uneasily. She was too nervous to eat. Too easily, she imagined the door to the cabin crashing open and a posse storming inside.

"Come on," Conner urged. "We've got to keep our strength. We've got to start making some plans for tomorrow."

"I know. You're right. But I don't want to think about reality. I want to pretend this escape is a movie."

"A movie?"

"You know, an adventure, with two innocent people on the lam. And at any moment, a director will yell, *Cut!* And we can go home and live happily ever after." But the exhausted ache of her muscles felt much too real. The residue of fear still haunted her consciousness. Hopefully, she said, "I'd like to hold hands and walk into the sunset."

"I've always wondered what happened to people when they did that. A sunset. What's on the other side?"

"You're much too literal, Conner. It's a fantasy. A dream." Far preferable to the nightmare she was living. "Happily ever after. Then, boom, the credits roll, and the audience goes home."

"I'd like that," he said.

"But it's not going to happen, is it?"

"I'm afraid not. We've screwed up big-time. In real life." He reached over and patted her shoulder. "But we're going to figure it out. Now, tell me about the boutique. What do you remember that might be a clue to his identity?"

In her mind, she heard the discordant notes of the blues, and then came the tinkling bell over the door. The heavy footfalls. "He had a heavy tread."

"Was he wearing boots?"

"I couldn't say for sure. Probably."

"What about his voice?"

"Just a whisper. It could have been anyone. Then the salesclerk returned and he ran out the door."

"You never saw him?"

"No. But I had a feeling. It was like that first night at Roger's cabin, before you came back with me. There was a sense of hatred and anger. I was scared, and that was exactly what he wanted me to feel. Helplessness . . ."

"Like with Otis?" he questioned. "Was it like the evil you felt from him?"

"Kind of." Confused, she said, "But Otis couldn't have possibly been the man in the boutique. He's in California."

"He could get here on a private jet a lot quicker than we could taking the commercial flights."

"But that would be easy to trace. He'd leave a huge trail of clues. Even Norm could follow it."

"Don't forget, Otis has people working for him, secretaries and receptionists. He's probably got transportation people, too. If not a chauffeur, a driver with a limo service. He's got to attend all those premiere performances and opening nights. And all the glitzy parties. Got to be in the right place at the right time. As well as entertaining his clients."

"How do you know all this?"

"Gina, I live in Aspen. A good proportion of the population is celebrities. They don't do things like the rest of us. It's a different life-style. One that almost *requires* an entourage." He shrugged. "Anyway, you can count on the fact that Otis has employees. Arranging a cover-up wouldn't be all that hard."

"Would they lie for him about something this important?"

With an indulgent smile, he ran the tip of his finger down her cheekbone. Fondly, he tweaked her nose. "Hey, city girl, you're supposed to be the cynic. Don't you know that money can buy anything?"

"Even a murder and a cover-up." She knew it was true, but she didn't like to believe it. "Or it could have been his accomplice, if we go back to the two-person-murder theory. Or what if Otis hired somebody to kill Roger? He was the one who mentioned organized crime. What if he's hired that same person to come after us?''

''It's possible.''

A professional killer. A shiver raced through her. It was difficult to imagine such a man, someone who exchanged human life for cash payment, someone who dealt in the business of murder, who accepted a contract and performed an execution. ''This is beginning to sound like a different kind of movie.''

''Gangsters, bootleggers, G-men—gunning down bad guys without ever wrinkling their double-breasted suits.''

''I don't like that kind of show.''

''Then let's think of an Elvis movie,'' he said.

''Please don't mention Elvis. He's the one who got me into all this trouble.'' *You looking for trouble?*

''You're speaking of Elvis in the present tense,'' he said in a teasing tone. ''Do you know something I don't? Is the King still alive?''

''Could be.'' Gina realized that she was smiling as she reached for the peanut butter. Though she still didn't feel safe and secure, Conner had succeeded in allaying some of her fears. ''If Elvis is alive, I know his identity.''

''Who?''

''Your friend Jerry fits the bill.''

''Jerome Sage? I've got to remember to tell him you said that. He'd get a hoot out of it.''

''Think about it, Conner. He's the right height, the right age, and he comes from the South. Not only that, but his career in writing musicals didn't really start until after Elvis was declared dead.''

''But Elvis didn't write his own material.''

"Well, maybe that's something he learned to do in later life. You have to admit that Elvis was able to take any old song and make it his own. The man did have style."

"Wise men say," Conner sang, "only fools rush in..."

The next lyric had to do with falling in love, and Gina waited for it. When Conner said nothing more, she realized how much she wanted to hear those words from him. *Falling in love.* She was closer to him than she'd been to any man. Ever before.

He'd seen her at her worst, at her most vulnerable. He'd seen her in handcuffs, he'd heard her cry. With other men, Gina had always been able to hold much of herself in reserve. She'd never paraded her emotions. Using her wit and fast talking, she'd kept herself safe. But not with Conner.

He knew her better than her own brothers knew her. Far better than her cousins, Alex and Dean. The thought of them brought her back to hellish reality, and the smile slipped from her lips. Right now, she didn't have the option of falling in love.

"Conner, what are we going to do?"

"We'll find the gun."

"And if we don't?"

"I don't know." He shrugged. "When I go out on a rescue, I never know what I'm going to find. But I've got to keep hoping. I've got to believe we're going to find survivors. Not victims." He took her hand in his. "You're a survivor, Gina."

"Then why am I so scared?" She grasped his hand and clung tightly to him.

"Nothing wrong with being scared. It's natural. But we've got to keep hoping. Okay? Never think of failure as an alternative. Ski fast. Ski hard. And win."

"Is that what your coaches used to tell you?"

"Yeah, and sometimes it worked."

"It often worked," she amended. "You were a world-class skier. A professional."

The fine wrinkles around his blue eyes deepened as he gazed at her. "This is different. We're playing for more than a title or a trophy."

"Much different." They were playing for their lives.

"I wish I could say something that could make this easier for you, that I could promise that everything will be all right. There are times when . . ."

"What, Conner?"

"This sounds kind of dumb and conceited. But when I was on the Olympic team, representing my country, I felt so proud and strong. I could've taken on the world. Back then, I could've promised that I'd make things right for you, Gina." His shrug was self-deprecating. "I miss being a hero."

"You're my hero," she said. "And you don't even have to win a gold medal to prove it."

"I would, you know. If that's what it took."

"I know."

He leaned toward her. His hand slipped around to the back of her neck. His gaze held a heartbreaking tenderness. And his lips were gentle as he kissed her. It was such a poignant moment that she wanted to weep, to allow the tears of happiness and regret to spill from her eyes until they were both afloat on a sea of emotion.

He pulled away from her. "Unzip your bag, Gina. We're sleeping together tonight."

She didn't object. More than anything, she wanted to perform the ultimate expression of trust and caring. For him. For her hero.

While she unzipped her bag and his, then fastened the two into one, he stripped off his jeans and sweater. Down to his long underwear. And then he pulled his white thermal undershirt over his head, revealing his strong arms and muscular chest, with its thick, dark coat of hair. She longed to touch him, to feel his vibrant flesh beneath her caress. He was so beautiful, like a sculpture of the perfect male, like Michelangelo's statue of David or Rodin's "Thinker."

He peeled off his thermal drawers and stood before her in all his masculine glory. "Now you . . ." he said.

She stood and stripped down to her black bra and panties. The heat of her passion was such that she didn't even feel the chill in the room. As she reached for the front hook on her bra, he stayed her hand. "Let me."

As he freed her breasts, Conner lowered his mouth to suck at the soft white flesh, to tease her nipples with flicks of his tongue until they were hard, sensitive peaks. She moaned as incredible sensations rocked through her body. When he delicately slid her panties down her legs and performed the same delicate manipulation at the juncture of her thighs, Gina thought she would die from the sheer pleasure of his touch. He trailed kisses up her body to her lips, and his hands massaged her, finding the pleasure centers and stroking until her knees went weak.

He eased her into the sleeping bag and lay beside her. Their bodies met, generating warmth and desire.

Gina knew that making love would never again be this wonderful. She looked into his eyes, studied his handsome, strong face, and she wanted to tell him that this was the best moment in her life. The most pure. The most perfect. But she was incapable of speech.

When he thrust inside her, she cried out, helpless against the emotions that exploded in her heart and her soul. Though she wasn't a virgin, it was as if she'd been saving herself all her life. For him. For this moment. For this ecstasy.

He drove harder and deeper, until neither of them could stand it anymore. With a gasp, they reached the intense, exquisite moment of fulfillment.

As Gina lay snuggled in the crook of his arm, she realized that whatever else happened to them, she would be all right. She had experienced perfection.

She closed her eyes and slept. Her dreams were soft pastel fantasies as she relived the moments of gentle, marvelous pleasure. She was floating, drifting on cloud pillows of goosedown. It was warm. There was sweet music, harp music. Images of flowers and sunlight and dancing butterflies played across her mind.

Then, suddenly, a sharp cramp clenched her body. A shadow fell across her vision of happiness. The music became discordant. She was running as hard as she could, a dark form pursuing her. A man in a ski mask, coming closer and closer. She couldn't escape. Her arms and legs were exhausted, weak, and she struggled through layers of sleep to consciousness.

Her eyelids snapped open. She was lying on a flattened, uncomfortable mattress in a dank one-room cabin. The sleeping bag tangled around her, confining her, and she kicked ferociously until her legs were free.

On the low hearthstones beside the fireplace, she saw Conner feeding another log into the dying embers.

"I couldn't sleep, either," he said.

With some dismay, she saw that he was wearing his thermal underwear. "Conner, I don't want to talk about the crime, or being on the run. I hate it."

"So do I, Gina." He poked at the fire, causing a shimmer of sparks.

She sat up, holding the sleeping bag to cover her nakedness. "For right now, I want to forget about the people who are after us. I don't want to think about the man in the black ski mask, the killer. I want—'' she hesitated shyly ''—I want you to make love to me, again.''

He turned toward her. Though his face was hidden in shadows, she knew he was smiling. ''I don't need a second invitation.''

She straightened the sleeping bags as best she could, and he joined her. Though their second encounter was less urgent than the first, the slow ascent to pleasure resounded in new, brilliant tones. They were a symphony, she thought, with the most blissful crescendo imaginable.

She curled up against his chest and matched her breathing to his. Through the small cabin window, she could see the pink of approaching dawn. Gina wanted to hold on to the night, to find a never-ending darkness in Conner's strong arms.

''Are you hungry?'' he asked.

She thought for a moment. ''I guess so.''

''The water's hot.'' He wriggled out of the sleeping bags. ''I'll make the coffee.''

She liked that he had volunteered to prepare and serve the coffee. This was a good precedent. Her idea of the perfect man was one who cooked.

Sitting bolt upright in the sleeping bags, she reminded herself that Conner was not the ideal mate for her. Despite the wonderfulness of their lovemaking, they would not, could not, have a relationship. She thought of the fable of the city mouse and the country mouse. Neither one could live in the other's environment. And that was the way it would be with Conner. He couldn't live with her in New York. No way. Her apartment was barely large enough for one person. And she wouldn't move to Aspen. Give up her career? Not likely.

But oh, my, last night had been wonderful. *Just one night. That was all it was. The best night of her life.*

If he asked her to stay with him, she really didn't know what she'd say. *No. I'd say no.*

She gathered her clothes and bustled to and fro in the small cabin, preparing to face another day, another disaster. When Gina had finally pulled herself together, she sat with Conner on the hearth, close to the fire, and sipped the bitter instant coffee he'd made.

"Are you always this energetic in the morning?"

"Yes." She bristled. "Something wrong with that?"

He shook his head. "Breakfast is peanut butter on bread."

"Yum."

They ate in silence. There were so many things to say that Gina didn't know where to begin. When Conner finally spoke, the sound of his voice was a relief.

"You know what I don't understand?"

"What?"

"Why is the killer attacking you? First he sets up this perfect frame. Then he comes after you like a psycho stalker. He almost seems like two different people."

"Maybe it is two people. One to plot the crime. And the other, the guy who's after me. That's what Norm and Alex seem to believe, except they have you and me cast in those parts."

"Well, Norm's misguided. And Alex? Well, Gina, it seems to me like Alex has a personal grudge against you."

"No kidding!"

"When you were kids, did you break his crayons or something?"

"I can't understand it," she said. "I come from an upper-middle-class, white-bread family. Roger was the most exciting person in the whole bunch. Everybody else is so staid and conservative, I can't imagine anyone, even Alex, working up a hatred this passionate over nothing."

"Traditional family," he said.

"One hundred percent. I'm the only woman past the age of twenty-five who isn't married with children."

"Living in Manhattan," he said. "Having a career. I think Alex is jealous."

"Don't be ridiculous. He's a lawyer. He makes tons more money than I do."

"But you work in the arts."

"On the fringes," she said. "And when it comes right down to it, Alex is probably a better artist than I am. He does watercolors as a hobby. I think Lydia has told me a thousand times that if Alex decided to pursue an artistic career, he'd be famous."

"Do you think she encouraged him?"

"Absolutely. Lydia thinks the sun rises and sets on her oldest boy." She sipped again at the awful coffee, then set it aside. "Kind of strange, isn't it? Dean actually has a fairly successful career as a musician, and Lydia pooh-poohs it."

"I hate to say this, Gina, because I know you like her, and so do I, but Lydia seems to be at the center of this. She was Roger's wife, and stands to benefit financially from his death. Wendell Otis worships her. Her two sons are devoted."

"Motive," she said. "Lydia is the key to figuring out the motive. Obviously, Roger wasn't the best of husbands. Someone might have killed him to protect Lydia."

Conner nodded. Now they were getting somewhere. "That gives us a list of suspects. Otis, Alex and Dean."

"Alex?" she questioned. "But he's with the district attorney's office. He's not going to commit a murder. We might as well suspect Norm."

"Okay, we'll add Norm to the list, too."

Conner wasn't sure why, but it seemed right to suspect Norm; maybe because he'd been so anxious to pin the murder on them, and Conner felt their friendship had been betrayed. The timing was surely propitious for Norm. If the sheriff had been in town, the whole investigation would have been handled differently.

Gina agreed to add Norm. "If we don't waste time suspecting Dean. He's probably the only person in Aspen who could stand to be around Roger. Remember how he went up to the cabin, looking for a souvenir, something to remember his stepfather."

"Or to destroy evidence," Conner said.

But she felt protective of Dean. When she thought of him, she didn't see the grown-up keyboard player with long hair. She recalled a little boy with big, sad eyes. He always tagged along with the older cousins, wanting desperately to be accepted.

When Gina was seventeen and Dean was twelve, he'd had a crush on her. Once, she remembered, he'd sneaked up behind her, kissed her neck and pulled her hair. Had she laughed at him? Had she teased him? Gina didn't remember.

Poor Dean. Always the younger brother. Never the favorite. Never the shining star, like Alex. Sure, Dean was eccentric enough to try every new or outlandish fad. But murder? Could he kill his stepfather? Or maybe he'd think he was sending Roger to another plane of existence.

"Don't forget," Conner said, "Roger had just cut Dean from performing at the Pisces party. Otis said Lydia had gone to the cabin to plead the case for her son."

"It was good of her to do that. I always feel as if Dean gets shortchanged and Alex gets all the attention."

"Gina." He compelled her attention with his voice. "We also have to consider Lydia herself as a suspect."

"I hate this. These people are my family."

But Conner didn't see them swarming around to protect her. Alex wanted her arrested, under lock and key. Lydia thought her niece had been trying to seduce Roger. And Dean? Who could tell what went on in his head? The kid barely showed any emotion at all.

"What about the hit man?" she asked, hopefully. "Roger could have been killed by a professional hit man."

"We'll add Michael Penrose to the list."

The sun was shining full through the window, and Conner recognized a familiar urge. He wanted to be outside. Morning was one of his favorite times of day. At his own cabin, he liked to watch the sunrise. He'd stand on his porch with a cup of steaming-hot coffee in his hand. The instant brew made a poor substitute, and this dank little place was nothing like his cozy home.

"Go ahead," Gina said. "I'll put on my boots and be right behind you."

He wasn't surprised that she'd read his mind. Last night, when they made love, he'd discovered a compatibility with her that ran deep and true. Her energy matched his own. And her passion was unbelievable. She was the perfect woman for him, and it was too damned bad that she lived in New York City.

He opened the cabin door, and the mountain cold blew over him, rousing his senses and making his thinking processes crystal-clear.

Gina stood beside him, gazing through the forested land. "Run down the list for me, Conner."

"Lydia. Alex and Dean. Wendell Otis. Michael Penrose. And Norm."

"I met Norm's mother when I was skiing," she said. "She's an aggressive little woman."

"That's an understatement." He watched a shimmer of snow as it spilled from a branch of a ponderosa pine. "I'm not a psychologist, but there seems to be an obsession with Mother in this gang of suspects. Otis had a picture of his mom in a heart-shaped frame. Lydia was up at Roger's cabin, fighting for Dean.''

"What about Alex?"

"Oh, man, he's the worst. He still lives with his mother."

"Like Elvis," Gina said. "He adored his mother, Gladys. He bought her that famous pink Cadillac, even though she didn't know how to drive. And a house. And Graceland was for her. When she died, he went into seclusion for nine days. At her funeral, he threw himself on the casket and sobbed uncontrollably. She's buried right beside him at Graceland, you know."

"I know."

"I don't understand this feeling men have for their mothers. But Elvis is a perfect example."

"And so are half the psycho serial killers who attack women. It seems like they're always trying to love Mom or to kill her."

Gina slanted a gaze at him. "How do you feel about your mother?"

"I like her. She's outdoorsy and independent, does a lot of traveling with my dad. But sometimes she takes off by herself. They're in the Orient right now." He raised his eyebrows. "Do I pass the test? Does that sound sane to you?"

"You could be covering up. When you were skiing professionally, did you ever look into a television camera and say, 'Hi, Mom?' "

"Never. I was much too shy to do anything but wave."

"I remember that," she said. "I used to watch you on the tube and think you were just so wonderful. And I guess, after last night, I was right."

Conner drained the last sip from his coffee mug. "How did the conversation come around to this? I thought we were talking about the murder."

"We've got our list of suspects," she said. "Now what?"

"Evidence. We need hard proof, so that Alex—if Alex is not the murderer—can take it to court. We need a murder weapon. Elvis's gun. But where should we start looking?"

"That seems obvious," she said. "We'll start with the mother. Lydia's house in Starwood."

"Tonight's the Pisces party," Conner said. "I don't expect that she'll attend, but Alex probably will. It's a big-deal event, all the local political types go there."

"Then we'll go to the house tonight, while Alex is gone." Gina looked up at him with wide, seductive eyes. "Conner, do you know what that means?"

Had he missed a clue? "No, I don't get any special meaning from that."

"We have almost all day. With nothing to do."

He wrapped his arm around her shoulders. "I have some pretty good ideas of how we could fill the time."

Chapter Eleven

The last embers in the fireplace died at midmorning, but Gina and Conner needed no heat other than the flames generated by their passion. Inside their sleeping-bag cocoon, she stretched out on her side next to him, lazily twining her fingers in his short brown hair.

She should be tired. Instead, she felt pleasantly awake, motivated to once more face the difficulties that lay before them.

"I should chop some wood," he said.

"Why? Are we coming back here?"

"We might. Besides, it's the right thing to do. We used up all the firewood that was left here. It's a courtesy to replenish the supply."

With slight alarm, she asked, "We're not expecting company, are we?"

"I hope not." He crawled from the sleeping bag, gave her one last kiss and began dressing. "Aren't you planning to help?"

"You know I'd love to," she lied, stretching out on her back and luxuriating in the warmth of the sleeping bag. "But, gosh, what could I do? I don't even see an ax."

"Right here, by the door. It was under one of the beds when we got here, but I moved it, in case..."

He didn't have to complete the sentence. Gina knew that they needed protection. After her encounters with the killer, in the boutique and on the ski slope, there was reason for caution. But she hated to think of it, to have fear intrude upon their idyll, hated to think of Conner armed with an ax, fighting for their lives.

But that was the truth. They weren't carefree lovers on a winter vacation. They were fugitives.

When she left the sleeping bags, the air in the cabin felt cold and musty. She dressed in a hurry. "Okay, Conner—how can I make myself useful?"

"I saw a couple of long logs under a lean-to at the south side of the cabin. Help me drag them over to the chopping block."

"Isn't everything buried under two feet of snow?"

"We'll manage."

The first thing she noticed when they went outside was that the snow had not piled up too deeply around the well-sheltered cabin. The forest formed a natural snow block. The second feature that drew her attention was their tracks.

There had been only a wispy snowfall last night, and their skis had left a clear trail leading right to this door. They might as well have painted a big red arrow and a sign saying Look here!

"Not exactly a secret hiding place," she said.

"We'll have to hope that nobody gets this far. There's a lot of mountain out here, Gina. I don't think the sheriff's department will make that much effort. Not even for a manhunt." He winked at her. "Or a womanhunt."

After some effort, they wrenched one of the six-foot lengths of tree trunk loose from the others and hauled it to the front of the cabin. Then Gina was excused from further duty. She sat on the porch and watched as Conner broke the large piece into smaller chunks and split those.

The heavy exercise made him warm. He peeled off his parka and sweater and went to work, wearing only his white thermal underwear on top. His arms moved rhythmically. The muscles in his back flexed.

And Gina observed him with pleasure. Her enjoyment came from sheer animal attraction to his masculine strength. Men, she thought, could be so obtuse and irrational. But there were moments when they were utterly wonderful. His body, so hard and powerful, seemed to have been made for the purpose of protecting her. She felt delicate and precious and cared for. She almost felt safe.

"Your turn," he said, wiping his brow with the back of his arm. "Gather up this stuff and carry it inside."

"Are we in a hurry?" she purred.

"Actually, I'd like to get going. We can ski up and over that ridge, instead of going across the snowfields."

She nodded her agreement. Though it meant another hour of Nordic cross-country skiing, she preferred the extra time to the risk of avalanche. Within a fairly short time, they were ready.

Falling in line behind him, she allowed Conner to break their path through uncharted territory. The day was incredibly clear, crisp and beautiful, with skies of endless blue, and clean white snow. Though he stopped often enough to let her rest, this was a major trek. Her muscles tingled and she knew she'd be exhausted tomorrow.

They were all the way to the far side of the broad upper area when Conner yelled, "Over here! Quick, Gina!"

She didn't ask why, but followed. He scrambled toward a thicket of pine trees. She skied up beside him. "What is it?"

"Don't you hear it?"

She listened. There was a faint, mechanical whir. "A helicopter?"

"Damn! If they're looking for tracks, we've left a map to the cabin."

She ducked down in the shadow of the trees, reached out for his hand and gripped hard. This could be the end of everything. They couldn't ski faster than a helicopter could fly. In this brilliant light of day, there was nowhere to hide. She waited. Her fear clenched like a fist inside her, strangling the slim hope that they would succeed in evading the police. She waited to be caught. Waited for the dark moment when her freedom would end.

The chopper crested a far hill. Like a giant hornet, it hovered. Blades whipped the air. Though it remained at an altitude of a hundred feet, Gina could see the passengers inside.

"Kids," she said with relief. "There are a couple of children in there."

"We're okay," he said. "They're only sightseers."

But the danger had once again become clear to her.

GINA SCRUNCHED DOWN in the passenger seat of the Volkswagen and stared at her photograph on a flier that was a modern-day version of a Wanted: Dead or Alive poster. The eight-by-ten sheet featured a head-and-shoulders picture of Conner, and one of herself, along with a written description of height and weight and physical characteristics. It gave the phone number of the Pitkin County sheriff's office, in case anyone sighted either Gina or Conner.

It was four o'clock in the afternoon, and they'd ventured toward Aspen. Their first stop was in search of something more filling than peanut butter and granola. At the roadside tavern, Conner had found the flier, sitting in a stack on a table by the bar.

He'd fled immediately. Now they were on the highway, heading back to Aspen.

"So," Gina said, "this is what it's like to be famous."

"Infamous," he replied. "This is real damn annoying. I grew up in this town. I've got a reputation."

"Nobody will take this seriously. Nobody who knows you."

"What about people I don't keep in touch with? Like guys at the Park Service, and rescue teams from other towns? Not to mention my grade school teachers. Old Mrs. Pelikan from fifth grade." He grinned sardonically, refusing to be beaten by this new ploy. "What the heck! Old Pelikan will love this. She always told me I'd amount to no good."

She picked up on his mood. "What about me? This is a horrid photo. Look at my hair! And they have my weight wrong. Everybody in Aspen is going to think I'm heavier by seven pounds than I really am."

"Damn Alex." He groaned. "I'm never going to live this down."

"Maybe it's a sign, Conner. Maybe it's time for you to leave Aspen, anyway. To move on."

Gina offered her suggestion quietly but she was dead serious. After spending the day making love with Conner, she didn't want to leave him. Returning to Manhattan seemed like a miserable, lonely idea. They had become a part of each other. Whether or not she wanted a relationship, that was what she had. A bond had been forged. It was Gina and Conner against the rest of the world. And she liked the feeling. She was, quite simply, falling in love.

Pushing her suggestion farther, she said, "When this is over, you might want to live somewhere else. There's good skiing in upstate New York."

"Those are hills," he scoffed. "The Rockies are real mountains. Aspen has the best skiing in the country."

"But you'd be close to me. I could get a car. I could drive up and see you on weekends."

"I'd like that." He turned off the main highway and parked on a side road. Conner pulled off his glove. With his bare hand, he stroked her jawline and traced the outline of her lips. "I don't want to be two thousand miles away from you. Not ever again."

It was the closest he'd come to a commitment. She held his gaze, pleading silently with her eyes. *Don't leave me. Don't let me go. We've got to be together.*

She couldn't look away from him. His handsome face. His wonderful, strong body. He was the perfect man. How could she ever live without him?

But she couldn't plan. They had no future until this nightmare ended. They hadn't declared their love for each other. Because of the intense situation, sorting out emotions was impossible. She broke the silence. "Would you consider it, Conner? Moving to New York?"

"You could move here," he countered. "There's a lot of art in Aspen. Galleries. Festivals. You could set up your own auction house."

She surprised herself by saying, "I might."

"You would?" A smile lit his face from within.

"Yes, Conner." What had she just said? She must have lost her mind to think she'd give up her career and start over in Aspen, a town she didn't even like, a town where she was an outsider, a town that had branded her a criminal.

But when he leaned toward her, stretching the limits of his seat belt, and kissed her on the lips, the mountains glowed. The cold vanished and the snow shimmered like a blanket of diamonds.

"We shouldn't even be talking about this," she said.

"You're right. We have to get out from under this. I'm blaming Alex for this. With those damned posters everywhere, it's going to be harder than hell to blend into the crowds.''

They both sat back in their seats, stared through the windshield and considered the possibilities.

Their initial intention had been to drive to Glenwood Springs, or Basalt, or some other neighboring town, and lie low until dark, when they would search at Lydia's. Now that plan was out of the question. Alex had undoubtedly papered the entire area with fliers.

"Where can we go?" she asked. "It's really not safe to keep driving around."

"I'm thinking," Conner said. "We can't go to Tommy's. They've probably got his place staked out. And I don't want to get my friends into trouble."

"What about somebody who is famous enough to be almost above the law?"

"Jerry Sage," he said. "You're right. Even Alex would hesitate before pestering the famous composer with the reputation for wanting to be left alone. Not many people know that Jerry and I are friends. We don't travel in the same circles."

"Can we trust him?"

"Let's find out."

Using every precaution they could think of, they drove toward Jerry's home, but not right up to the door. On the chance that the police had an ID on the Volkswagen, they left the car a few blocks away and approached on foot. His home nested in a forested area where the natural landscaping gave the impression of mountain solitude without the inconvenience of uncleared roads. The nearest neighbors lived a couple of hundred yards away.

Conner watched the house and the street for a good five minutes. There seemed to be no surveillance. Not only was

Jerry an unlikely person to associate with Conner, but this wasn't the sort of area for a stakeout.

They had a few points in their favor, he thought. Tonight was the Pisces party, and half of the sheriff's department would be moonlighting as guards at the entrances and exits.

He shepherded Gina to the front door and rang the bell.

When Jerry answered, he hustled them inside. "Come on, come on in here, right now."

Shooing them in front of him like a couple of naughty chickens, he got them into the sitting room with the baby grand and sat them on the long sofa. Then he paced in front of them. Even his eyebrows scowled. In his slow southern accent, he drawled, "What the hell did you think you were doing by resisting arrest?"

"Saving my butt," Conner replied.

"You got yourself in one hell of a mess, son. And dragged this pretty little lady along with you."

"It's the other way around," Gina said ruefully. "If anyone can be blamed, it's me."

"You need a lawyer," Jerry said. "I can put you in touch with someone."

"Wouldn't do any good."

"The hell it wouldn't. A smart lawyer would get those charges reduced and have you out on bail in no time."

"Maybe so," Conner said. "But we can't take the chance of being locked up and unable to investigate. The circumstantial evidence is stacked against us and Norm Garrett isn't looking for any other suspects. We've got to find the killer. Or else be prepared to stand trial."

"I don't know about that, son."

He regarded them thoroughly, staring hard enough to see into their brains. His upper lip curled, and Gina was struck once again by his resemblance to Elvis. Abruptly Jerry turned away from them, went to the piano bench and lightly played a chord. "Why don't y'all tell me about this evidence? Then we'll see what I can do to help."

Conner deferred to Gina.

She took a deep breath and started talking. "I went to Roger's cabin to see his collection of Elvis memorabilia. The night before, we'd had that little altercation—"

"When you knocked him flat on his ass," Jerry put in.

"You could say that."

"I did say that." He played the opening phrase of Beethoven's *Fifth*. "I'm going to play a little while you're talking. Helps me think."

"Anyway," Gina said, "when I got there, the cabin was empty. The phone was dead."

Her sharp memory recreated the room in her mind. "The Elvis record 'Blue Hawaii' was playing on Roger's jukebox stereo. There were gloves on the coffee table. An Elvis whiskey decanter and two used glasses in the kitchen. On the desk, I found an envelope with my name doodled on the outside. I opened it up and found it contained forty thousand dollars in cash."

Jerry played "We're in the Money."

"I went upstairs. In the bedroom, I saw Roger's clothes, discarded across a chair. In the other room there was a brass statuette of Elvis. When I picked it up, it was bloody."

"And you left your fingerprints behind," Jerry concluded.

"Correct. Anyway, I tried to leave. I went down to start my car, and it was dead."

"What was wrong with it?"

Conner supplied the answer. "Loose coil wire to the battery. Could have been a coincidence. Or someone could have purposely disabled the car to strand Gina at the cabin."

She continued, "I tried to cross-country ski away from there. But the blizzard had moved in. When Conner found me, I was half-frozen. We went back to the cabin."

"And what about Roger's body?" His long fingers skipped lightly across the ivory keys, playing "Rhapsody in Blue."

"We found him the next morning, in the woodbox. He was wearing the white Elvis jumpsuit. He'd been shot in the chest, but no murder weapon has been found yet."

Jerry drew the conclusions: "All the evidence they have is a package of money with your name, a brass statue with your fingerprints, and the fact that y'all were there at the cabin that night. What about the glasses and the decanter. Any prints on those?"

"By the time Norm Garrett arrived in the morning, I'd broken the glasses and cleaned up." She frowned. "I don't think I even mentioned the decanter and the glasses to the police. I'm sure I didn't."

"You should have."

"It's too late now." She sighed. She couldn't very well telephone the sheriff's office with clues when she was the chief suspect.

"What about the money?" Jerry questioned. "What was that all about?"

"I don't know," Gina replied. "Norm Garrett has decided that Roger was going to bribe me into some kind of sex thing."

"A forty-thousand-dollar one-night stand?"

"Who knows what they're thinking? Oh, yes, and Norm found a suggestive note from Roger to me, saying something about how he had what I wanted. Obviously, he was talking about the Elvis memorabilia, but Norm made it sound like a sexual proposition."

"Then you took your trip," Jerry said. He played "California, Here I Come." "Find out anything useful from Mr. Wendell Otis?"

It was Conner's turn to explain. "Otis admitted that he'd been at the cabin earlier that day. And so had Lydia Philo."

"Lydia?" Jerry's eyebrows raised.

"He's obsessed with her. There's a shrine to Lydia in Otis's bedroom. Otis didn't think Roger was worthy of his wife."

"He got that right. Roger Philo was a philanderer."

"Protecting Lydia could be the motive for murder."

"Unless..." Jerry played a tremulous chord on the baby grand. "Unless Lydia whacked him herself."

"Jerry!" Gina protested.

"I've been thinking about it since the last time we talked, and it seems like women are committing more and more of the murders these days." He plunked out an unidentifiable melody on the piano. "Can't say that I approve. Though I do like a strong female with a mind of her own, murder is going too far. Still..." His voice was pensive. "Ladies killing their husbands makes for damned good opera, don't it?"

"But she couldn't have physically done it herself," Conner said.

"Let's try this scenario," Jerry said. "The eternal triangle. Lydia argues with Roger and knocks him unconscious with the Elvis statue. Then, she convinces Otis to dispose of the body."

"And they set up the frame," Conner concluded.

"It doesn't work," Gina said. "Otis told us that he followed her all the way back into town."

"Could be he's lying," Jerry suggested. "I never did like that Wendell Otis. He's too dang healthy."

"What if he was telling the truth?" she asked.

"Alex could have been the killer," Conner said with obvious relish. "He supposedly has an alibi, but it's not airtight."

"The stepson killing his father," Jerry speculated. "But why did he happen to go up to the cabin and do it on that particular day?"

"Suppose he talked to Lydia," Conner said. "And he realized how distraught she was. So, Alex zips up to the cabin to give Roger a hard time. And ends up killing him."

"I like this theory," Gina said. "And it explains why Alex is so determined to have us arrested."

"But the timing's a problem. There's the scene with Lydia and Otis, then a phone call to Alex, then Alex drives up. And all this happens before you arrive at four o'clock."

"She could have called him from the cabin," Jerry said. "Maybe the phone was working then."

"But Otis would have seen Alex driving up the road toward the cabin." Conner's face lit up. "Maybe that's it. When I was talking to him, I had the idea that he hadn't told me everything. Maybe he neglected to mention the arrival of Alex."

Jerry played the first notes of "Frankie and Johnny," and said, "I do prefer the crime-of-passion idea. With Otis and Lydia working together."

"I don't." Gina pushed herself off the sofa and paced the room. She didn't want to consider Lydia as the murderer. She admired her aunt. Gina had grown up with Lydia as her role model for a successful, sophisticated career woman.

Besides, when she thought of Lydia as a suspect, the death of her uncle became somehow more tangible and less abstract. Lydia was a real person. Gina had been to her wedding. She'd received Christmas cards and birthday presents from her aunt. How could she think of Lydia as a murderess? How could she possibly imagine her in jail?

"The problem," Conner stated, "is that we don't have proof for any of this. We need the gun."

"The gun?" Jerry asked.

"According to Otis, Roger owned a couple of Elvis's personal handguns. But we didn't find them at his cabin."

"Elvis's handguns? Now, that's something I'd like to see. I always did have a fondness for Elvis," Jerry reminisced. "Not just because we come from the same part of the country. But because of his style, especially in gospel and ballads. Boy, oh, boy, that man could sing."

He played the opening to "Memories," and when he sang the first verse, Gina could only stare. Jerome Sage sounded exactly like Elvis Presley.

He lifted his fingers from the keys. "Okay, kids, I agree that y'all ought to try to solve this before you get yourselves locked up by the cops. However, supposing that you do get yourselves arrested, you use that one phone call to contact me, and I'll find a good lawyer to get you out on bail."

"*If* they'll set bail," Conner said. "Because we went out to California, they consider us to be likely to flee."

"That's a load of bull, courtesy of Alex Philo. He's not the most popular man in Aspen right now. Lots of us heard about what happened at the airport, and most all of us think Alex was way out of line."

"Maybe even a murderer," Conner said.

"I like Alex as a suspect." Jerry rubbed his chin. "He's mean as a copperhead, and twice as slimy. But this speculating ain't getting us nowhere. What do y'all want me to do to help?"

"We need someplace to hang out until the Pisces party tonight. Can we stay here?"

"No problem. But I hope you're not planning to attend the party. You're not exactly anonymous these days."

"We're not going to the party," Conner said. "But we're going to take advantage of the fact that everyone else is there so we can search for the murder weapon."

Jerry held up his hand, forestalling further talk. "Sounds like breaking and entering to me. And if you don't mind, Ms. Bonnie and Mr. Clyde, I'd rather not know precisely where y'all are going to commit your next crime."

"That sounds terrible." Gina's voice was worried. "This has kind of snowballed. When we started out, we were completely innocent. And now..."

"It'll be all right," Jerry predicted. "Now, is there anything else I can do? Are you two hungry?"

"Starving," Gina said. "Have you got meat?"

"Honey, I got practically nothing else but meat. That's one of those things I got in common with Elvis. I love a high cholesterol diet. Greasy burgers and burnt bacon and everything with gravy."

He led them into the kitchen where he slapped a couple of burgers on a grill. The fragrance of sizzling beef filled the air.

Conner was halfway through his burger when he remembered to say, "You know, Jerry, there is another way you might help us."

"Shoot."

"Michael Penrose is the main entertainment for the party and Roger arranged for him to perform. According to Otis, Michael Penrose has connections with organized crime."

"That's right," Gina put in. "We think Roger might have been killed by a hit man."

"How come? If Michael Penrose got the job, why would Roger get hit?"

"I don't know. But it's worth checking out. Then I could stop suspecting members of my own family." She smiled at

Jerry. "Could you, please, arrange for me to talk to Michael Penrose?"

"I can get him over here. No problem. He's already called twice and left messages. Looking for a new song, he says." Jerry washed down a bite of burger with soda pop straight from the can. "Don't even know how he got my phone number. Probably Roger. I'd probably be mad at him, if he was still alive."

"Why?" Gina asked.

"Since I write musicals, every singer in the known world seems to think I've got hit songs lying around, waiting for them to make famous. They don't understand that my music comes as part of the whole story. The American Revolution is going to have different music than hippie protestors in the mid-sixties." He got a faraway look in his eyes. "Or the story of Lydia."

Gina was about to argue with him when she realized that Jerry wasn't talking about Lydia herself. His imagination had been caught by the idea. Before Gina's eyes, he was transformed from good old Jerry, Conner's skiing buddy, to Jerome Sage, the brilliant composer.

"A woman who's driven to kill the man she loves," he mused. He hummed a few notes. "She's a country-bred gal. From Memphis. And she betrays her niece to keep herself out of jail. This story is really about you, Gina. How y'all get framed." He set down his burger and gazed into space. "And Elvis. Man, if I could work Elvis into the story, I'd have something."

Conner interrupted his train of thought. "About Michael Penrose."

"I'll get him here." Jerry returned to reality. "But tell me, how am I going to introduce you? Should I say, 'These are a couple of my fugitive friends. You might have seen their likeness on some wanted posters around town'?"

"I have an outfit for the Pisces party," Gina said. She'd thrown the blue jumpsuit into her almost empty backpack. "If I pin my hair up on top of my head and put on makeup, he'll never recognize me from that old photo on the poster. You can just say I'm a friend of yours."

Jerry picked up the telephone. "I'll do it."

JERRY MADE the arrangements, and Gina went to an upstairs bedroom to change. After a blissfully hot shower, she got herself dressed in the midnight blue jumpsuit with the border of white lace at the plunging neckline. She twisted her hair up in a knot and was putting on the finishing touches when Conner came into the bedroom.

He stood and stared at her. He didn't have to say a word. She could read the appreciation in his gaze.

"Beautiful," he murmured as he pulled her into his arms. He whispered in her ear, "You're so beautiful, Gina."

Her reaction to him was immediate. In their long day of lovemaking, he'd learned the secrets of her body. He knew exactly how to touch her. She pressed hard against him.

"I don't want to mess you up," he said.

"It's okay. Go ahead. Mess me."

"I'd love to, but Michael Penrose is going to be here any minute." He stepped back from her. "Know what, city girl? That outfit looks like a lady's version of an Elvis costume."

She glanced down at herself. "You're right. It's a jumpsuit. My God, Conner, do you think Elvis is contagious?"

"Whatever he is, I owe him. If it weren't for Elvis, I never would have met you."

"And you never would have been accused of murder," she reminded him.

He nuzzled below her chin. "You're worth it."

"Worth all the bad things that have happened?"

"Gina, I—"

They were interrupted by the doorbell, and she left the room. Time to track down another clue. Time to meet with Michael Penrose. Gina stood at the top of the staircase and primly patted her hair into place. She couldn't quite believe that she was all dressed up and ready to talk about a hit man.

Michael Penrose was an extremely good-looking man with a deep, deep tan. His coal black hair was smoothed back into a small ponytail. When Jerry introduced Gina as a friend of his from New York, Michael hardly wasted a glance on her. He was focused, one hundred percent, on Jerome Sage.

"I brought along a CD," he said. "Some of my more recent work. But you know what I need to progress in my career."

"Let me take a wild guess," Jerry said, sarcastically. "Y'all need a hit."

Gina looked up sharply. A hit? As in hit man? But the double entendre went right over Michael's head. He snapped his fingers and pointed at Jerry. "A hit song. That's right. And I'll wager you're just the man to do it for me."

"That's a bet you'd lose," Jerry muttered under his breath. To Michael, he said, "Tell you what. You give me that CD. I'll take it into my sound room to play it, and then I'll be back out."

"You don't want me to come with you?"

"Most definitely not. I don't want anything to distract from your voice."

Michael snapped and pointed again. "Gotcha."

As Jerry lumbered from the room, he tossed an order over his shoulder. "Michael, y'all talk to my friend while I'm gone. Y'hear?"

"Sure thing, Jerome. Whatever you say."

He tossed a dazzling white smile in Gina's direction, but his eyes were vacant and disinterested. Apparently, since she couldn't do anything to further his career, he didn't have much to say to her. But he kept on smiling.

"I'm looking forward to the party," she said. "A lot of important people are going to be there."

"A lot," he agreed.

"This is a wonderful opportunity for you. The Pisces party is such an 'in' thing. How did you happen to hear about it?"

"Well, it was Roger Philo. Too bad about what happened to him."

Michael sounded as if he were talking about an inconvenient stubbed toe, not murder. "Was Roger your agent?"

"We'd been talking."

"At one time I thought he'd scheduled his stepson, Dean, to play at this party." She decided to appeal to Michael's ego. "You must have done something spectacular to change his mind."

"Must have."

She was getting nowhere with him and she didn't have all day to chat. Gina cut to the bottom line. "Did you have one of your *friends* talk to him? Did you apply some muscle?"

The smile fell from his face. "What do you mean?"

"We've all heard the rumors, Michael. Some of your *associates* in Las Vegas have nefarious reputations."

"Nefarious?"

"They're crooks. Aren't they, Michael? Organized crime?"

"That's a lie!"

His fingersnap and point became a threatening jab, close to her nose. His eyebrows lowered angrily. Gina might have been frightened if Conner hadn't been right upstairs. Her mountain man, Conner, could flatten this city lizard like a semi passing over road kill.

Gina gave him an ingenuous smile. "Gosh, I'd like to tell Jerry he doesn't have anything like that to worry about."

"Jerry?" His tanned forehead pulled down in a frown.

"Jerome Sage," she reminded. "My friend."

Michael Penrose released a gusher of profanity, then said, "I don't know how these rumors got started. But they're lies. All of them are lies. You tell Jerome—Jerry—that I've got no ties to organized crime."

"Really?" Gina conveyed cool disbelief in her tone. "Then how did you get Roger to change his mind about booking you?"

"Out of my own pocket. I gave him forty thousand dollars' worth of reasons to sign me for this gig."

Gina's eyes widened. That explained where the money had come from.

Chapter Twelve

When Jerry Sage dragged back into the room, holding Michael Penrose's CD as if it were a particularly nasty piece of garbage, Gina excused herself and raced upstairs to the bedroom where Conner was waiting. "The money," she said, "I know about the money. It was a bribe from Michael Penrose. Isn't that wonderful? One piece of this stupid puzzle is solved."

"Gina, slow down."

She plunked down into the center of the king-size bed. "Come on, Conner. Let's enjoy this. We have so few answers."

"Here's another question. Why was your name doodled on the corner? Michael Penrose had no reason to write 'Gina' on the envelope."

"Neither did Roger." She thought for a moment. "The murderer might have written my name, as part of the frame."

"That's good thinking. Very good." Conner mused, "I wonder if Norm bothered to do a handwriting analysis. Probably not. He hates forensics."

"Now can we celebrate?" she asked.

"Another question. We know where the money came from. But what was Roger planning to do with it?"

"I couldn't tell you. Must be a problem. What does one do with nasty bribe money?" In high spirits, she grinned. "Michael Penrose said he gave the money to Roger only a couple days before he was murdered. Can you imagine? He paid all that cash for a chance to sing."

"Question number three—where did he get that kind of money?"

"He doesn't have any links to criminals."

"And you're sure about that," Conner said sarcastically, "because he told you so."

"Even if he was lying—and I don't think he was—there was no need for a hit man. Think about it this way. Michael was happy with the arrangement, and Roger accepted the bribe. The only reason for a hit man to come after Roger would be to get the money back. And it was still there, on the desk in the cabin. In plain sight."

"I'll buy that," he said.

"Everything's falling into place. I can feel it. We're going to have this all worked out." Reveling in hope, she bounced back on the bed with her arms spread wide. Then she hugged herself. "We'll be free. No suspicion. No more hiding out."

"It's great." But a twinge of regret crossed his mind, and Conner felt a tight little pain in the area of his heart. "You're anxious to get back to New York."

"That's not it." She sat up quickly. Her eyes scanned his face. "Conner, I want this disaster to be over. But I don't want... I don't want *us* to be over."

"I know." He forced a smile. God, he was an idiot. Why had he even brought this up? "It's okay. You have a life. I have a life." What was he saying? Why couldn't he shut up? "We both need to get back to our lives. I understand."

"No, I don't believe you do." There was an urgency in her tone. "I don't want to leave you."

"We don't need to talk about this now. We've got to concentrate on tonight. Lydia's house. Searching for the guns."

But he was drawn toward her. She looked so damn pretty, kneeling on the bed. The blue and the lace at her neckline complemented the ivory skin at her throat. And her dark eyes shone. He was compelled to touch her, and to wonder what it would be like to make love to her here, on this great big bed.

After the morning's activity in the cabin, Conner couldn't believe he was even considering sex again.

His hands slid down her sleeves. He wanted to tell her how he felt, to make some kind of declaration so that she'd understand how important she was to him, how she'd changed his life. God, he didn't want to lose her. Instead, he said, "You need to change clothes. We've got to get going."

"I know." She lightly kissed his lips and went to the adjoining bathroom to change back into clothing that was more appropriate for breaking and entering.

There was a rap on the bedroom door and Jerry entered. "You owe me for this one, Conner. Y'all owe me big."

"Why?"

"Not only is this Michael Penrose an untrained singer with the personal poise of a sick cat, but Gina got him so shook up that he started crying. Y'hear me, son? He was crying, blubbering all over about how everybody has the mistaken idea that he's involved with the criminal element in Las Vegas because he dated a gal whose father was in one of the families there. Whatever the heck that means." Jerry took a deep breath. "He said he could produce statements from nuns that guaranteed he was okay."

"Sorry, Jerry."

"Doggone right you are!"

"How'd you get him out of the house?"

"I promised him singing lessons for the next week," he muttered.

"Excuse me?" Conner chuckled. "You must think he has some talent if you offered to do that."

"Maybe a little shred of talent, but it's buried under that slick Vegas phrasing. Kind of reminds me a little bit of you-know-who."

"Elvis?"

"Yeah. But he ain't telling anybody I'm doing it. And that goes for you, too."

Conner grinned. "Okay, Phantom."

"Don't you go comparing me to the Phantom of the Opera. I'm a hell of a lot better-looking."

Gina reappeared from the bathroom. Before Jerry could chastise her, she glided up to him and took both his hands in her own. "You've been wonderful, Jerry. I thought the famous Jerome Sage was a cold and brilliant recluse. But you're the warmest, kindest friend anyone could ever have. No matter what happens, I'll always think fondly of you."

Totally disarmed, he squeezed her small hands and said, "Gina, you are an inspiration."

She hugged him. "Thanks for everything."

When they went back into the night, preparing to search, Gina felt the chill all the way to her bones. The Volkswagen started up with no problem and she huddled in her seat waiting for the car to warm up. "I guess we have to scratch an unnamed hit man working for Michael Penrose from our list of suspects. That's too bad."

Conner murmured his agreement. "This wasn't a crime for profit. Unless somebody in Roger's immediate family is going to earn big bucks from his death. But both Lydia and Alex seem pretty well fixed. That leaves Dean."

Gina surprised herself by nodding. "Yes, it does. He must have been outraged about being jerked off star billing at the

Pisces party. And if anybody in the family needs money, it's got to be Dean."

"Let's not write off Alex. Okay? Maybe he's living with his mother for financial reasons. I don't suppose you know if his divorce was costly."

"I think it was a lump-sum alimony settlement. No kids, but she got the house. The family rumors are, of course, sympathetic to golden Alex. I've never even met his ex-wife, but I've heard that she was a social climber who was unhappy because Alex wasn't doing well at his law firm."

"They probably expected him to work," Conner muttered, "rather than accusing people and slapping them under arrest."

"He's not diplomatic," she said.

"Probably not good at negotiating settlements." He threw the car into gear and chugged away from the curb. "We're too early to show up at Lydia's house. Let's swing past Dean's place first. It wouldn't hurt to see if he's got the gun there."

"Do you know where he lives?"

"I know the apartment complex. A couple of my other friends live there and they complain about Dean playing his music too loud."

Aspen at night was quaint and beautiful, lit by the glow of streetlamps that shimmered on the gingerbread trim of Victorian houses. It looked old-fashioned, but the streets were not quiet on this Saturday night. Along the sidewalks, they spotted several glamorous outfits worn by people who would be attending the Pisces party, but had probably gone out to dinner first. Through the rolled-up car windows, Gina heard chiming laughter and sensed the aura of excitement.

For an instant, she envied the glitter of Aspen and wished she could be one of these people, hobnobbing with celebrities and skiing with millionaires. But Aspen didn't mean that to Gina, not anymore. This glamorous resort town meant being near Conner. She'd rather stay with him in a rough-hewn one-room cabin than go to a party any day. In his arms, she was truly happy, she was beautiful and she had all the excitement she could stand.

DEAN'S APARTMENT COMPLEX, which was a far distance from downtown Aspen, was also not as picturesque, not by a long shot. There were several square buildings, lumped together. Conner parked, and they approached two different three-story buildings before they located one with Dean Philo's name on the registry by the center door. "Apartment 106," Conner read.

As they circled to the rear of the building, Gina was feeling guilty. "Are we going to spy on him?"

"We're just going to make sure he isn't home before we sneak inside and open his door with a credit card."

"Do you know how to do that?"

"I'll figure it out. I'm getting good at this criminal stuff."

"Why wouldn't he be home?"

"He'll be at the party. Everybody goes to the Pisces party. It's a good place to meet people, and the food is free."

"I thought invitations were hard to come by. The sales-clerk at the boutique envied me for being able to go."

"Never thought of that." Conner shrugged. "I've always been invited."

As they rounded the corner of the building, they heard the loud thrum of music, and Conner motioned for her to stand still. Lights shone from the uncurtained windows of the last apartment.

"Is that his place?" she whispered.

"I think so."

She followed as Conner crept to the window ledge. Though the sound of their boots on the crunchy snow was anything but quiet, Dean's music hammered loud enough to drown any other noise. They stood beside a small spruce and Gina whispered, "Let me look."

Somehow it seemed less of an intrusion if she was the one spying on her cousin. Either way, she felt bad. Unlike Alex, Dean had done nothing to hurt her. When he telephoned her, he'd been trying to help.

Conner backed out of her way.

Gina took off her cap and slowly peeked inside at the typical dismal clutter of a bachelor pad. Every flat surface was covered with papers, used mugs and stacks of tape cassettes. It was such a mess that she almost overlooked Dean himself. He was hunched down in the center of the sofa, staring at blue flickers on the television screen while music blared from huge speakers. His blue jeans had huge holes at the knees. His hair looked unkempt and unwashed.

Gina ducked out of his line of vision. "He's there."

"Probably decided not to go to the party."

"What if he wasn't invited? Poor Dean! That would be terrible! What if he wasn't even invited to the party where he should have been the star?"

He pulled her away from the window. "Roger could have blocked his invitation if he thought Dean would cause trouble."

You looking for trouble?

They walked back to the car, their opportunity to search Dean's apartment for the gun thwarted.

"It's just as well," Gina said. "Spying on Dean makes me feel creepy. Besides, the mess in that apartment is frightening. Are all men who live alone such pigs?"

"I'm not, anymore. But there have been times when I've lived in places that should have been condemned by the public health authorities."

In the lot opposite the one where they had parked, Conner pointed to Dean's van. It was covered with a dusting of snow. "Looks like he hasn't been out in a while."

"Poor Dean!" she repeated. "He must be so bitter. Roger kept promising him the world, promising he'd be bigger than Elvis, then snatching it away. Do you think he did it deliberately? Did he hate his youngest stepson?"

"With Roger, it was hard to tell. Most of the time, I don't think he was malicious. Roger loved making a deal. He was blind to other people."

"So," she concluded, "when he got the bribe from Michael Penrose, he simply changed his mind about Dean. Because it was more profitable to book Michael. That's awful."

They climbed back into the Volkswagen and drove to Starwood. The plainness of Dean's apartment made a sharp contrast with these elegant homes. They parked on a terraced road, looking down on Lydia's home, and saw two cars at the entrance.

"They haven't left," Conner said,

"Maybe they're not going to the party. It really is a little soon after Roger's death to be socializing."

"Alex will go," Conner said. "Especially if he's gotten some flak about how he's handled us. Alex will make an appearance and show everybody how terrific he is."

She cracked open her car door. "Let's get closer. Maybe we can see what's going on."

Strangely, Gina had no reservations about spying on her aunt and Alex. It seemed logical, necessary and right. She and Conner hid in a leafless aspen grove that was uphill from the house. This was the southern exposure and they could see through windows on two sides.

Jerry would have loaned them binoculars if he'd had them. Instead, both Gina and Conner were equipped with opera glasses. Like a couple of Pavarotti spectators they flipped open the lenses and peered at the house.

Gina pointed. "Right there. In the dining room. It's Alex. Oh, my, he's dressed in a tux." She lowered her glasses. "Would you have worn a tuxedo to this party?"

"Yeah, it's black-tie."

"Do you own a tuxedo?"

"Doesn't everybody?" He grinned. "It's getting a little snug around the middle. Must be over five years old. There were all kinds of fancy-dress affairs when I was on the Olympic team. Fund-raisers. That kind of thing."

"Somehow, I'm not surprised." She turned her attention back to the house. "So, I guess you were right. Alex is going to the party."

"And there's Lydia," he said. "She's dressed, too."

"You're kidding!" Gina focused on an upstairs bedroom, the bedroom Lydia had once shared with Roger. Her aunt stood at the sliding glass window, which opened onto a small balcony porch. She almost seemed to be posing. One hand rested on her hip, the other lifted a wineglass to her lips as she gazed out into the night.

The widow, Gina thought. Was Lydia contemplating her future without Roger, trying to put a brave face on her social obligations, despite her tragedy? Or was she looking forward to a good time? "At least her sequins are black."

"When they leave," Conner said, "how are we going to get inside? Do you know how their security system works?"

"Not only that. I have a key."

Conner's eyebrows raised. "How'd you get a key? Your purse is back at the police station."

"It was in the inside pocket of my parka. I'd meant to return it to Lydia when I brought back the Jeep, but Dean didn't want to go inside. He took me back to the hotel and I forgot."

"Good for you."

They snuggled together to wait on the hillside. The headlights of a car flashed as someone else pulled away from Starwood, heading to the Pisces party.

"Look," Conner said teasingly, "it's Demi Moore and Bruce Willis."

She didn't even turn her head. Celebrities had ceased to impress her. The events of the past few days had put much of her life into perspective. When basic freedoms were threatened, nothing else seemed important. "Who cares."

Right now, she and Conner were two fugitives, displaced people hiding out in one of the nation's most affluent neighborhoods. The playground of the stars. Though she was in danger, though she had nothing, no money, no food, no security whatsoever, she felt more complete than she ever had before.

When Alex and Lydia left the house and drove away in the Bentley, she and Conner sidestepped down the hill. Gina used her key on the front door and immediately punched in the proper number sequence to disarm the alarm system. "There," she said. "We've broken and entered. Now, where should we burgle?"

"We're not stealing anything, Gina. We're looking for a gun."

"In the bedroom," she said definitely. "Don't most people hide their handguns beside the bed?"

"I'm not sure if the same rule applies to murder weapons, but let's give it a try."

They climbed to the second floor. Gina had never actually been in Lydia's bedroom before, and when she pushed open the door she stared in awe. It was posh, luxurious and in perfect taste. In one corner was a black Jacuzzi, surrounded by blue tiles that perfectly matched the carpet. Plants and flower arrangements were large and dramatic, featuring Wedgwood blue, white and dark maroon. There was an overstuffed chair and a love seat. And, of course, the huge bed, with a spread that perfectly blended all the colors in the room.

Gina made a quick mental comparison with Roger's cabin; the two places were like night and day, perfect taste versus tacky. Under her breath, Gina mumbled, "How did they ever stay married? Even for a week!"

While Conner searched the bedside furniture, Gina went to the dresser. On the perfectly dusted and cleared surface, two objects seemed out of place. A photo album and a bright red hatbox. She lifted the cover. Inside, there were packets of letters, tied with satin ribbons.

Gently Gina removed the top packet and untied the ribbon. Love letters. Still in the envelopes. All the letters in this packet were addressed to Lydia. And they were from Roger.

Gina checked a postmark. It was from less than six months ago. She opened the letter and read. Roger's neat handwriting flowed across the parchment page in wonderful, sensitive prose.

Gina checked the signature, amazed that Roger had had such sweetness within him. He referred to a party that he and Lydia had attended, where she'd been, he said, the most beautiful woman in the room. Her eyes, he said, were dark promises of enchantment. And he called her his sorceress, his reason for breathing, his lover and his life.

In another letter, which had apparently accompanied a gift from a local boutique, he apologized for being a fool, a jester. He lived for those moments when he would hear her laughter.

Conner emerged from the walk-in closet. "I haven't found anything. What have you got there?"

Gina held the letter against her breast. She averted her gaze, not wanting Conner to see the mist of sentimental tears that had gathered in her eyes. Had Roger really written these sweet, adoring phrases? He'd been a big, crass man who'd made obnoxious advances toward her. However, in these letters, Roger Philo was the most considerate lover she could imagine.

"Gina, what's wrong?"

"Roger's dead, and I never really knew him. I think I would have liked him, Conner."

"What caused this change of heart?"

She looked down at the letter and read, "My darling, when I saw you across the room, a senseless jealousy tore at my heart. I want you all for myself. I want all your laughter and all your tears. Yet, I am proud of you, so very proud that you are independent. I love you, dearest Lydia."

Her voice caught in her throat. "Roger wrote that." She pointed to the red hatbox. "This box is full of letters. I never dreamed he was so kind and wonderful to Lydia."

"That's why she stayed with him," Conner said.

"Exactly why," she agreed. "In private, he was a different man. I feel awful for the terrible things I've said about him, the anger I've felt. This wasn't his fault. He's dead, Conner. But I've been blaming him."

Conner gently embraced her, comforting her regret and her pain.

"When I think of Roger," she said, "all I can see is his death. The horrible wound in his chest. The garish Elvis costume. And he was so much more."

Though Conner stroked her hair and offered assurance, he himself would shed no tears for Roger Philo. The letters, Conner thought, reeked of phony self-indulgence. Too often he had seen Roger in action, picking up other women, drinking too much, being a fool. Sweet apologies could only excuse so much lousy behavior.

Conner had attended some police workshops on domestic violence, and Roger fit the pattern of an abuser. The guy would slap his wife around, then apologize lavishly, and she'd forgive him. Until the next time.

Though Conner didn't think that Roger had ever hit Lydia, his actions had been abusive enough. In Conner's opinion, she was well rid of her husband.

Someday, he and Gina would talk about these things. Someday, he would show her the way a man should be with a woman. But for right now, she was too upset, almost unhinged about the closeness of this murder. It was her family.

She pulled away from him and wiped her eyes. "I'm okay. We should hurry. Find what we need and get out of here."

"They'll be at the party for hours," he said.

"I wish I could talk to Lydia. To tell her how truly sorry I am." She reached up to put the lid back on the box. "I shouldn't read any more of these. It's prying."

"Are there any clues?"

"Actually, he does mention Elvis several times. Elvis songs and goofy Elvis movies."

"Does he say anything about Wendell Otis, or any of our other suspects?"

"I haven't seen anything."

"You might look," Conner suggested. "There might be a motive hidden in one of those letters."

She settled down to read and he went into the downstairs area of the house. It was a huge place, with lots of drawers and cabinets, but Conner had an edge in making this search. Neither Alex nor Lydia would expect anyone to be looking here. They considered themselves above suspicion.

So Conner checked the obvious spots first. The drawers of a desk in the study. The niches in an antique wardrobe closet. Kitchen cabinets. The breakfront in the dining room.

Gradually, he made his way into the rear bedroom on the first floor that belonged to Alex Philo, the assistant district attorney, golden boy, and all-around son of a bitch.

The huge room was tidy as a hotel room. Alex's house-keeping habits were nothing like those of his slovenly brother. Either that or maid service came with the room.

One wall held a desk and entertainment unit. No photographs, Conner noted. Apparently Alex didn't care to be faced with the memory of his ex-wife, or to enshrine Lydia in a heart-shaped frame. A floor-to-ceiling bookshelf held legal textbooks and a miscellany of manuals and how-to books.

With a certain smugness, Conner mentally compared it to his own bookshelves. In addition to his skiing and ski adventure stories, he had several fiction books. A lot of Jack London, Clive Cussler, and everything ever written by Douglas Adams. In this sterile bedroom, there were no novels to stir the imagination of Alex Philo.

Conner went through the desk quickly and checked the bedside table. Then he went into the walk-in cedar closet, where rows of fine suits lined one wall. The shoes were racked neatly on the floor, except for two boxes at the far end. When Conner inspected them more closely, he saw that they had been tied with twine. The weight of the boxes in his hand indicated they were not empty.

In the first he found a turquoise-handled Colt .45. In the second was a single-shot derringer inlaid with pearl. They were almost too pretty to fire. Elvis's guns.

Conner did not touch the weapons. He didn't want to mess up the fingerprints. But now what? Now that he'd found the murder weapon in the bedroom closet of an assistant district attorney, what could he do about it? Unsure about fingerprints, he used a bathroom towel to pick up the two boxes and carry them down the hallway.

He heard the sound of water running in the kitchen and rounded that corner. "Gina, look what I—"

Staring back at him was Lydia Philo. She was dressed to kill in black sequins. Her manicured fingernails showed bright red against the handle of a long knife.

"Conner!" she said. "What the hell are you doing here? What's that in your hand?"

Gina must have heard the noise in the kitchen because she came barreling down the stairs and raced up behind Conner. She held the photo album that had been on the dresser in Lydia's bedroom. When she saw her aunt, Gina hesitated, then set the album down and started across the room. "Lydia, I'm so sorry."

Conner caught her hand. "Gina, she has a knife."

"Don't be silly, Conner. It's a breadknife. What do you think she's going to do? Saw off my crust?"

Lydia appeared to be ready for just that. As Gina approached her, she raised the knife threateningly. "Keep away from me, Gina. Don't touch me."

"Lydia, I'm sorry. I've misjudged you. And Roger, too."

"You killed Roger," she said. There were no tremors in her voice. None of the characteristic hesitation in her speech. "Alex told me. And I believe my son."

Though Gina was flush with the flowery sentiment expressed in Roger's letters, she wasn't a fool. At least Conner hoped not. He hoped that Gina had the sense not to mention that she'd been prying into Lydia's private papers. Nor would it be wise to tell her that, in his opinion and Gina's, Alex was no better than a playground bully.

"Please," Gina said gently. "Listen to me."

"I'm calling the police. Right now."

Conner took matters into his own hands. He set the boxes on the countertop and strode across the room. He caught

Lydia's wrist and disarmed her easily. Then he unplugged the phone.

She threw back her head and screamed. It was a long, loud, piercing wail.

"Nobody can hear you," Conner said. "That's one of the drawbacks of being too rich and living in Starwood. You put too much distance between yourself and your neighbors."

"You bastard!"

"Maybe so. But right now, Gina and I have to leave." He paused. "I don't suppose I could trust you not to call the police the minute we step out the door."

Lydia threw back her chin and gave him a disdainful glare.

"I didn't think so," Conner said. "Then you pick, Lydia. Would you rather be tied up or knocked unconscious?"

Gina stepped forward. "Stop it, Conner."

"We need to leave, Gina. Right now."

"But I want to talk to my aunt. I have to explain."

"She won't listen," he said.

"She will," Gina said urgently. "You care about the truth, don't you, Lydia? You want to know who murdered your husband."

"Of course. I loved . . . Roger."

"Will you listen to me?"

Lydia inhaled deeply, drawing herself up to her full regal height. She straightened her shoulders, clad herself in poise. The only evidence of her screaming was two spots of crimson on her pale cheeks. "You may speak, Gina."

Conner watched as the two women came together. The contrast between them was remarkable. Gina was volatile and passionate, as flammable as the red in her hair. Her aunt maintained an ice-cold blond sophistication. It must take a ton of self-discipline and willpower, he thought, to keep up that front.

She was a clever woman, a former actress. In many ways, he had to admire her.

All the male suspects they had considered, with the exception of Norm Garrett, who was an outside shot at best, had been influenced by Lydia. Whether or not she was the mastermind who had engineered her husband's death, she had to figure into the picture somewhere.

"I suppose," she said, "I should thank you for fixing my Jeep. What are you using for transportation these days?"

"We borrowed a car from one of Conner's friends."

"Tommy Kuhara, I expect. He and Conner have always been close."

"As a matter of fact—"

"Say, Lydia—" Conner interrupted before Gina could give the make, model and license plate number of their getaway car "—why aren't you at the Pisces party?"

"I had planned to go. To keep up appearances and let everyone know that I was all right. But when we got to the door, I couldn't manage it. Roger had arranged...so much of the party. I didn't want to be there without him. I dropped off Alex and came right back here."

"Then I don't suppose you heard Michael Penrose sing," Gina said.

"How do you know him?"

"I met him over at Jerry Sage's house."

"Jerome Sage?" She cast a sidelong glance at Conner. "Oh, yes, he's another of your...friends, isn't he?"

He didn't trust this woman in the least. She was pulling information from Gina without even trying. "We've got to be going, Gina."

"Wait," Lydia said. "I would like Gina's opinion."

She gestured to the bulletin board above the disconnected telephone. There were three photographs of Roger. "Which outfit should I bury him in?"

One picture showed Roger in a navy blue suit, another a casual sweater and Levi's. The third photograph was Roger wearing an Elvis suit with turquoise-and-silver designs. The picture was similar to the one at Otis's house.

Conner wondered what kind of game she was playing. Her smooth face did not register shock, concern or guilt. She was one hell of an actress, far better than Conner would have guessed from seeing her occasional performances at the local community theater.

She speculated, "He really doesn't look bad in the Elvis suit, does he?"

"Not really," Gina said.

"When I first heard about his costume, I was... embarrassed," she said. "But then I decided it was appropriate. It was...Roger. I think I will have him buried in this very costume. If the cleaners can get the blood removed."

Gina swallowed hard. "When is the funeral?"

"Day after tomorrow. And we will not be having a burial. There will be a memorial service with an open casket. Then, Roger will be...cremated." She glanced up. "By the way, Gina, your parents will arrive tomorrow afternoon. We will expect you to attend the funeral."

"Lydia, I don't think that will be possible. I want to explain to you about everything that's happened. I've been framed. And now the killer is coming after me."

"Roger would have wanted you there."

"I can't be." Gina was losing patience. "Warrants have been issued for my arrest, and for Conner's, too. We're fugitives."

"Oh...that."

"A minor inconvenience," Conner said. His temperature was rising. Lydia couldn't be this stupid. She was toying with them, stalling, he thought. Maybe Alex was on his way back here right now. "We need to leave, Gina."

"Please stay," Lydia said. "I am . . . lonely."

"No," Conner said, "we won't. Gina, have you forgotten that Alex wants to lock us up and throw away the key?"

"Not my Alex. I don't believe that's true. He simply did not want for you to leave town." She bestowed a haughty smile on Conner as she explained, "Alex would never hurt Gina."

"Alex ordered Gina to be arrested. He personally instructed the arresting officers to put her in handcuffs."

"A misunderstanding."

"Dammit, Lydia. How dumb do you think we are?"

"I don't know, Conner." She whirled to confront him. "How dumb are you?"

"You're protecting him, aren't you?"

"I have no idea—"

"Come on, Lydia. I found the murder weapon in the back of Alex's closet. Two guns. A Colt and a single-shot derringer. Did you put them there?"

Her eyes darted left and right, searching for excuses. "I might have done so. Roger often left his Elvis . . . souvenirs lying around the house. And how do you know these guns are the murder weapon?"

"Forensics can test the weapons. They'll know which one fired the bullet."

"That can't be!" She was shrill. "You brought those guns here! That's why you came to my house!"

"Fingerprints, Lydia. I haven't touched them. Gina hasn't even seen them."

"How dare you come here and accuse my son?" She drew back her hand and slapped Conner full on the face. "I've lost my husband. I will not lose my son, too." She turned on her heel. "I am calling the police."

Conner made a move toward her but Gina stopped him. "Let's go. Let's get out of here."

"If she makes that call, we're fried."

"You can't knock her out or tie her up. We don't need to add assault to the other charges against us."

Gina turned to her aunt, who was standing erect and still in the center of the kitchen. The shimmer of black sequins on her dress betrayed the trembling of her slender body. "I've always admired you, Lydia. I'm sorry for everything that's happened, but I won't go to jail to protect Alex."

"You'll go to hell, Gina Robinson. Spreading lies. Accusing innocent men. This is your fault. All your fault."

"Five minutes, Lydia. That's all I ask. Give us five minutes to get away from here."

She took Conner's hand and they ran to the door.

Chapter Thirteen

He watched them flee. They burst from the house and charged up the hill, running as fast as they could.

Tonight, he was hidden by the darkness. There was no need to wear a ski mask. A blanket of clouds had slipped across the Pisces moon and dimmed the starlight. If Conner and Gina hadn't raced into the aspen grove above the house, hadn't passed within twenty feet of him, he might not have seen the shoe boxes Conner carried beneath his arm.

The guns. Elvis's Colt .45, and the single-shot derringer he'd used to murder Roger.

He'd wiped them clean, perfectly clean. But forensic investigations had become so sophisticated. There might be a piece of lint. A hair. A mote of dust that was uniquely his own. A single fiber that would convict him.

He needed another plan, another idea.

Climbing the hill, he saw them leap into a yellow Volkswagen with Nordic skis on a rear rack. He memorized the license plate.

This was almost too easy. He could call in an anonymous report, saying he'd seen the people in the fliers. The police would put out an all-points bulletin for the license plate. Then they would be apprehended and delivered to the justice that awaited them at the Pitkin County jailhouse.

But they had the guns.

Cops weren't the answer. Gina and Conner had a way o slipping through the fingers of the law. Flying to Califor nia. Escaping from the courthouse. As they pulled awa from the curb and headed toward town, he ran to his own vehicle.

They looked like they were fleeing, instead of going to th police with the murder weapon. And they had cross-countr skis. Perhaps, he thought, they were still in hiding.

He would follow them.

The legal system had failed him, again and again. Look ing for proof? He'd give them Gina. Accidentally dead, and presumed guilty. Case closed.

Then Conner would be next.

Maybe he'd get lucky, and he could do them both at once

But first, he would deal with the gun. He had to dispos of the weapon. Then he would see that they got what wa coming to them.

GINA DIDN'T SAY a word to Conner as they drove throug Aspen, the most dangerous place in the world for them t be. Slowly, the Volkswagen rolled along streets that wer congested with merrymakers and Saturday-night traffic.

"Damn." Conner braked hard to avoid hitting a coupl who skipped off the curb and strolled onto the road with n more sense than a pair of well-dressed raccoons. His hand gripped tight on the steering wheel. His jaw clenched. It wa obvious to Gina that he was angry. Furious, in fact.

"Conner, I—"

"Don't talk to me, Gina. Not right now."

When they reached the state highway, she assumed the were returning to the cabin. She had to say something "Maybe we should take the guns to the police station an turn them in to Norm."

"Why don't we put nooses around our own necks and ave them the trouble?"

"But you found the guns in Alex's bedroom. That's got o count for something."

"As Lydia pointed out, we could have put them there."

"Conner, it won't do any good to go back to the cabin nd hide." She pointed through the window at the cloud over. "The weather's getting bad. If it starts snowing, skig across that snowfield is going to be difficult."

"Let me handle this, Gina."

"But why?"

"You're too much in the middle to be objective. You lon't want to believe that anyone in your family killed Roger. And, if that's not ridiculous enough, you're thinkng of Roger himself as some kind of really great guy and vonderful husband."

"Those letters—"

"Don't start, Gina. You don't know what you're talking bout. He might have been your uncle, but I knew him. And e was a sorry excuse for a human being. He cheated on our aunt. He lied to his own stepsons. He tried to swindle Otis, and probably everybody else he came in contact with. don't care about his sensitive letters. I don't care if he was he reincarnation of William Shakespeare—Roger Philo was lime."

The vehemence of his tirade surprised her. Though she'd een his temper before, Gina had grown accustomed to hinking of Conner as caring and gentle. Now she felt the azor's edge of his anger, directed toward her, cutting her to he bone. Though he hadn't accused her of anything, she eard the message underlying his words: She wasn't part of his Aspen life. She didn't fit in.

Her anger rose to combat the hurt that spread within her, oisoning her judgment. "Maybe I am an outsider here, but that's just fine with me. However, I'm certainly entitled to an opinion of my own stepuncle.''

"Does getting close to people bother you, city girl?''

"That's right. I like the impersonal streets of Manhattan. There's more privacy in those crowds than here in Aspen, where everybody pokes into everybody else's business.''

He didn't respond. He drove cautiously, a hair under the speed limit, and kept an eye on the rearview mirror.

"And another thing,'' Gina said, filling the silence. "My aunt Lydia couldn't have possibly been involved in the murder. Did you notice what she said?''

"The jumpsuit,'' he said.

"That's right. Lydia looked at the photograph of Roger wearing that silver-and-turquoise design and she said they might bury him in that very outfit if they could get the blood out. But Roger wasn't wearing that jumpsuit when he died.''

Gina gave her head a violent shake, immediately erasing the mental picture of Roger's mutilated body, stuffed into the woodbox. "It was a sunburst design. In gold. Lydia didn't know which outfit he was wearing when he was killed. So, she's innocent. She wasn't there when he was murdered.''

Conner turned his head and glanced over his shoulder. "Gina, I think we're being followed.''

"What?''

"Watch the headlights of the car behind us.''

She peered around the edge of her seat and looked through the small rear window of the Volkswagen Bug. When Conner eased up on the accelerator, the car behind them matched the slower speed, keeping a constant distance of about thirty yards. Conner went faster. His pace was matched by the other vehicle.

Her anger had blinded her for a moment. She'd forgotten the jeopardy of being pursued. "But it can't be the police. They'd pull us over."

"It's not a patrol car," he said.

There was a worse danger. Gina's breath caught in her throat. The stalker! The man who had come after her twice. Had he found them? Was he following? Everything else paled in comparison. If the murderer was after them, they were truly running for their lives.

They couldn't stop and ask for shelter because the fliers identified them as criminals. There was no one they could turn to. Even Lydia had threatened to call the police.

Her only hope was Conner. He was the only one she could trust. "What should we do?"

"I'm going to pull off and see if he stops."

The idea terrified her. Each time she encountered him, he'd gotten closer. At Roger's cabin, he'd been a presence without form or shape. On the ski slope, he'd worn a mask and kept his distance until he swooped down for the attack. And then, in the boutique, she'd heard him whisper, she'd seen his hands through the thin fabric of the curtain that separated them. If she came face-to-face with this monster, the consequences might be horrific. The end result might be death.

But when Conner pulled off at an exit and parked under the bright lights of a gas station, the other car kept on going.

Gina was breathing in shallow gasps, hardly daring to move.

"Are you all right?" he asked.

"Did you recognize the car?"

"No."

Their being followed could have been a coincidence, Conner thought, but he doubted it. There was some reason

they'd been tailed. He would have to be extra-careful on th
approach to the cabin.

He looked over at Gina, who was trembling beside him
He hadn't meant to frighten her or to hurt her. Yes, he'
been angry at Lydia's house, when Gina had allowed her
self to be convinced that her aunt was nothing but an in
nocent bystander. And Roger was a saint? He'd wanted t
drag Gina back to reality, to have her on his side, knowin
that even if Lydia had not killed her husband, she was par
of the motive for his death.

But now, seeing her so scared and trying not to be, he fel
like a jerk. "I'm sorry, Gina."

Her huge brown eyes shimmered. "It's not your fault."

But it seemed like it was. He was supposed to be the bi
hero, but his only solution was to run and hide. "We've go
to go back to the cabin."

"Why?"

"There's too much we don't know. Imagine this, Gina
You're locked in a jail cell, no one else around, and you'r
visited by our main suspect, Alex. He could be the mur
derer, the guy who keeps coming after you. And mayb
when you're locked up and helpless, he arranges some kin
of accident."

"And ruins his career?"

"If he's accused of murder, his career is over." H
paused. "Think about it, Gina. All this plotting an
scheming is typical of Alex. If he pulls it off, he'll feel smu
and superior."

"So confident that he hid the murder weapon in his ow
closet."

"We can't turn ourselves in. Finally, the advantage is o
our side. We've got the guns. But we've got to figure ou
how to use them."

He drove carefully back to their hideout, checking the rearview mirror, watching. When they set out on the skis, light snow was falling. The snow was good, Conner thought, because it would cover their tracks. But it made the trek across the avalanche chute even more perilous. They had to ski close together, couldn't take a chance on losing visual contact. But they made it.

When they'd settled inside and he'd built a fire, his mind veered away from the danger that surrounded them. He thought of Gina, of what would happen to them when this was over.

She was already curled up in their sleeping-bag nest. But he was hesitant to join her. What if she didn't want him beside her? When they'd argued, her first response had been that she was going back to New York. She might be really anxious to leave Aspen. And he couldn't say that he blamed her.

"Gina?"

"Yes, Conner?"

"When this is over, I don't want you to leave. I want you to stay here with me. At least stay in town."

"And what would I do for a living?"

"You could work at one of the art galleries. Or open your own place. With your New York contacts, you'd be great."

"Quit my job and move to Aspen." She sounded doubtful, but he caught a hint of amusement in her voice. "That's so irresponsible."

"I'll be the responsible one," he said.

He went to the sleeping bags and slipped inside. Her body was warm, and she eased against him. Her touch was comfortable and right. The firelight gleamed in her hair. "Let me take care of you, Gina."

"Why?"

"Because I love you."

On that starless night, their passion was a slow dance, reminiscent of the first time they'd met, in the tavern, and he held her in his arms. In spite of the anger and hurt and fear, the small cabin filled with the warmth of their love.

Close in each other's arms, they slept deeply.

It wasn't until morning, when they sat on the porch, drinking bitter coffee, that Conner came up with a plan. "I'll go into town alone," he said. "You stay up here with the guns. That's my bargaining chip."

"Why can't I come with you?"

"This way, they won't have both of us. I can make demands. I can get some follow-through."

"What kind of demands?"

"I can see their complete police report, the forensic information and the alibis. I can insist on talking to the district attorney, instead of Alex. Maybe even contact that lawyer Jerry was talking about."

"You're right," she said. "If they have both of us, they don't have to do a damn thing. Norm can lock us up and tell everybody that he's caught the murderers."

"Exactly."

She kissed him on the cheek. "Okay, do it."

Conner hated to leave her alone, but he thought this was the best way. And up here, in the cabin, she'd be safe. Nobody could hurt her.

Still, when he was ready to depart, he felt reluctant. "If I don't come back by tomorrow," he said, "I'll send someone to bring you out."

"I'll be okay," she said.

He skied out, swiftly crossing the dangerous snowfield.

Their tracks from last night had been mostly obliterated by the snowfall, but the weather today was sunny again, and he made parallel streaks across the snow. The markings were good, he told himself. If he needed to send someone else up here to find Gina, the way would be clearer.

Conner fired up the little Volkswagen and drove toward Aspen. The sun shone brightly on the snow. It was peaceful, a beautiful Sunday in the mountains. The ski slopes would be jam-packed with tourists, but the locals would sleep in. They'd had their party last night. Today would be a time for rest.

With his heart beating like a snare drum, Conner parked outside the police station. Before he could think about the consequences, he marched into Norm's office, where he found the deputy sitting amid a clutter of paperwork. "You've got to listen to me, Norm."

"It's about time." He leaned back in his chair. "I wondered how long it would take for you to get your sorry butt into town. Where's Gina?"

"Someplace safe." Norm seemed congenial, friendly.

"Hey, Conner, I'm sorry about everything. Especially those stupid fliers with your pictures on them. That was a dumb idea, but I was mad. Dammit, you shouldn't have pulled that escape. I told Chas and Leon that they were going to have some serious explaining to do when the sheriff gets back."

"You're sorry?" *What was going on here?*

Norm took a gulp of coffee and wiped his mustache. "Want to help us with the manhunt that's going on right now? That would be something, huh? You could be the one to catch Roger's murderer."

"You've got another suspect," Conner concluded.

"As much as I hate that forensic stuff, it's damn useful in turning up physical evidence. They found a couple of hairs on the body, and fibers from a sweater. So, we got ourselves a search warrant. When we went through the suspect's belongings, we found gloves with blood spatters, and a black ski mask with the same. It was Roger's blood, all right."

"Have you made an arrest?"

"Here's the bad news. Can't find him."

Gina! He'd left her in the cabin. Alone.

GINA WASN'T GOOD at sitting and waiting. She'd done more contemplating in the past few hours than in the rest of her life. When this was over...

Should she quit her job and come to live here? With Conner? It sounded good. It sounded like what she wanted to do. But what a change!

Of course, she'd been the one who insisted on a committed relationship. But now that he'd made the offer, she just wasn't sure. Not that they were talking about marriage or anything. He hadn't asked her to marry him.

He'd said that he loved her. And she felt that he meant it. Because she loved him, too.

But it was awfully irresponsible to quit her job at Berryhill's. It was a great career, authenticating fine art and antiques. And Elvis, she reminded herself. Authenticating Elvis.

That wasn't her favorite assignment, but she was eternally grateful to the King. He'd brought her here, where she'd met Conner. Maybe, someday, they would honeymoon at Graceland.

When she went outside to gather up a few more sticks of wood for the fireplace, she was humming the tune to "Heartbreak Hotel," Elvis's first hit. Then "Don't be Cruel." That was the song Roger had picked for her.

Stepping back inside the cabin, she immediately sensed that something was wrong. There was a small plop as a stone was tossed into the center of the sleeping-bag nest she'd shared with Conner. A stone? Sharp-edged. A reminder of Roger.

"Dean?" She dropped the firewood and turned around.

He was leaning against the wall behind the door. "Hello, cuz."

"What are you doing here?"

"It's time that you face justice. You killed Roger, and you're going to have to pay."

"What are you talking about?" He was his usual cool, emotionless self. "I didn't kill him."

"But all the evidence points to you. Alex told me all about it. There was the money in the envelope. The statue with your fingerprints. You went up to his cabin for a party. There was even that Elvis whiskey bottle, with the two glasses."

"Wait!" She'd broken the glasses and put away the decanter. She hadn't remembered to tell Norm about them. There was only one person, besides Conner, who knew. That was the person who had set up this elaborate frame. The killer.

Panic raced her pulse. After all the questions, the clues, the suspicions, the answer became clear. Dean. It was Dean.

He cocked his head to one side and studied her. His inspection was cool and clinical. He reminded her of his mother. "What are you thinking, Gina?"

"Nothing." She had the answer. But if he knew, he would kill her. Her heart sank. He meant to kill her anyway. That was why he'd come here, tracked her down.

"You know," he said.

She didn't bother to deny it. "Why, Dean? Why did you kill him?"

"I didn't mean to." He pushed his hair out of his eyes. "I didn't go to the cabin planning to kill him. I was going to talk to him about the Pisces party gig, make him change his mind."

"Was your mother there?" Gina feared his confession. The more he told her, the more reason he had to kill her, too. But she wanted to keep him talking, to keep him distracted. The guns were hidden at the foot of the sleeping bags. Only five feet from where she was standing. If she armed herself, she might have a chance. "Was Lydia at the cabin then?"

"She was there. And so was that weenie Otis. I saw their cars at the bottom of the hill when I put the van in the garage. Then I listened to what they had to say."

"Lydia was speaking up for you." She inched closer to the guns. "Wasn't she?"

"Yeah, sure. But she backed down to Roger. Like she always did. He was her man. Her main man."

"Why didn't you go inside?"

"Because I'm sick of the scene. Lydia gets all weepy, and Roger apologizes, and she forgives him. I've seen it played a hundred times. And I hate it."

"But she cares about you, too."

"How do you know that? How do you know what it's like to be me?"

"I wouldn't want to be you, Dean." Her temper flared. "It must be hell."

"What do you mean by that?"

"I couldn't stand to sit in a filthy apartment, staring at a television screen while the damned music plays too loud."

"How do you know about my apartment?"

"I was there. I was spying on you."

His laughter rang with eerie overtones, too high-pitched for his voice. "Spying on me. Well, that's pretty funny. I've been watching you, too. I followed you everyplace. Even last night, when Conner figured out that I was on your tail. I stayed way back. But I managed to find the Volkswagen. It wasn't until this morning, when Conner made those nice tracks, that I knew where to look."

An alarm went off in her brain. "Conner. Is he all right?"

"Are you worried about your big ski hero? Don't you think he can protect himself?"

"Tell me, Dean."

"Why should I? You can figure it out. You're one of the smart ones, one of the family success stories. Like Alex."

"Did Alex know? Was he covering up for you?"

"Mister True Blue? The golden boy? What do you think, Gina? Alex wouldn't cross the street for me. He sure as hell wouldn't risk his career. In fact, he was going out of his way to be hard on you—so nobody could accuse him of playing favorites because you were his cousin."

"He didn't think I was guilty?"

"No way." Dean's eyes shone from behind his mane of hair. "He was trying to protect you. Like Conner. Like everybody. They all love little Gina, with her pretty red hair. It's me they hate."

"I don't think so, Dean. It's—"

"Shut up, Gina. I know what they're thinking. I'm the bad boy, the one who's never going to make anything of himself."

He took a step toward her, and Gina made a dive for the guns. She came up empty-handed.

Dean laughed again. He stuck his hands in his parka pockets and came up with both pistols. One in each hand. "Are you looking for something, Gina? Looking for trouble?"

Her hands clenched into tight fists. There was no way to protect herself. The ax was outside, by the woodpile. "What are you going to do?"

"First, I'm going to stand here and watch you crawl around on the floor. You look real cute when you're groveling. Does Conner like for you to do stuff like that? Does he like to have you crawl around?"

She scrambled to her feet. "You go to hell, Dean."

"Maybe I will. But I'll probably get out of that rap, too." He put the derringer in his pocket and gestured toward the door with the big Colt .45. "Let's go for a walk, Gina."

"I'm not going anywhere."

He came at her in two fast strides. Before she could react, he backhanded her so hard that she fell to the floor. And he stood over her, his hair dangling around his face.

"When are you people going to get it? You've got to do what I say. Do I have to kill all of you?" He grabbed her arm and yanked her to her feet. "Now, let's go."

She stumbled outside into the brilliant sunlight. Her jaw ached where he'd hit her, and her mind was foggy.

"Start walking," he ordered.

Numbly she followed the path made by Conner's skis going out and Dean's skis coming in. In the trees, the snow was ankle-deep, except for drifts that came up to her knees. She didn't have a cap. With only her sweater and turtleneck, she was freezing.

She turned and looked at him. He had slipped into his cross-country skis and was managing easily in the snow. "Where are we going?"

"To your funeral."

"You won't get away with this."

"Sure I will. When they find your body, they'll think your death was an accident. If I have to shoot you, they'll think it was suicide. Either way, I'm doing Alex a favor."

"I don't understand."

"If you're dead, not poking around and stirring everything up, Norm and Alex will be happy to blame you for Roger's murder and close the case. That way, everything can go back to normal in Aspen."

"What about the guns?"

"Nobody will ever find the guns. I'm taking the guns with me and getting rid of them. It's the only evidence."

If only there was something else. She needed a reason for him to keep her alive.

"I should've dumped them before," he continued. "But I like these guns. So I hid them in Alex's closet. I figured nobody would look in there. Nobody would suspect the golden boy."

"I did." She tried to think. Oh, God, where was Conner? Had Dean killed him already? She had to get out of this. "We could work together, Dean. We could put the blame on Alex."

"I'm not falling for it, Gina."

She stumbled to the edge of the snowfield, then turned toward him. "I can't go out there."

"Keep walking."

"Dean, that snow on the ridge is about to slide. It'll be an avalanche."

"If you're lucky, you won't feel a thing."

But she could be buried alive. She could suffocate slowly. "Please, Dean. Don't."

"If I kill you, Gina, it's going to be slow. It's going to hurt a lot. And you're still going to be just as dead. This way, it's fast."

She waded into the snowfield, plowing through crusted snow that was up to her thighs. Every step was a struggle.

"Keep going!" he yelled. "That's a good girl! Keep moving!"

She sprawled on her face, freezing-cold and exhausted.

Dean's laughter was loud enough to trigger an avalanche. "I wish Conner could see you now. You look like hell, Gina."

Conner was alive! "You didn't kill him."

"No, I was saving that for later. After I had the guns back. Besides, you're the big suspect, cuz. You're the problem. You're the star."

"Let me go. Please, Dean." She had to warn Conner. "I'll do anything you say, anything you want."

"I'm not some stupid twelve-year-old you can boss around." His voice was loud, too loud. And angry. "Try running across the field, Gina. Maybe you'll make it to the other side. Maybe you can get away."

She forced herself to move a little farther away from him. Maybe she could get away.

"That's enough!" he yelled. "Turn around and look at me!"

Not a chance. She was twenty feet from the edge of the trees. She might be able to crouch down and double back. Burrow through the snow. But she was cold, so damned cold. Her hands were like ice.

"Gina! Turn around! I want you to see this!"

His voice boomed. She felt the cracking beneath the snow, the beginning of the avalanche.

"Hey, Gina. I'm holding the gun over my head. I'm going to fire it. Hey, look."

She tried to remember every survival method she'd ever known. She ducked down, curled into a ball. She had to protect her face, to create a pocket of air in case she was buried.

"Dammit, Gina!"

She started. His voice was closer. He'd skied out onto the field beside her.

"Look up at me!" Dean hollered. "I want to see your face when you know you're going to die!"

There was a roar. A rumble that was louder than a freight train, as the massive wall of snow cracked loose. She heard Dean's screams, glanced up in time to see a boiling mass of snow. Then she was thrown, dragged and tossed in the fury of the avalanche. She crashed into something. She was still being thrown, but more slowly. The snow roared past. She was on the fringe, on the edge.

Her left shoulder throbbed with pain and it was dark when the still-moving snow covered her face. With her right hand, she thrust upward. If she didn't get out of here fast, she never would. The avalanche snow set like cement when it stopped.

She broke the surface. Sucked down a gulp of air.

Thinking of Conner, thinking of freedom, she fought clear of the snow and the debris of shattered trees.

Overhead, in the blue ether skies, she saw a shadow block the sun. A helicopter. Her eyelids closed and she lost consciousness.

SHE WAKENED WITH A JOLT. Her eyes wide with terror. An avalanche. She'd been buried in an avalanche.

But she was alive.

And warm, blissfully warm. The soft light before her eyes formed into a shape. "Where am I?"

"In the hospital," Conner said. "You're going to be okay."

He held her right hand. Her left wrist was in a cast. When she tried to move, her shoulder throbbed painfully. Everything ached.

But she was alive. And Conner was here. She gazed up at him, thinking that he was the most wonderful sight in the world. "Was I unconscious?"

"You have a concussion. Matter of fact, I promised the doctor I'd call as soon as you were fully awake."

"Wait," she said softly. Memories flooded back to her. "Dean. What happened to Dean?"

"He's dead. We found the body. Broken back."

"He killed Roger."

"I know, Gina. Norm actually had the evidence. He was going to arrest Dean when I showed up in his office."

"Then we're not suspects?"

He gently stroked her cheek. His fingers rested on her lips. "We're free."

Her eyelids fluttered closed. Tired, she was so very tired. And there was something in the back of her mind. Something she needed to tell him. "Lydia," she said. "Does Lydia know about Dean? Does Alex?"

"They both know. Neither of them had anything to do with the murder. It was Dean, acting alone."

"Yes," she said. Poor Dean, always alone, with his music playing too loud. "But I don't feel sorry for him. He tried to kill me."

"I shouldn't have left you there at the cabin. I'll never leave you again."

Oh, my, that sounded so wonderful to her. "A lifetime," she murmured.

"I'd better get the doctor now."

Her eyes snapped open, and she suddenly felt fully conscious. "I'm going to be all right, aren't I? No permanent damage?"

"Not that anyone can tell."

"Oh, good. Because I have a lot to do."

"There's time." He smiled down at her. "Plenty of time."

"Don't patronize me, Conner. I have to get busy if I'm going to open an art gallery in Aspen. I'll need to lease a place—maybe Lydia can help me with that. And, of course, I'm going to need to use a lot of my contacts from Berryhill's. When I go back to New York to get my things, I'll—"

"Slow down, Gina."

"Easy for you to say. You already live here."

She tried to sit up, but the effort was too much for her. She fell back on the pillows with a long sigh. There was something else, something very important, that she had to do.

"Oh, yes." Now she remembered. "I love you, Conner."

He leaned close and kissed her cheek, whispered in her ear, "I love you, city girl."

She was awake. And content. She truly believed that, eventually, everything would be all right. The aches and pains would go away. Her memories of Roger and Dean would gradually fade. Now, she was safe and warm and deeply in love. Conner was her hero, and she never would leave him again.

This September, discover the fun of falling in love with...

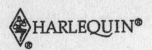

Harlequin is pleased to bring you this exciting new collection of three original short stories by bestselling authors!

**ELISE TITLE
BARBARA BRETTON
LASS SMALL**

LOVE AND LAUGHTER—sexy, romantic, fun stories guaranteed to tickle your funny bone and fuel your fantasies!

Available in September wherever
Harlequin books are sold.

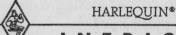

HARLEQUIN®

I N T R I G U E®

As part of Harlequin Intrigue's "Decade of Danger and Desire," we invite you to

RETURN TO THE SCENE OF THE CRIME

Four of your favorite authors reprise the stories that *you* made some of the most popular Harlequin Intrigue titles over the past ten years. In these *brand-new* stories, you can pick up the loves and adventures of the characters you first met in the original novels...and delight in meeting some new ones.

In September, don't miss any of the
RETURN TO THE SCENE OF THE CRIME books:

TANGLED VOWS: *A 43 Light Street novel*
by Rebecca York
(based on SHATTERED VOWS, 1991)

WHO IS JANE WILLIAMS?
by M.J. Rodgers
(FOR LOVE OR MONEY, 1991)

CRIMSON NIGHTMARE
by Patricia Rosemoor
(CRIMSON HOLIDAY, 1988)

THE DREAMER'S KISS
by Laura Pender
(DÉJÀ VU, 1990)

Watch for details on how you can get the original novels on which these stories are based!

RETURN TO THE SCENE OF THE CRIME

RTSC